Ellie

The Unexpected Influencer

Emily Jacobs

Cover design by: Emily Jacobs
Illustration by: @topicalparadise_
Edited by: @pinktartandolly

For Victoria

My inspirational, moon loving, big hearted sis.

"Surround yourself with people that push you to be your best self!"

1

Today is my birthday. I have survived thirty years on planet earth. It should have been my first wedding anniversary too. That was until I caught Bob face deep in a vagina that wasn't mine. Only five months after he said "I do." Twat.
I thought my *love luck* had changed when I met Bob – clearly it had not. Birthdays shall never be the same, they will always be a reminder that I am the big D - Divorced.

My apartment door thuds "HALLOHA," screams bestie and all-time legend that is Ruby Richardson.

I open it. As per, Ruby looks effortlessly trendy – she is the definition of slay in her yellow cord dungarees complementing her flawless black skin. She smiles warmly holding a gigantic unicorn balloon.

"How's my all-time fave birthday girl?" Ruby pats me on the shoulder and strides past into the small open plan living space I call home.

"I'm fine," I shrug.

"Really, you are FINE Miss Ellie Benson?" Ruby challenges my definition of 'fine' whilst scanning over my comical appearance.

My long red hair is piled up in a messy topknot, sour cream dip dribbled shamelessly down the front of my black onesie. I can confirm this is the reason for my unfortunate stench. Ruby gives me a look. The Look. *The don't lie to your best friend look.* I burst into uncontrollable tears. She follows me to my sofa, covered with a tatty purple throw and hugs me tight. I must confirm I am an ugly crier. No glistening tear rolling elegantly down my cheek. I wail, I snort - it has been said I resemble a baby elephant. I blow my nose and clear my throat - I shall avoid all mirrors for the foreseeable future.

“Cry it all out” Ruby encourages rubbing my back looking around. Her eyes land on the empty wine bottles huddling sinfully together around my over flowing silver bin. But, given my bout of snot and tears she chose not to comment. If my landlord was to pay an unexpected visit I would be out on my arse.

“Tonight, we celebrate in style. Birthdays are precious Ellie, don’t waste a single one because of that - thing.” Ruby couldn’t even bring herself to say Bob’s name. In the beginning she referred to him as a parasite, then she started feeling sorry for parasites.

“It’s going to be epic; restaurant is all booked. Me, you and Matt – just like old times.” Ruby wiped my tears with a tissue and a twinkle of excitement in her eyes. Ruby did nothing half arsed. Always full arse, which makes me realise I can’t say no. Even though I had planned to drink copious amounts of cheap prosecco and watch Lucifer from start to finish, again. Each crime scene I would imagine Bob begging for his life as Lucifer showed his true self. Too far? *Probably*. Verging on slightly psycho? *Perhaps*- but it helps me feel better imagining Bob literally shitting in his pants that Lucifer is the devil. And the fact Tom Ellis is hilarious and exceptionally pleasant on the eye is a bonus.

“You ARE coming out tonight and you ARE going to have FUN Ellie!” Ruby ordered.

Fun. I can’t remember the last time I had genuine prolonged fun. These days fun is found at the bottom of a bottle. I almost cry again.

“I’m a fat mess, working as an undervalued secretary to a group of dip shit consultants fighting to be alpha and I have a pile of red letters waiting to be opened.” I point at the white envelopes stamped with the words *overdue, urgent and do not ignore* in bold red lettering.

“And to top it all off I have a resting bitch face that makes men out run Usain Bolt." I rant.

"You know Ellie; you can't let love in if you don't start loving yourself," Ruby whispers softly. I open her present to see a beautiful MK black tote bag. Inside it is a self-help book – subtle as a sledge hammer.

"Love, love, love, thank you," I hug the beautiful bag like I'm embracing a new born baby. Then I read the back of the book jam packed with ideas on how to love yourself.

My tears have been building up. I haven't cried for weeks, months actually. I am generally not a crier. But today if the tap doesn't get fully opened, I fear I may explode. I cry as I cannot explode – it would not be a pretty sight. All I have consumed for two days is pizza, prosecco and those Percy Pigs from Marks and Spencer's. Recipe for an exploding disaster.

An hour later I am a presentable thirty-year young woman. Ruby could easily swap her successful PR job for counselling. She lifts my mood by her presence and as an extra birthday surprise, tidied my flat while I showered. One is definitely adding cleaner to life goals.

"Tonight, is going to be epic Ellie. I love you!" Then she was gone. Away for her Saturday morning meeting to keep some very *influential* influencer happy.

I had a slurp of coffee fantasising how I would have been celebrating if Bob hadn't cheated. Five-star hotel, champagne, baby making sex... *Must change mind-set. Stop giving Bob room in your head. He is not worthy!* I pull off a strip of eyelashes hanging like a suicidal spider down my face. Since becoming a divorcee, I have piled on three stone more rapid than snow falling during an avalanche. If I'm witness to one more skinny bitch bragging about the heartbreak diet, I may eat myself to death. *He left me and so did the fat, lost my man and three stone, heartache was worth it....* Blah blah blah. I am a comfort eater – end of. Carbs and chocolate are both my biggest comfort and greatest enemies.

Since Bob ruined my life not only am I carrying more blubber than an Antarctic seal – but my tolerance of people in general is at an all-time low. My abruptness has catapulted into new levels of rude and my motivation for life has plummeted. I overheard my mum telling her friends at a coffee morning I had been diagnosed with verbal diarrhoea-ism! I mean - really mum? That's not even a fucking condition, but Betty and Violet were soaking it up - eyes filled with sympathy for poor Nancy. Speak of the devil. Incoming call from mum. FaceTime. Probably reminiscing about squeezing my naked 9lb 6oz out her hairy fanjita thirty years ago.

"Darling you look horrendous," my mum held her hand over her mouth dramatically. Signalling for my dad to come and see.

I laughed, *I looked horrendous*. Her face was caked in fake tan. Her dyed blonde hair set in pink rollers and she had on a pink silk nighty with a boob almost popping out.

"What?" she snapped sorting her spaghetti strap.

"Bet you looked worse thirty years ago, drug free labour and all that – did the bowling finals go OK?" I ask. Mum ignores me, which meant she lost badly, and signalled my dad again.

"Happy birthday Ellie," smiles my dad in the background raising his blue mug. He still couldn't get his head around the twenty first century technology. Video calling freaked him out. And since retirement he still couldn't have a cup of coffee without adding a shot of Whisky. And he drunk a lot of coffee. To be fair I think my mother could drive any human to drink.

"Thanks Dad."

"Why haven't you accepted my follow request on Instadaram?" Mum interrupted looking more annoyed than hurt.

"Insta-GRAM Mum!" I correct her, for the millionth time.

"That's what I said. Well why haven't you? You only have 241 followers you could do with an extra one." My mum added blowing her newly pink painted nails. Ruby should never have explained Instagram to her. Her username should have been @davidhasselholfstalker because that's why she set it up.

"I'm on a social media detox," I lie. Although I do feel I need a SM detox. Instagram is the first thing I check in the morning and the last thing I check at night. I mindlessly scroll through the endless feed of old school friends and celebrities. Most friends are married with multiple kids yet still a size zero and holding down a successful career. Jealous? Never. OK total lie. I am. It makes me feel like shit. However, I still do it. *I fear the day that technology will surpass our human interaction. The world will have a generation of idiots.* I hear ya Albert. I am an idiot.

"Are you listening Ellie?" snaps my mother who still has to wish happy birthday to her only child. We had celebrated early with a spa day last weekend. Some quality mother and daughter bonding time that drove me to buy two bottles of wine instead of one.

"All ears Mum." I made myself a coffee while nodding occasionally to confirm I was listening.

After what felt like hours, hearing in depth about my uncle Raymond's successful kidney stone removal and the neighbour's daughter coming out as a lesbian, I agree to go to Aunt Patsy's ballroom bash in six weeks. Not only is my petite busy body Aunt celebrating her sixtieth birthday, but also her retirement from some fancy financial company that she gave thirty years of her life to. Gives me a target to lose weight for. It's going to be a big extravagant party in Edinburgh, big enough m that I can easily mingle into the background. I have successfully avoided all family gatherings since getting divorced. I fear the question, "so what happened with you and Bob?" Or worse, "can I have my wedding gift back?" *Eh, Bob's a dickhead and your gift has either been smashed to shit or sold on eBay.*

My dad gestures hand strangling throat when my mum mentions Violet and IBS.

"Bye Mum, love you" I cut her off before I hear the unnecessary details regarding Violet's bowel trouble. I hit the red button with Nancy still talking. Thanks dad I mutter, grateful for the warning.

This was not how I envisioned my life at thirty. I ditch the coffee and pour a glass of white wine in my unicorn mug. It is my birthday after all, and no one is here to tell

me not to. I gulp it down. Then cry.

2

"How does today make you feel?" Matt asks flicking my cheek.

"Like acid reflux Matt. It is - my birth-day, wedding day, jump off a bridge, pray for zombies to end the world, so I don't have to jump off bridge day!" I reply in my best bitter sarcastic tone.

"Hasn't someone brought their A game in the dramatics!" Matt hugs me then slaps a present, carefully wrapped in a blue plastic bag against my stomach.

"Skint as per. Happy birthday Els." He nods to the photograph I pull out the 5p carrier bag. I smile, it's perfect and in a bright yellow frame. I love yellow.

The photo is a trip down memory lane. I must have been nineteen. Ruby and Matt are pushing me in a shopping trolley (stolen yet returned, so technically borrowed) my feet in the air, swigging the cheapest cider money can buy, my vibrant red hair long and wild. Visually it combines a scene from Absolutely Fabulous and a wild Lioness perfectly. We all look so happy, so young, so carefree - my tripod of friends. I fancied Matt for months at high school before realising he was gay. Devastation was an understatement. But once I got over the fact that his penis liked penis, we became inseparable mates. I was surprised Ruby hadn't ditched us. Matt and I are foul mouthed underachievers and Ruby - the well-presented, beautifully spoken, kind, kick arse career woman. #MyInspiration.

Matt has signed the photo with a black marker pen at the bottom #SQUADGOALS

"Go get dressed unless you're going out in... whatever the fuck you call that. Curtains, floral bin bag?" Matt points at my house coat.

I ignore his insult and go to my bedroom. The prosecco pops open – music to my ears.

Sara Blakely should be crowned. Spanx is absolute genius. I salute you – so does my silhouette. I'm happy with the black jumpsuit that arrived by post. Loose enough that I can breathe and sit down- always a plus. Yet tight enough not to look like I am wearing a bin bag. Yay! The biggest bonus - I don't need to slug around the shops looking at outfits I can't fit or afford. Happy birthday to me. I twirl in my new heels leaving my bedroom and the bundles of washing littered all over the floor and bed. I really must use remaining annual leave to catch up on housework. What a waste of fucking time. But it is required. I have no clean pants. Tomorrow it will be the black bikini bottoms.

"If I wasn't gay." Matt gives the thumbs up of approval - rocking his skinny black jeans and lemon flamingo patterned (looks nicer than it sounds) Armani shirt. Make-up was sprawled all over my wooden kitchen worktop. By day Matt was King Barista in a retro vibe coffee shop and by night (or more specifically weekends) he was make-up artist to his friends.

"Sit." Matt orders patting the bar stool in my kitchen, selecting a double wear foundation. I poured us both a prosecco as Matt blasted "50 Cent – In Da Club," through the speakers screaming loudly 'go shorty it's your birthday!' Matt insta storied our glasses clinking. A Boomerang – is there any other way? Tagging @itismeellieb Happy Birthday Sexy Bitch #THIRTYANDFLIRTY #foreverfriends #letsgetsmashed

"Happy birthday Ellie." We gulp in unison. *Thirty and Flirty*? I sound desperate. God, perhaps I am. I met Bob weeks after my twenty-sixth birthday, we were engaged by my twenty-eighth, married on my twenty – ninth and then divorced 'officially' just five weeks before my thirtieth year on this planet. So, the only penis I have seen in four years is Bob's penis. Nothing to shout about, but we had a rhythm going - sex on a Tuesday,

Thursday and Sunday. Occasional blow job when I couldn't be fucked having sex (after compulsory bottle of wine) - BJ got results quicker. Sex became comfortable, if not slightly robotic. I am worried I no longer have the wow factor in the bedroom, or worse I am portrayed as damaged goods. When potential suitors find out I am a divorcee will they ask themselves, what is wrong with Ellie Benson?

"Make me smoking hot!" I pout pushing all Bob related thoughts away. Or attempt to pout. Instagram is flooded with girls effortlessly pouting their plump sexy lips. Given the 'hell no' look on Matt's face clearly, I can't add 'perfect pouter' to my resume.

"Ellie by the time I'm finished you could be celebrating your 21st," Matt laughed with a click of the hips and fingers.

"However...."

"Fuck Matt – it's my birthday" I remind him. I was going to add that I should be celebrating my first wedding anniversary for the sympathy, but we had made a pact not to talk about Bob's pathetic loser-vile existence. He is dead to me.

"However..."

When Matt said *however* an insult was sure to follow. He tried to make it like a compliment sandwich - two compliments with a negative squashed in the middle but the negative still far outweighs the compliments.

"Your hair is so long and bouncy, real beauts Ellie..." he starts.

"But beautiful hair aside. It is time to take the plunge. You need to jump back on the healthy eating train." Matt pats my stomach with no remorse.

"Maybe a personal trainer?" Matt perked up still unfazed that I wanted to smack him.

"YES a PT would be amazing," I agree.

"I think so too," he gave my cheek a playful nip.

"If I had disposable income, and motivation, but I just can't justify putting it on a credit card, not when I am two months behind on council tax. The price of beauty is not a cheap one. And the growing pressure to appear like you'd been spat out a Kardashian's vagina is insane. I feel sorry for the teenagers today. Especially the poor pouters. Fuck you, social media."

"Take that as a nooo then." He whispers under his breath, rolling his eyes, before looking emotionally wounded. Matt is the only person I know that can give an insult then play victim.

We finish the bottle of prosecco, laugh at dancing dogs on YouTube and decide in our next life we shall be reincarnated as an A-lister's chihuahua. We scroll through their lavish lifestyles – shocked to discover their weekly grooming costs more than my yearly beauty maintenance.

My flat buzzer goes in the nick of time as I rugby tackle Matt's mobile from his hands. He was just about to call his Ex – Leo. Leo is a coke snorting dickhead. Matt deserves way better. But when alcohol starts travelling through his blood stream, everything goes to shit, Matt forgives Leo's sins and begs for cock.

"TAXI!!!!" Ruby bellows through a crackled receiver.

"Let's go."

"Thirty and flirty!" Ruby pouts as we climb in the taxi. Ruby has indeed mastered the art of pouting.

"The thirty and flirty vag needs action," Matt points at my lady parts.

"Are there no boundaries in our friendship?" I ask throwing my hands up.

"You did get waxed?" Matt continues pointing, he looks panicked. My friends are fully aware the only action it has seen in months was from a young chatty nurse doing my smear test. And that was an embarrassing memoir! I had used Ruby's niece's talc powder to freshen up. What I did not read was 'glitter talc'. My vagina was sparkling like a disco ball. I lay legs apart oblivious to my sparkles talking about how guns should be made illegal in America. *Glitter talc should be branded with a bright neon sticker.*

Matt and Ruby stare at me, wide eyed. Imagining the worst. A ginger neglected afro.

"Jeez, I got waxed! Happy?!" I snap. I have got waxed but not for any man. I feel cleaner being hair free. My hair free lady parts are for me, thank you very much.

"We will be happy when it's drowning in cock." Matt declared, Ruby nodded. The poor taxi driver drove through a red light. We jolt forward as he slams the breaks. He mutters an apology with a red face.

I shift the cock chat back to Matt with a smirk. Ruby threatens him within an inch of his life not to contact Leo. Ever.

"Keep the change" Ruby paid the cab as we pull up in Glasgow City Centre, it is a warm sparkly evening. The night is alive, with people laughing, chatting, bustling around. Different wafts of perfumes and aftershaves all intertwining make me smile, I haven't been 'out out' in a long time.

Then I think about money as I stare at the girls entering the lush restaurant – dripping in designer gear and diamonds. *Hookers* I decide to make myself feel better. Not cool, I know, but I feel better. Back to money though – at least the so-called *hookers* could buy rounds of drinks without worrying it may affect what they would eat prior to pay day. Maybe I have found a solution to lose weight. Spend every penny I have so I can't buy food. *Food for thought.*

I used to have savings. Granted not much, but it was a small safety net that kept my anxiety at bay. Every last penny went towards the bloody wedding. My dad is old fashioned and insisted on paying for as much as he could, so I cut costs down by paying for what I could.

My current financial situation is in simple terms -pure shite. Living month to month. Pay away day as soon as my wages hit the bank. Currently -

£320 cash. Two weeks till pay day. Includes buying basic life survivals like food, prosecco and glossy magazines. Oh, shit and travel.

£365 left on high interest rate credit card.

£290 left on my other credit card currently sitting with a balance of £4759.

I am sure I could get my overdraft extended to avoid using credit cards. Must cancel scale and polish to save dosh. Teeth are overrated anyway.

"And birthday girl, as I said before tonight's on moi." Ruby smiles grabbing my hand.

"I'll buy the chips and cheese when we stagger to our Uber." Matt held his hands up with his 'you're welcome' face.

"Have a lovely evening." A bulky security man growls opening the glass door.

Dim light flooded majestically from the grand chandelier in the reception. Soft soul music echoed over the chatter of beautiful people. A fantastic cream and baby pink rose wall was in the foyer. Girls were pouting and selfie-ing the shit out of it. "10-year anniversary" the large expensive looking cream and gold balloons said.

"It's a big night tonight. The restaurant is celebrating their 10th anniversary," Ruby said noticing my mind churning over the word 'anniversary'.

"Ruby are you sure we can't just get a beer and burger somewhere?" I nudge feeling a little daunted by the romantic setting ...and fat. Ruby was born for these places; she is graceful and charming – I am not. I had already told Ruby that I wanted to do NOTHING for my birthday but she persisted for weeks. I agreed to a dinner with her and Matt. She has pulled out all the stops, this place is something else.

"Shut up Ellie. Champagne and steak." Matt gasped at the

thought of trading this for some beer and burger meal deal. Leaning his elbow onto the reception desk, hand under his chin - he runs his eyes over the boy who couldn't have been past twenty-one. The boy looked flustered.

"We have a reservation for Ruby Richardson." Matt smiles seductively. The boy's face is now full tomato.

"Charmain shall take you to your table." He points at a small dark hair girl without making eye contact.

"Sorry - he's a dick." I whisper to the boy Matt had burning like a Bunsen Burner. He smiles back awkwardly.

"He's still in the closet." Matt whispers confidently.

Ruby is air kissing the manager, *Tim - General Manager*. I read his shiny gold name badge. He is small, balding, porky and clearly fancies the pants off Ruby. They obviously know each other but I can tell Ruby is in work mode.

The smell of food wafting towards us is mouth-watering. We walk through the exquisite modern dining area. Hunger is kicking in. I cannot wait to eat my body weight in delicious fancy food. I say a prayer in my head that the food portions are substantial and not equivalent to a hamster helping.

"Thanks Ruby." I hadn't wanted to do anything for my birthday but I feel happy. Happy to be out with my two-favourite people. Happy I wasn't spending what should have been my first anniversary alone.

"Promise Ellie, this is going to be the best night of your life." Ruby points in awe at a tower of champagne. God knows how many glasses all stacked up on top of one and other taking form like a Christmas tree. Champagne flowing down. Beside the champagne tower an exquisite five tier cake is displayed on a circular table decorated in delicate pinks and creams.

"Now that's some seriously cool PR." I agreed with Ruby photographing the moment. "Insta gold," she adds, taking a few more photos on her mobile.

“Tim told me; they are cutting the cake at 9PM when the owner arrives. She’s doing a speech while we all receive a Moet from the display. Gold dust to get in here tonight” Ruby looks pleased with herself.

“Let’s make it one to remember.” I smile taking a seat at our private booth. Complimentary Champagne on ice awaits us at the table. Tim really does fancy Ruby. Charmaine pours us all a glass and passes the A La Carte menus.

“Cheers guys,” I raise my glass. Heart full.

“To our kind, funny, beautiful Ellie, thirty years young. The world is brighter with you in it.” Ruby taps her glass against mine, boomeranging the moment. My eyes well up. Her words are so beautiful.

“To a memorable drunk and disorderly night,” Matt adds lowering the tone. Then his face changes. Like a vampire in transition – bright and glowing to full on pale vamp in a matter of seconds. Dead-to-me Bob has just walked into the building. And he is not alone.

Happy fucking birthday.

3

My heart races so fast. I panic – could my heart pop out my chest? I realise I need to breathe when I hear Ruby shouting for a paper bag. I'm hyperventilating like a scene from Casualty. Except I am not acting. Shit this is horrible.

God please, please don't draw attention to me mid panic.

"I a-m o-k." I finally stutter, sweating profusely. I sink low in the dark blue suede booth taking a long deep breath. I don't want Bob to see the new fat(ter) me. I pop my head up to see them being seated across the room.

"That bitch was at my wedding." I down a glass of champagne like it was cheap ass cava and pour another. The image of her hair free vagina in my marital bed still haunts my thoughts. I can be in the supermarket, casually strolling down the veg aisle then BANG, her vag is there, in the form of a small pert cauliflower. Sunday morning strolls around the park, then BANG - her vagina is there, imprinted in my mind - sucking the 'super' out of super soul Sunday. Ruby and Matt are gawking like bunnies in headlights. First at Bob, then each other, now me. My breathing is back to normal.

"You couldn't write this shit," I snap, anger now creeping up. In animation movies steam would be whistling violently out my ears.

"You couldn't." Ruby agrees shaking her head.

"Well you could. Would actually be a good story," Matt nods visualising my drama in print.

"Jok-ING! he quickly added receiving the look of death from us both.

There are moments in your life that define you as a person. Overwhelming inner strength to do the right thing. It's OK I tell myself; THIS IS OK. A list of reasons why I wanted Bob to drop dead ran through my head -

It is my birthday. √

It should have been my first wedding anniversary. √

I wasted four years falling head over heels in love. √

Invested my life savings, time and energy into getting married. √

He cheated on me with a family friend after five months of marriage. √

Made me question everything about myself. Looks, humour, rate in bed. √

Publicly embarrassed me by changing his profile picture to him and her. √

The reason why I am sitting at forty-two pound's overweight making Bridget Jones look anorexic. √

"THIS IS NOT OK, FUGILY FUCK!" I can't decide if I want to laugh or cry. I snort when I laugh. I snort when I cry. I snort chuckle, exasperated while holding my head in my hands.

"Double fugily." Matt said matter of fact.

It is true, Bob is no Tom Hardy. Matt gave him a five out of ten when he first *accidentally,* deliberately bumped into him in the supermarket. He is three inches above my five foot three with thinning blonde hair, a round face with small-ish features compensated for by his amazing body. If he walked about topless twenty-four seven, he would be much closer to a ten. Once upon a time he was my gym-obsessed gentleman so I didn't see the flaws. I loved the bones of him. Now I wish he was bones- rotting in the dirt while worms feed on his flesh. OK I don't wish him dead. But I do wish him to move the fuck out of Glasgow and delete all social media accounts.

"At least I can wear heels now." Every cloud and all that. I drink some more.

"And jokes aside Ellie, did you really want your gravestone to read here rests Ellie Hickinbottom?" Ruby reminds me of my ridiculous marital name.

"Matt burst into fits of laughter, "Ellie Hickinbottom."

Ruby takes a draw of her vape. "The fugiliest of all fugels." Stressed or drinking Ruby vapes. She is a secret vaper. I hold out my hand. She passes me the vape, I take a draw too.

"Madam you can't do that in here," advises Charmaine appearing like a puff of smoke. She points at the vape like it's a joint.

Ruby apologises with a tight-lipped smile and takes another draw as she walks away.

Fugily has to be up there with one of my fave words. The combination of fucking and ugly to strip it of vulgar-ness is genius. But be under no illusion, fugily is an insult. Unless it's one of those *hit by a bus looking dogs*– the so ugly but cute kind. Those dogs are fugily but in a complimentary way.

I am in a trance so Ruby orders me a fancy pasta dish, its name, I could not pronounce even if I tried. Matt orders three Jagerbombs. Charmain looks confused. Her face screams *one that eats in such a place does not do Jagerbombs*.

"OK what's the plan?" I ask Ruby. She always had a plan. I was hoping Tim could sneak me out the back door. Bob and his bitch are in full view of the exit. I can't decide if I want to leave without him seeing me or if I want to attract his attention? I could show him how much fun I was having without him. Perhaps I could find a man, maybe the hot barman and beg/pay him to snog me before I exit. I pop my head up again staring across the room, they were laughing. He should not be laughing! He should be drowning in guilt. Prick. Anger flares again.

"Let's enjoy our food, then stuff any remaining alcohol in our bag and get the feck out of here. I'll get one of the staff to keep them occupied while we leave." Ruby had another draw of her vape.

"OK. OK – good plan," I am a beautiful thirty- and flirty-year old woman in her prime. I do not need nor do I want Bob's attention. I wouldn't mind a snog off the hot barman though. Maybe tonight I will put my resting bitch face aside and focus on getting laid.

Thankfully the food arrives promptly. Looking, smelling and tasting amazing. Bob's presence couldn't deter me from this plate of deliciousness. My replacement, Rachel, the scrawny Barbie lookalike was no doubt munching on a salad with a sparkling water. Boring. Skinny. Bitch. *(Jealousy makes you nasty, nasty makes you fat – and all that.)*

"Got anything new going on at work when you go back?" Ruby asks trying to distract me.

"No. Same shit different day." I beam with sarcasm. I don't hate being a secretary but I don't love it either. Trouble is, I am a good secretary. It's a comfortable job.

"You need to start writing again Ellie." Ruby urges assertively. Ruby is a go-getter, passionate about people following their passions; she is my biggest inspiration.

"I should." I agree. After school I studied business at college to fill a two year 'I don't have a fucking clue what to do with my life' gap. During this blurry time other than drinking excessively I realised I love to write. I wrote about everything and anything whilst dreaming about having my own magazine column. I never got there.

"They are kissing!" Matt interrupts.

I strain my neck back to glance over. I have the urge to cry. But I won't. No, I will not cry on my birthday *again.*

"Filter Matt! Filter!" Ruby shoots Matt an evil death stare.

"My bad," he tops up our glasses.

"How's that tall, dark, sexy, fit as fuck fiancé doing?" Matt changes the subject.

"We love Jamie," I raise my glass.

"He's alright, thanks." Ruby giggles into her glass blushing.

"Set a date for dress shopping yet?" I am so excited to be Ruby's chief bridesmaid.

"Yes! Just got the boutiques booked, today actually. It's next month, will message you all the info, but tonight's not about me, what's your plans for this year Ellie? Let's set some goals for you to smash." Ruby gave me her undivided attention. My mind was fuzzy from the alcohol and the only thing I can think about is Bob sitting meters away from me.

"Hoes before bros - self-love ladies." Matt stretches his arms and flicks his hair pompously. To the outside world Matt was your eccentric, speak your mind gay with a wicked eye for fashion and an opinion on everything. To the people that really knew him he was all of the above but also the softest, loyal, most honest person that any friend could wish for. I am grateful he is mine.

Food was done. We skip dessert, deciding to finish the bubbly then make an exit for it. The restaurant is now packed, every seat filled with well dressed, deep pocketed humans. Laughter ripples throughout the warm room, couples are gushing at each other, kissing, gently stroking each other's cheeks – it was making me nauseous. A band is playing on a small, pink marble floored stage. Gentle jazz music, a middle aged, perfectly Botox-ed lady is singing with a husky memorable voice. Her voice danced beautifully over the room. The lighting dimmed further.

"I need to pee," I announce. I would not be able to hold it for much longer.

I feel intoxicated already. Mixing drinks was a no-go for me. And shots. Well that's just asking for trouble. But it is my birthday. I promise my soon-to-be pounding head I will drink a big glass of water before bed.

Ruby and I walk arms linked to the toilets. Bob is now close enough for me to see the dimples as he smiles. I find myself dropping to the floor. I crawl, to make sure he doesn't see me. Then I hit a shoe. A small black shiny shoe.

"You cannot crawl along the floor." Charmaine says while carrying Jagerbombs towards our table.

"You scare the shit out of me." I answer back staring up at her vicious scowl. She did. She has truly mastered the death stare. Impressive.

"Sorry." Ruby apologises taking my hand and helping me to my feet. The toilets are just a metre in front of us. Standing up, the room spins. I stop for a moment trying to get my balance. I stand up straight and try to focus. I close one eye to stop seeing three of everything. I do the thing I keep trying to avoid and look across to their table again. I see her crying, wrapping her arms around him.

"YES!" She's screaming holding up her left hand. A big diamond ring, sparkling like sunlight hitting the turquoise ocean. How bloody romantic. Surrounding tables are clapping, toasting the newly engaged couple.

The expression *I saw red* was never truly one I understood until this very moment. He had proposed on my thirtieth birthday, on what should have been OUR first anniversary. For a moment the only people in the room is me and them. I see the horror on Ruby's face as she tries to grab my hand.

It's too late - I am marching. On a totally un-thought out mission, resembling Mrs Trunchbull in the Matilda movie. My eyes are burning. I want to cry but my sadness acts as a catalyst for temper. My heart is racing. I clench my fists. I know I can't hit them. Can I? I know I am drunk. I know I should pee and leave. I know I will regret this. But I don't care. In this moment it feels so very right. He deserves a showing up. They both do.

They are unaware I am hovering over them. Their lips locked on each other's. I pick up their wine glasses. Red wine thankfully – I pour.

"This was £389!" Rachel screams jumping up patting her white designer top. Her face red with embarrassment as the room grows quieter. Domino effect until silence falls, even at the back of the restaurant. Some brass customers take to their feet for a better view. Bob stays sitting, jaw hitting the table. I start on an uncontrollable non structured rant. Shouting and crying through my words and snorts.

"Oh, and I lied. It doesn't make you an Olympian style Greek god having a small penis it just means you have a small fucking penis. She is only after you for your money, heard you got a big bonus at work - clearly, she is out of your league...and that IS NOT a compliment Barbie – it just means you are technically a prostitute. ...AND HOW THE FUCK CAN YOU EAT CARBS???" I scream looking at her pasta dish then her waist. How unfair.

"Oh Ellie, you have always talked – and ate - too much." Bob smirks arrogantly patting his head with a napkin and pointing at my stomach with his other hand.

I pull my hand back and punch him with all the force I could muster. His nose starts to bleed. My hand hurts.

"Ouch mother fucker." I shake off my aching hand. I should have kicked him in the balls.

I feel dizzy and sick. I've drunk too much, too quick. My mouth is possessed by some warrior alien, hell bent on getting every last issue off her chest. I see the security guards entering as I am still shouting at Bob. Everything is in slow motion. I lean down to itch my ankle. My bangle catches on my heel. I STUMBLE...I FALL...I CRASH....

I am the star of my own horror movie – the photogenic, insta-gold champagne tower is tumbling down round about me while everyone stops what they are doing and stares. I say a silent drunken prayer that I am hallucinating.

Maybe I should have insisted on staying at home…

I ponder the thought watching the glasses fall and shatter around the five-tier love heart cake I had been admiring an hour earlier - I pass out.

4

My mouth is dry. So dry. The metallic taste is curdling my stomach – or it could be the basin filled with vomit. I want to hurl *again.* My head is pounding. I can just about open my eyes. I squint at the unfamiliar surroundings. It smells damp. Concrete walls, bars on a locked gate. A blue itchy blanket at my feet.

A tall, ruggedly handsome man in uniform pulls a bunch of keys from his pocket and unlocks the gate keeping me contained. He hands me a plastic cup of water. I down it like a ravishing beast, vowing never to mix drinks again. I feel like I've Zumba danced around the desert.

"I am so very sorry," I point to the basin. *Dear god please have ensured that I was on my own when this happened.* I panic discreetly checking my jumpsuit and the bed. It is a total pain in the arse to take my jumpsuit on and off for the toilet. Fortunately – I did not piss myself. Well done me.

"Let's go Ms Benson" he speaks kindly but firmly. He looks tired. Must be the end of his shift. I would have loved him naked in my bed but THIS – this is disastrous. WAKING UP IN JAIL, has to be the lowest point in my life. Totally tops the time I woke up in Botanic gardens naked. Or fell asleep on the train and ended up hours in the wrong direction of home. I feel worse than the time I stole a small jar of coffee from Tesco express, purely because I forgot my purse and could not be fucked doing the journey home and back. I really needed caffeine. *Holy shit, I am a bad person.* I feel like Eleanor Shellstroop in the Netflix comedy The Good Place. This is FORK FORK FORKING AWFUL!!!

Fear starts to consume my hungover brain – it is working overtime to piece the night together. My own shit storm of a jigsaw puzzle. Flashbacks flood my mind - flickering on and off like a glow torch in need of new triple A's. I hold my now, swollen, slightly bruised right hand. I remember. *I punched Bob. Shit. I actually punched the twat. In front of everyone.*

Day one into my thirtieth year and I exceed my mother's expectations. Although the actual words have not come out her mouth, *I know* she blames me for Bob's affair. Telling me, I should have cooked more and been an all-round better housewife. I'll admit, I am a messy bitch, but he knew that prior to putting a ring on my finger. As a proud feminist all for gender equality, I made him do the dishes every other night. Should I blame washing up liquid for catapulting my man into the bed of another woman?

"Did you bring me here?" I ask flirtatiously noticing no wedding ring. He is so hot. Maybe he is gay. Don't get the gay vibe. Wish Matt was here. Think I may still be drunk.

Instant regret for trying to flirt as I catch my reflection in a window. Ellie the shameful slut. Bra visible, boobs pushed up, hair a riot, makeup smudged. Heel of my shoe broke.

"Heel of my shoe! Oh god. The champagne tower!" I remember. Horrified. Embarrassment cripples my thoughts. My face lights up the same fiery red as my hair - I can actually feel the heat evaporating from my cheeks. Cringe with a capital C.

"Yes, I brought you here after a medic helped you." Hot policeman points to my ankle.

"Butterfly stitch." He continues with paperwork. An older lady with white poker straight hair and judgmental piercing eyes is typing behind the desk. I pay my tax lady. I have well and truly paid one nights B & B in this establishment. I'll presume the cup of water was breakfast. I think these thoughts, but do not have the balls to say it out loud.

"I am not a prostitute." I decide to say in my poshest voice giving her a royal wave. She looks at me like I am the spawn of

Satan.

"You are being issued with a restraining order in regards to Robert Hickinbottom and Rachel Henderson," he hands me a letter.

"You have to be fucking shitting me?" I snap, grabbing the paperwork to read it. *Bob ruined my life and I am getting a restraining order.*

"Nope - no shits," he half smiles. I can't work out if he is joking. I don't laugh. Though I may throw up.

"Listen - he hasn't pressed charges; neither did the restaurant thanks to your friend. A restraining order is a civil order and does not give you a criminal record." Hot policeman hands me a pen and points for me to sign.

"How very generous of him." I reply with heavy sarcasm. *He is lucky I am not charging him for adultery.*

Ruby on the other hand. I owe the biggest apology to date. The restaurant – her manager friend. Double shit.

I am going home to put on my onesie, register for online supermarket shopping and never leave the house again. EVER! Ellie Benson will cease to exist. Or...I could change my name, move to New Zealand and start a fresh. The new reinvented moi shall pose as a tee total, tofu munching, yoga loving, moon worshiper. Yes, I like that plan. I'll stick with Plan A until everything is in place to put plan B into motion.

I take my bag and fumble inside, my house keys, lipstick and a half-eaten sandwich. No mobile or purse. Shit, shit, shit. Too embarrassed to ask hot policeman if he knows the whereabouts of my essential personal belongings, I stay quiet. Once I move to New Zealand, I will renounce my mobile,and delete all social media accounts. Life problems solved.

I hang my head low like when my mother used to give me a telling off as a child. I stare up meeting his dark inviting eyes. He looks like he wants to laugh. Don't blame him, I'd laugh at me too.

"Thank you." I smile handing him back the pen. He ushers me toward the door. We walk silently down a corridor. He strides in front distracting my mind for a moment. I notice his muscular shoulders and arms through his white shirt. His long legs, tight buttocks. Pretty much walking perfection with his killer jawline and dark messy hair. The sexiest part, he clearly is not aware of just how gorgeous he is.

"Through the door to reception and you're free to go," he smiles standing aside, hand pointing to the exit.

I hold my hand out. He smirks but kindly shakes it to avoid further humiliation. Why the fuck did I go for a handshake? *Thank you very much for arresting me officer, it was a pleasure spending the night in your cell.*

I feel my face burning up again. I stay quiet turning towards the door.

"And Miss Benson. Off the record, he deserved that punch."

I pause with my hand on the door. Grateful for his words. Shame melting ever so slightly.

I turn to say thank you. But he is already half way up the corridor.

Outside I see a grey estate parked in full view of the police stations exit. My dad gives me a jolly wave inhaling a cigarette deeply, eyes closed as he blows the puff of smoke out the window. His thick white hair perfectly side combed. My dad has been a non-smoker for almost five years now – *if you ask my mother.* "Thanks Dad." I open the passenger door and climb in. I take a cigarette and light it. It has been a while. Two months, three weeks and five days *not that I am counting.* We both smoke in silence down to the last draw.

"Sorry Dad." I push up the visor to escape my reflection.

"Sorry for?" He starts the engine and puts on his thick black rimmed specs.

"Everything." I sigh dropping my head into my hands. After a few moments he lets out a heartfelt chuckle. An inappropriate belly laugh in my moment of despair.

"Losing Bob is the best thing that ever happened to you. He is a boring little man with an ego that could sink the Titanic. I raised a glass when I heard you had left him." He nodded turning up Radio 2.

I smile. Looking at my dad, Albert Benson. His navy woolly jumper pressed against the steering wheel courtesy of his belly. I notice in particular his deep-set wrinkles - frown and laughter lines etched in his weather-beaten face. I realise in this very moment that time doesn't stop. Obviously, I have always realised time moves on, I am not an idiot, not all the time. But it's so easy to forget that we are growing older one day at a time. Time is precious. I ponder on my intellectual philosophy as the sun shines through the windscreen. I know in time I may laugh about this very weekend, but not today. Today I am overcome with, *the fear*!

We drive in silence back to my flat. Both smoking one more cigarette each. On route we pass the people I so want to be, *I am going to be.* The Sunday morning joggers, the women that plan and prep all their nutritious meals for the week ahead. The size tens.

"Don't be over thinking anything Ellie," my dad parks the car outside the entrance to my flat and points to the dashboard. My mobile and purse are both there. I am so relieved. Slightly less anxious now I don't have to cancel and order new bankcards or think about the whole drama of getting a new phone. And, I am at a very high level in bubble pop. Would take me months to get back to my high rankings.

"Matt and Ruby did try to get you home last night, but you wouldn't wake up. Your mum called Ruby when you didn't answer her text," he laughs again. My dad had enjoyed the drama.

It gave him time off from Nancy to smoke a full pack of Richmond's.

We sit in silence for a moment before my dad laughs again. He jumps out and strolls round to open my door with a joyful smile before hugging me tightly.

"Think you'll be needing these more than me today," he laughs again, handing over the remains of his cigarette pack. I hug him tighter. I wish I could bottle these hugs for whenever I need them. A tear trickles down my cheek.

"I love you Dad." I whisper. We don't tell each other often enough. But today feels like a good day to say I love you.

He kisses me gently on the head reminding me to shower as I smell of vomit.
"If your mother catches a whiff of any smoke, I AM blaming you." He toots the horn and speeds off.

I stumble up two flights of stairs to find Leo leaving my flat. He makes no effort to hide his amusement at the sight of me.

I forget for a split second about last night and march in. Clearly Matt was in despair at my horrific ordeal. I'm banged up in a cell and he's banging someone he shouldn't, in my house!

"MATT!" I scream throwing the door open. I am going to confiscate his key.

He doesn't even look up. He's sprawled out on the sofa in *my* pink fluffy dressing gown, in *my* unicorn slippers watching something on his mobile. Hand over his wide-open mouth.

"EHH HELLO!" I shout slumping down on the sofa next him punching his arm.

"Fuck – Ellie." Matt sit's up straight and turns his mobile upside down. He takes my hands in his and looks me straight in the eye.

"Don't freak out…" he starts.

I'm freaking out that Matt is advising me not to freak out. What else could have gone wrong?

"Last night, the punch – the fall – the security guards.... it's gone viral. You are racking up more views per minute than if Kayne announced he was getting a penis enlargement." A very hung-over, tired Matt starts crying. He always cries after Leo leaves. These are not tears of sympathy. This is tears of deflection, crying about his problem but kidding on it's about mine.

This is bad, very, very bad. I must have been Hitler's assistant in my last life and karma is finally catching up with me. Immigrating to New Zealand will have to be put into motion sooner than I thought.

I want to cry but I can't. I am paralysed with The Fear!

Who knew rock bottom had a basement!

5

The door knocks. I drag myself from the comfort of my bed as someone thuds it again and again. I have spent the weekend in bed binge watching hours of Richard Attenborough. A Birthday box set from my cousin Joel that I had no intention of ever watching. Thank you, Joel for your surprisingly enjoyable educational gift. It served as a great distraction to *The Fear,* that is still consuming me.

“COMING!!!” I scream. I am sore, still hungover and hungry.

“Thanks.” I sign for a letter. I can’t decide if the young, spotty, postman is looking at me with empathy or disgust. I shut the door realising I am wearing nothing but my oversized comfy grey bra and pants. Rolls of stomach on display. Must have been disgust. *Sorry dude.*

I open the letter praying it’s a gigantic inheritance cheque from some long lost relative.

Dear Ms Benson,

On Saturday the 2nd of May, your actions in our establishment caused monetary damage as outlined below, (rounded off to the nearest pound).

£1420 – Champagne tower

£899 – Bespoke anniversary love cake

£620 – Cost to cover complementary meals/drinks for tables that had glass splinters fired their way.

£345 – Deep clean of carpets

Total =£3284

Despite being verbally abused on your departure we are not

pressing charges, thanks to your friend Ruby fully explaining the situation. However, as I am sure you will agree – you ELLIE BENSON are liable to pay the £3284. Or legal action will be taken.

We expect this to be paid in full by Saturday the 13th of June. Payment methods are shown over the page. It is fine to pay in one lump sum or instalments.

Due to the unexpected, alarming coverage your outburst received, as a gesture of good will the restaurant owner has arranged for six weeks' therapy (free of charge) with one of the most sought-after therapists in Scotland. All information required is over page.

I appreciate your co-operation, and hope you understand, given the awful press we received for our 10-year anniversary (as a result of YOUR actions) you are not welcome at our establishment again. EVER.

Kind Regards

Timothy Branson

General Manager

Well fuck me.

6

Therapy Session One – Thursday 7th of May

Birthday Balance - £3284

Instagram Followers – 242 (accepted mums friend request)

Happiness Ranking – 0/10

I shower, turning the heat lower than normal. I feel faint. My body still aches, I have bruises on my thighs and buttocks. Now more yellowish in colour than the purplish blue they were five days earlier - result of my drunken tumble. I took a pair of scissors and cut the wire to my BT (ridiculous I know) and my mobile data has run out. For once I am not complaining. Although I totally forgot that cutting of my internet would stop my Netflix and Amazon Prime, hence my gratitude for cousin Joel's DVD box set to distract me from the fucking disaster that was my birthday.

I cannot bring myself to watch the YouTube video and have every intention of deleting all social media accounts once my mobile data renews. I am dreading going back to work on Monday. Maybe they will be clueless. I can only pray.

At least my hangover has finally departed. I know this as I am considering rewarding myself with wine tonight. It is 7AM. I have my first obligatory therapy session. The owner was planning on pressing charges, however, Ruby's theatrical performance regarding my mental health due to Bob's betrayal was Grammy worthy. Matt said she gave Angelina Jolie a run for her money. So, the owner insisted a therapist could work wonders on me. *Free,* therapy sessions as a smoke screen to soften the blow that I have to pay £3284 within six weeks. May have to order mask, fake gun and consider robbery.

I should have stayed at home – thee most expensive birthday to date. It's all Bob's fault. I hate him. I don't need therapy. I am fine. Just a tad bitter. But I am going, because I *have* to.

Due to utter embarrassment I haven't ventured further than the corner shop since my overnight stint in jail. But today I have no option – off to therapy it is! The sky is empathising with my mood; although warm, it is dull and damp. The sky looks sad, like me. I forgot my umbrella too. Typical - given it's that sort of rain that seems like nothing but then soaks you through to your pants. I am sweating and I've only walked five minutes. I throw my hair up in a bun when I reach the bus stop, realising the time spent bonding with my curling wand was in vain. Frizz had set in. Finger, live electric socket – you get the picture. For the first time, in as long as I can remember, I have left my additional limb alone - on my bedside table. Not that I would have insta storied this moment anyway, caption; *Frizz monster in oversized black rain coat en route to be cured #thirtyintherapy*. I am a miserable cow. There is no denying it.

I decided against the black wig, sunglasses and hideous leopard print coat suggested by Matt – and opted to squeeze into my slim black jeans, red converse and black top branded with #BESTLIFE. The slogan intended for the therapist to realise I am OK. Surely someone that should have a top branded with #SHITLIFE wouldn't be walking about bold as brass with #BESTLIFE? I reflect on my mumble jumble thoughts and realise my thinking is bullshit. Instant regret for wearing this top to an obligatory therapy session. I decide I will turn it inside out before actually seeing the doctor. Sarcasm is the lowest form of wit after all. So, they say. I myself am partial to a dose of sarcasm but this is not the time nor the place.

It is hot on the bus, and busy. I graciously give my seat to an elderly lady, even though she looks physically in better shape than me. I'm grateful she appeared as I was just about to loosen my jean button for fear it may go pop. It's only a ten-minute journey into town so I am happy to stand, and do something I haven't done in a long time. I observe - I people watch. Normally I would be checking every social media app on my iPhone, then WhatsApp and perhaps a quick game of Bubble Pop. I realise very quickly I am not the only person people watching. A group of young teenagers dressed in tight tracksuits and baseball caps are staring at me and their mobiles, whispering amongst each other. Maybe I am imagining it. Maybe not.

"On yerself hen, get him telt. Best Life. Belter!" He gives me a thumbs up and a big wink before taking a slurp of Irn Bru. I feel my cheeks turning pink but I give a lame thumb up back whispering "Yayyy." I am most definitely buying a bottle of wine tonight. The young man with the yellow neon cap has confirmed it.

"Fucking small penis..." Another boy smacks a hand on his thigh. Then they all go into fits of laughter. Hysterically cackling uncontrollably like a bunch of hyenas. I presume this would be the moment I catch my bangle on my heel. I actually wish I had worn Matt's suggested disguise. My vibrant hair and rounded arse are just too distinct. Maybe I should dye my hair. That's it! What colour would match green eyes and pasty skin - I will think about it.

The bus stops. I practically run off. My face crimson. Ruby had to fly to London on a work trip. She has given me strict instructions to be honest with the therapist. She is so adamant that the therapist will help me, I am beginning to think she had deliberately orchestrated it all. I'm tired and over thinking things.

I arrive outside the building; a brass plaque reads *Dr Kendrick. Nothing is impossible.* Stupid quote really. Obviously jumping out a plane ten thousand feet off the ground was impossible, if you did not own a parachute. The office was in the Merchant City and had won awards. Once inside the main entrance I see the toilets. *Thank you, toilet location!* I quickly run to turn my #BESTLIFE t-shirt inside out. I take down my hair to cover the label. I couldn't quite decide which would be dissected as worse, my slogan of choice or leaving home with clothes on the wrong way. Fuck it, time was no longer a luxury I had. I cannot be late. Once in the reception area I have a good look around. Very fancy indeed - all glass with different shaped velvet sofas and seats. Reds, yellows and oranges. Warm. Inviting. It smelt like Christmas. I notice a candle burning. Sweet Fig and Cinnamon. I would have opted for the fresh cotton scent myself.

"Miss Benson!" greets an over enthusiastic girl from behind the glass desk. She looks happy. The sort of happy you would presume to be after paying for therapy.

"Ellie, please." I smile walking towards her.

"Dr Kendrick will be with you soon. Tea, coffee, water?" she asks.

Wine, Magners, gin –.

"Water would be appreciated," I said warmly knowing alcohol would not be an option at 9:30AM on a Thursday. I have three days left of my holiday and instead of lying in bed. I am here. A consequence due to my actions. My actions suck.

The happy girl came back with my water and showed me to another door when a buzzer went.

"Ellie, please come in," greeted a short, slender woman much younger than I was expecting. My age, possibly younger. This unnerved me. Though, she was dressed as I had expected – smart and classy. She looked understated yet sophisticated in a plain grey pencil skirt and a white silk blouse. Teamed with the footwear you would expect from someone charging two hundred pounds an hour - Black Louboutin's.

"You're American" I say. More of a statement than a question. Her brown hair is pulled back in a simple ponytail.

"That I am. Chicago born and raised. Lacy Kendrick," she smiles pointing to a comfy mustard coloured sofa.

"Before we begin Ellie, please know this is a safe space, anything you say is completely confidential."

"Even if I say my ex-husband is dead, and stuffed under my bed" I joke.

"Is he?" she asks - face poker straight. I notice a huge diamond ring. Square cut and screamingly expensive.

"No, no he is not. Very much alive," I smile. *Help me God.*

She takes out her notepad and pen and sits elegantly in a black swivel chair across from me.

"So how are you feeling today then Ellie?" Doc asks writing something on her pad. What, I don't know as I haven't even spoken. How am I feeling? Doc, as I will refer to her in my head remains quiet, waiting patiently for my answer.

"Erm, not one hundred percent but I'm not ready to jump off a building." I joke breaking eye contact.

"On a scale of one to ten where would you rank yourself on happiness?" her words cut me like a knife. Happiness. Happy. To be happy. Genuine feeling of light sunshine, not a pit wrenching emptiness full of hurt and betrayal.

"Zero," I say honestly after a few moments.

"Lovely," she smiles scribbling something down. It wasn't 'zero' it seemed more of a sentence. Maybe was along the lines of *miserable unhappy cow – session one, let her realise how unhappy she is.*

"Lovely?" I snap, my eyes welling up. How on earth could she take this as *lovely*.

"Well Ellie Benson - the only way is up!"

7

I feel surprisingly lighter after therapy. Sadly, not literally or Dr Kendrick would be charging by the minute. I had cried, I had laughed, I had shouted - session one has confirmed, in *my words,* that I am merely a fat hamster. Eating, shitting and sleeping as nature requires – whilst running on a wheel, repeating the same patterns and expecting to arrive at a new destination.

On the plus side, I feel lighter having burdened a total stranger with my emotional baggage. On the downside - I feel pathetic realising I am a warthog, bathing in a mud pool of self-pity. With that said, I have decided to do a Ruby and go full arse cheeks into the next six weeks. I will do everything the Doc tells me. I am jumping off the hamster wheel, washing off the mud – ready to wave bye bye to rock bottom's basement.

I don't like the word *homework.* It makes me feel nauseous thinking of high school. The detentions I received due to lack of homework gave poor Nancy a red face on parents' evenings. Especially when they produced Matt's letters with her perfectly forged signature backing up my excuse. I actually softened the blow for her. One could have expected a teenage rebel to grow into a dysfunctional thirty-year-old divorcee.

Nevertheless, I had homework. And I was going to do it this time. No excuses. No procrastinating. I was going to follow the simple steps I had been tasked:

Step one - Buy fresh notepad and pen you love.

Step two – Write down five things you have never done, but want to. Depressingly Tom Hardy doesn't count. Seemingly not an achievable/realistic goal.

Step three – Before bed write a list of things you are grateful for that day/in general. Gratitude is my new attitude.

Step Four – Complete one of step two's list every week.

Step Five – Repeat step three every single day. Writing DITTO DOES NOT COUNT

I have all the steps written down on a plain piece of paper. I fold it in half, then again, stuffing it in my jean pocket.

"See you soon Ellie" Dr Kendrick smiles. She opens the door appearing pleased that she's reduced me to tears. *Sadist.*

"Next Thursday." I smile. Unless I win the lottery. If good fortune is to come my way, I will be sipping strawberry daiquiris in the Bahamas with a gigantic bowl of deep-fried mozzarella bites. Bliss.

It is just after 11AM, I say goodbye to Miss Happy Pants at reception, visit the loo to turn my top the correct way and dig my sunglasses from my new black tote bag. The sun is shining through the drizzle, lighting the sky up with a beautiful rainbow. I stroll up through George Square, marginally avoiding being shat on by a pigeon. A toddler is having more fun feeding the birds than eating the flaky sausage roll his mother just gave him. He's a cute little thing. Flop of blonde hair and chubby cheeks. I want kids. I wonder if I will be able to keep a man long enough to impregnate me. Bob was always so cautious; I was on the pill and he used condoms. Now I think of it, probably so I didn't catch Rachel's crabs. I am fully aware my biological clock is ticking; my mother reminds me of it daily. Normally by a not so indiscreet text.

Mrs Freeman's daughter just had a baby. They called him Fred. I am jealous Mum x

Readers Digest, P49 tips on falling pregnant. For when you get a man Mum x

Hope I live long enough to be a gran, Love you Mum x

The latest -

By the time I was 30 you were 10, Just a thought, happy birthday Mum x

The downside of being an only child. Wish I had a sister that got pregnant with triplets straight out of high school. I bet you fancy Nancy wouldn't be stressing about my ovaries then. My *sister* would have kept our mother occupied with puke and dirty nappies and I, divorced, failure of a daughter, would be off the hook.

I stroll. I am in no rush, my only quest before meeting Matt for dinner is to buy a notebook and pen. I trail around a few different places before finding myself in a Waterstones book shop– thanks to a very pleasant woman working in Greggs. After seeing bird feeding toddler with a sausage roll it prompted me to get one of their delicious vegan ones. OK two. Randomly the girl serving came around and hugged me. Queue and all. I obviously welcomed the kind attention knowing it was merely a case of mistaken identity. I didn't want to embarrass the poor girl. She asked what I was up too, so I told her my shopping requirements. I can see why she pointed me in this direction.

Who would have thought there would be so much choice when it came to notepads? I had never paid attention before. After a solid thirty minutes going through all the stationery and notebooks of every shape, size and colour, I narrow it down to two.

In my left hand I have 'BE THE BEST VERSION OF YOU!' in bold white letters on top of a sparkling gold cover. Love it. Maybe it's a sign to read Ruby's birthday gift.

In my right – '*UNFUCK YOURSELF*' in black italic writing on a plain white cover. Love it also. Simple and to the point. A slogan I can relate too. With my life in turmoil, some would say I am *fucked.* Not the naked, passionate, orgasmic kind of *fucked.* The plain and simple your life is shit, *fucked.* And that is not the sort of *fucked* I want to be.

My lengthy decision-making progress is normally saved for the liquor isle, but I am surprisingly enjoying this. Shopping usually has the same appeal to me as drinking bleach - but that is normally because it involves me trying on clothes and looking in the mirror.

I love both A5 sized notepads, so I decide to splash the cash. I select a black ball point pen that appears to have been dipped in gold glitter and make my way through the shoppers to the till.

"Thank you very much." I say switching £22.99 for two notepads and a pen.

"You're welcome," a man replies robotically. He looks bored. *I was actually thanking my credit card that was paying for the extravagant but worthy present to me, from me.* He hands me a receipt without making eye contact.

"Next," he mumbles unenthusiastically. My cue to leave.

I make my way to the escalators reflecting on my customer service experience. Donny, as his name tag advised, was not rude but nor was, he polite. The man clearly hated his job, negative vibes oozed out his pores like puss. He was miserable. He reminded me of ...me, on a Monday morning. I push the thought of emails, coffee runs and the never-ending ringing switchboard to the back of my mind. I still have three days until I am back to the shithole that pays my rent. I refuse to give it head space, I dump my work thoughts in the corner of my brain alongside Bob and my horrendous birthday night and saunter towards the underground.

My mind wanders back to my morning bus journey. Face turning red at the thought. Ruby had promised me she would do everything in her power to get the embarrassing video of me off YouTube. I still can't bring myself to watch it.

Maybe if I looked like the sexy squad marching past the window, I wouldn't have minded being uploaded on the internet for the world to ridicule. The girls that just walked past had their heads held high, shoulders back, walking purposefully – immaculately dressed with just the right amount of make-up.

They walked like the sun came out just to shine on their day. Ironically, the other week I posted a quote on my Instagram page.

"Nothing sexier than a girl that has her shit together!" #ONIT #THISISME #ELLIEB

I do not have my shit together. My shit's been blasted into a billion, trillion pieces and scattered across the planet. The quote was posted purely for Bob's creepy old cousin that still follows me. He double tapped it so I knew he saw it. I had hoped at the next family gathering he would casually mention to Bob that I am doing well.

I am mastering the art of dissecting what my peoples' posts actually mean. Most commonly people post total and utter BS, fabrications of their reality - guilty! And often, as I have displayed, some posts are directed at just one of your followers. But instead of sending a text or DM to that *one* person, we casually message it to everyone in hope that *one* person gets the picture. Soon we will be able to get a BA on the politics of social media. However, my drunken rampage did not paint the picture of a girl that has her shit together so it was a total fucking waste of a post.

I hate myself. No, I don't. Yes, I do - My mind plays ping pong – I find the line between self-love and self-hate very thin. Doc said I must pay myself a compliment anytime I have a negative thought about myself. Then charge this compliment by going over my gratitude journal.

You have good taste in notebooks Ellie. I compliment myself taking the rudest one out my bag. Now seemed like as good a time as any to think about five new things I wanted to do whilst completing therapy. I open a blank page and write in my neatest handwriting.

I intend to do the following by Saturday the 13th of June. In no particular order of priority...

1 – Get a TATTOO. Of what, I have no clue. Not my name, or a butterfly. Must think about appropriate branding for my body. And where to get it. Note: Google least painful places to get a tattoo when back online. And check costings.

2– Get a SPRAY TAN. Booked to get several times before then cancelled for fear therapist will have heart attack on seeing me naked. Book tan and make commitment not to cancel. Hilary from work looks undeniably slimmer when tanned. Remember this.

3 - Take a YOGA CLASS. Not the one in a sauna or paramedics may be escorting me home.

4– Go to the CINEMA on my OWN. Enough said. Go me.

5 – Go on a BLIND DATE. Have always thought this seemed romantic but have never had the balls to do it.

I put my pen down and read over my list. I smile for the first time in days. Dare I say, I am actually quite excited.

8

"Shit happens." Matt says matter of fact. He is not taking no for an answer, adamant I am watching my epic fails sensation. At this very moment.

"And your internet is all back up and running," Matt dangles a key in my face. My eyes and mouth widened. I had taken my key off him – punishment for sleeping with Leo in my flat, while I was otherwise occupied in jail.

"I had a copy made ages ago. Just in case I lost it and you went ape. You are welcome!" He says proudly signalling for me to zip my lips.

"Sit." Matt orders pointing to the cosy corner sofa in the coffee shop. He locked the front door and turned the sign to closed.

I feel fearful, anxious, embarrassed, guilty, shameful to name a few emotions buzzing around inside - the thought of watching my drunken antics is making me squirm. Matt flips open his slim laptop; I almost choke on my gulp of coffee before bursting into laughter.

"It's not mine," he snubs unfazed. He clicks on the video saved to his desktop.

"Gross." I squirm at the cartoon cock with shaven balls.

"Thought you might have forgotten what one looks like." He nudged squeezing beside me.

"Fuck you!"

"Sorry hen, you're not my type."

Then I saw me. I wish it was still on the cartoon cock. A zoomed in picture of my face, red with anger holding two wine glasses above the heads of kissing Bob and Rachel. The video filmed by some arsehole spectator captioned my moment –

"FAT RED HEAD GIVES EX A ROASTING – watch till end to see her epic fail." What a charming little C U next Tuesday. I hope he or she catches an STD that has them itching till it bleeds. Did they really need to shame the fat?

"Over two million views already." Matt speaks with excitement. I want to hit him.

Kill me now. It must be circulating on social media like wild fire. I really am going to need to starve myself and change my hair colour. *Fat red hair soon to be skinny blonde in attempt to salvage her dignity.*

"Your face is priceless," chuckles Matt.

"At least try and scrape together a shred of sympathy." I beg wishing Ruby was with me and not kissing arse at some bloggers lunch.

"Ready?" he hovers over the play button.

"NO!" I close my eyes.

"Great!" Matt hit play.

I peak one eye open. I'm filmed from the left. Side on. Not my best angle, but it could have been worse. Rachel's back is to the camera, completely missing her face. Karma I am losing faith in you! Music has been edited in, the jaws soundtrack building up the suspense as I raise the wine glasses above their locked lips. It then goes into slow mo – the wine appears to be fighting gravity taking an extra five seconds to splash all over them.

Boom - action. It zooms in on Bob's shocked face. His mouth wide open, then goes back to slow mo as he shakes the wine from his hair like the bath scene from Beethoven. Then back to my smug, happy face. I punch the air with joy.

An emoji appears in the top right-hand corner of the video. DING. The bell from a boxing match sounds and a winning point goes under the dancing girl emoji.

Then I rant, I can vaguely remember the words I spewed from the wide hole on my head. It becomes apparent I am not speaking I am shouting.

"You cheating, wanking piece of shit" I start off with completely ignoring Rachel's screeches that I ruined her expensive silk shirt.

"Enough Ellie," Bob says quietly but firmly. I knew that low tone all too well. *Enough Ellie*, no more bread. *Enough Ellie*, no more wine. *Enough Ellie*, watch your language. It hit me like a bolt of lightning from the almighty Thor himself– I had strived so hard to be the Ellie that Bob wanted me to be, I had lost the Ellie I really was.

"Oh, and I lied. It doesn't make you an Olympian style Greek god having a small penis it just means you have a small fucking penis. She is only after you for your money - clearly, she is out of your league...and that is not a compliment Barbie – it just means you are technically a prostitute. ...."

In the video the dancing girl emoji appears again. I now have three points under her.

"Oh Ellie, you have always talked – and ate - too much." Bob smirks arrogantly patting my belly with his index finger.

Now there is a male dancing emoji that has just received a point following the loud DING.

I watch in frustration as I see Bob basking in the joy of my weight gain. He ate all the right foods, in all the right portions. I didn't. I have never been a gym bunny; he knew it from day one. I was his secretary – he knew my top drawer was filled with lots of sugary snacks. Nevertheless, despite my bad food choices he pursued me like a project - insisting I swap Cream Eggs for kale. I married him with my full heart. Then he cheated on me. *He left me*. There was no begging for forgiveness, or bulging apologetic sorry, he just left. He made me look like a fool. He was in the wrong, IS IN the wrong. Not me.

I watch him laugh at my blank sad expression, before telling Rachel I am jealous because I do not look like her. Bob gets another point for his seriously low insult. God damn you stupid dancing emoji. The video is basically portraying a boxing ring, DING top left corner for Bob. DING top right corner for me. *What sicko composed this?*

"Best bit," Matt's jumps up bouncing around like Rocky Balboa.

"Funny," I roll my eyes.

It is now I punch him. I punch, clenched fist, with every fibre of my being. The same right hook I got taught at Boxercise. I went for a block of six weeks, then Love Island started. I opted for the sofa, cheap bubbly and watching the sexy Megan Barton Hanson instead of bouncing around like a red sweaty tomato.

My points go up by three. Wow I can really throw a punch. No wonder my hand is still sore! Bob is holding his nose, blood sprouting into a napkin. Rachel is screaming. The combination of blood and red wine splattered everywhere – fit for a scene on CSI. In the background Charmaine is there shouting for security. No doubt blaming the Jagerbombs.

"Crazy bitch!" Bob shouts, also screaming for security. I am not an advocate of violence but I clearly show no remorse.

"Round of applause for your flawless make up!" Matt claps loudly as they zone in on me grinning like the Cheshire cat. Then, of course an emoji of a ridiculous smiling cat flashes on my face for a few seconds. *What is wrong with people!*

Matt pauses the video.

"See not so bad," he nods still mimicking Rocky. Badly.

"What about the last forty seconds?"

He twists his face in horror. "That, my friend, is the bad bit."

"My dignity is already flushed down the rat invested sewer. Fuck it. Hit play."

Rachel is now gushing around Bob gathering napkins to help stop the blood. I reach down to rub my ankle. My new heels had been chaffing against my skin. I have on a large bunch of hooped gold bangles. Large enough that they catch on my heel. I try to stand. I can't my arm is caught on my heel. I hop, I hobble. Not a good look. Security guards fast approaching. The three folds of my stomach is there for all too see. I look fat, fatter than I think I actually am. I have instant regret for my daily binge on carbs. Mr and Mrs carbohydrate along with their million carbs kids have fermented nicely around my belly and arse. My bad. The camera leaves me momentarily and shines on Rachel's face beaming like a child on Christmas morning. Even with the red wine staining her blonde locks and white top she still looks annoyingly pretty. Karma we are done.

"Who's laughing now bitch!" She cheers. Another point to Bobs corner.

Then it's back on me. Slow motion kicks in again. I am hopping, bangles caught around my heel, I'm stumbling backwards towards the champagne tower.

"You OK?" Matt asks semi sincere giving the sheer terror on my face.

I can't answer. My hands are over my eyes; I'm peeking through my fingers. I feel sick.

I fall buttocks first towards the glasses towered like a Christmas tree some security guard grabs my free arm to stop me actually landing on the glass shattering down but my foot knocks a glass from the bottom of the pyramid. The security men jump back, pulling my arm. I hop, stumble falling to the ground, lying on my back. Arse in the air. The laughing emoji's fluttering up the left side of the video. Then the champagne tower starts to tumble, crashing down, splinters flying everywhere. People screaming. Some laughing. My arse still in the air. I unhook my bangles; my legs drop on the floor like led weights. I close my eyes.

Then points start DING, DING, DING, DING up in Bobs corner

until eventually it appears like bomb has gone off on the video.

THE END, Thanks for watching guys - subscribe for more real-life epic fails.

I run to the coffee shop's toilet and throw up.

9

I feel numb, I sprawl over the sofa. The door is locked, the curtains are closed and the wine is poured but my mind just can't stop churning over the video. I keep getting flashbacks of the night, which is causing my heart to race, my palms to sweat and my breath to quicken. I focus on the rainbow canvas on my wall and take a big deep breath, saying each colour out loud till my breath returns to normal. I fucking hate technology and the twat that uploaded the video. This era sucks.

I have managed to shower and change into my black and gold star pyjamas. And, I did some basic chores. I washed clothes, I had too – I had no clean clothes, bikini bottoms had been substituted for pants for the past two days. I took the rubbish out too, including the mouldy cucumber, peppers, lemons and something I could not identify. I spend far too much time watching healthy recipes on Instagram, the ones with the time lapsed videos that make healthy, mouth-watering plates of deliciousness. Then I find myself marching into the supermarket with the required shopping list only to find the ingredients smelly and mouldy in my fridge a week later.... Ah well - it's the thought that counts.

Maybe I really should bugger off to New Zealand. I pick up my carefully chosen new notebook, deciding I would do what Dr Kendrick tells me and write down what I am grateful for every night. If someone had told me to write a list of everything I didn't like or a list of negatives about myself my pen would be leaving smoke.

First excerpt in my gratitude journal. Gratitude is my new attitude.

Friends, even though slightly unorthodox and rude I am grateful I have Matt and Ruby. People who have my best interests at heart.

Food and water. Sometimes I really forget how lucky I am to walk to a tap and just have instant access to clean cold water to drink.

Bubble baths! Again - thank you water! And thank you to Epsom bath salts and lavender oil for contributing to my relaxing bath time.

The corner shop. Even though slightly over priced, friendly Mr Ahmed has saved me a bus journey to the supermarket on many occasions.

My parents. For different reasons. But grateful for their love.

My hair. I like my hair. Grateful to my hairdresser for her magical bouncy blow drys for £15

My face is pleasant as well. At least I think so… thankful for my good skin and big lips. Hey Kylie Kardashian. Twinning. Not really, mine are real and I am poor. How is that fair.

Until recently – the internet. Love that you can be in your living room on Google Earth and see parts of the world you dream about. Thank you, Matt, for reconnecting me. May Google Earth New Zealand to choose my next abode.

Lipstick and my black charcoal teeth whitener. No matter how fat my arse is getting with red lippy and my killer white smile I feel more confident.

Grateful I make my own money and pay my own bills (maybe not always on time but better late than never)

Prosecco – maybe not appropriate to include this favourite bubbly, as it was no doubt the catalyst of my birthday drunken antics. But it tastes good and helps me give less of a shit. So yeah, thank you prosecco.

My bed. It is so comfy. I would stay in it all day if I could, preferably with a desirable man.

On the man note, I am grateful for the hot police officer that helped me feel less slutty and shameful on departing prison.

I take a sip of wine and reflect on turning thirty. So far, I've got pissed, punched my ex and spent the night in Jail. As a result, I owe £3284 to Tim and will always be known as the fat red head from Epic Fails. Scandal. Of. My. Life.

It is the last weekend of my holidays, and I intend on spending it in doors, out of sight from any other human.

Wine is giving me confidence to check my Instagram. I have not been on it for almost a week.

I log into my account username @itismeellieb

Password: BOBHASASMALLDICK

This must be a mistake. I exit app clear my phone, open app and log in again.

Holy shit – so many follow requests. Too many to count, I scroll through. Hundreds.

I screen shot it and send to my 'Besties' WhatsApp chat.

RUBY: Delete any posts you don't like, make your account Public and change your bio to… let me think.

ME: Really, let me think?

RUBY: Let me think about what you should put for your bio. Duh!

ME: ha-ha PSML

MATT: Buying followers is sad hen. Even for a unicorn x

ME: Piss off

RUBY: I am in a VIP meeting, goodbye children.

I started a new Instagram the week after Bob cheated on me. I had to. I did not want to have a daily reminder of what my life was. A good life, at least that's what I perceived it to be. My new Instagram posts are mainly of wine, mugs of coffee and funny motivational quotes I have Googled when pissed. There are also several selfies of me, mainly from the neck up. I have no idea why people would take an interest in me, Ellie Benson - but the obvious guess would be my social media tag @itismeellieb is plastered all over YouTube with the Epic Fail video that I will never, ever, escape from. Fuck you 21st videoing century. What happened to - *what happens on a night out, stays on a night out*!

I make my account public, instantly accepting my new friend requests. I have no Bio anyway so I will await Ruby's expertise.

I now have 1017 people following me on Instagram. *Holy crap.* I feel stupid for feeling happy about this. I do not know these people but my thirty-year-old ass feels a sense of accomplishment gaining popularity. Weird right? Why would random strangers requesting to be my social media friend make me happy?

Probably want to troll me. Fuckers!

10

Monday has snuck up on me. I have not been a fan of Mondays since I started working here three years ago. But I can't hate them that much because I have made no attempt to move my fat arse anywhere else. I could handle my shitty work that neither motivates or fulfils me because I had Bob. Sad really, I turned into one of the women I vowed never to be. My life revolved around him, our new house, planning holidays. I worked for money, nothing more, nothing less.

I close my eyes as the lift opens, silently praying nobody has seen my video.

They have most definitely seen the video - my desk is decorated. I have been off for precisely ten working days and my colleagues are still idiots. I've served them ammunition on a platter; small plastic wine glasses (depressingly empty) are stacked in front of my keyboard taking the form of a Christmas tree alongside a small penis keyring.

"Ha fucking HA!" I try to take it in good sport as I move my mouse to see my face as my screen saver.

"ELLIE." Wanda says sternly walking past my desk.

"Missed you too Wanda," I shout back turning on my computer. My screen saver has been changed - the *angry me* with the wine glasses ready to pour. After changing my screen saver back to my happy place - warm white sand and an inviting turquoise blue ocean, I open my emails. Backlogs of work to catch up on. Should have played the lotto – got to be in it to win it, and all that.

Jim, Benny and Dave are bent over in double as they watch my YouTube video on a mobile, no doubt for the hundredth time.

The suited and booted jerks are married, and close to the big forty, yet Ruby's five-year-old niece, Lena, behaves with more maturity.

"Honestly Ellie, you have literally made my month." Benny slaps me on the back, crying with laughter. He slumps down on his seat next to mine and pats away the tears with a tissue.

"You are welcome dickhead" I mutter with sarcasm thinking about an iceberg. I get goosebumps and feel colder instantly. Genius blogger - I read on some lifestyle blog you can control your face turning into a tomato with such visualisations.

The other secretaries greet office manager Wanda and walk past my desk. All say hello with big wide judgmental eyes. Jazz, the only nice one, has had a haircut – she reminds me of a pixie from Peter Pan.

"Well go you," she congratulates me before parking her bum on my desk. She taps my hand and winks at Dave making him turn a shade of pink. Jazz has heard me cry in the bathroom over Bob more than once. She often offered to punch him, but I doubted it would have had made any impact - my thigh weighs more than her whole body.

"Not all good, but thanks Jazz. I'll fill you in at lunch when Dave's big ears aren't flapping."

"Eh I can hear you ladies." Image conscious Dave rubs his ears.

"Exactly!" Jazz smiles seductively.

"Jail," Benny butts in then slurps his red bull.

"You ended up in Jail?" Dave asks with the widest smile I have ever seen on his face.

I could feel my face starting to beam. Ice, snow storm, swimming in the artic. It was no use my face went red.

"OMG ELLIE, you did? I was joking!" Benny put a hand over his mouth.

I give him the middle finger without making eye contact and

open my first email marked urgent.

“Still behaving like a lady, I see.” Dave chirps in, ecstatic about the entertainment I provide.

“Heard Mary gossiping about your tic tac testicles.” I reply just to confirm his assumptions. Mary is Dave’s wife, never seen or talked to her. Dave falls silent, confirming what I have always presumed – Dave has tiny balls to match his tiny penis.

Benny laughs loudly.

“Good to have you back jailbird.” He laughs again.

Shit this is my life. Surrounded by morons at their beck and call for shit pay and shit holidays.

“You should come to yoga with me tonight Ellie, change of scenery will help.” Jazz brought her hands into Namaste. Jazz looked like she will be able to bend in all ways necessary to perfect every yoga pose. I, on the other hand, am struggling to bend down to buckle my shoes. But Dr Kendrick’s words are ringing in my ears like a lunch time bell.

“Count me in,” I beam, fake smiling with tight lips. I am grateful I can spare the effort of having to Google yoga classes. By tonight I will have ticked yoga off my to do list.

“Awesome! Yoga buddy!” Jazz rubs my shoulder and bounces to her seat. The big boss enters like a thunder cloud. The room falls quieter. No more social chat - it is all work. Benny’s client calls, I pass him through and start catching up on emails before a shadow appears.

Big boss, Mr Brown is hovering over me. The fat, bald giant that has employed me for three years, yet never uttered a word to me. Other than “move” when I was blocking access to the coffee machine. But now he is here - with his minty breath almost disguising the prawn cocktail crisps I saw him shovelling down earlier. His name suited him today dressed in a horrendous chocolate brown suit. Mr Brown reminds me of a big turd.

"Sir?" I place my pen down and turn to face him. At this moment the thought of being sacked and going home to vegetate sounds delightful. I still have exactly seven hours and forty minutes before I can venture home.

"Meeting room three – 11AM" he barks.

"Am I getting a pay rise?" I asked nervously. Bad joke.

"NO!" he marches off shouting at tanned Hilary to get his morning cappuccino. Her bronzed slimming complexion reminded me to ask her where she gets such a glow.

Everyone looks at me with baited breath. Benny rubs my back reassuringly before answering his phone. I open my emails.

To: Jazz

Fuck - think I am getting sacked. Ex

To: Ellie

He wouldn't do it. Wanda would do it. She would take great joy in sacking you. You are not getting sacked. Weird. Jx

To: Jazz

Maybe he is setting an example of me. E x

To: Ellie

Maybe he fancies you? Jx

To Jazz

Currently throwing up in my mouth. Ex

To Ellie

Spit or swallow? LMAO Jx

To Jazz

Bugger off.Ex

Two productive hours pass fast. I get through 35 of the 204 emails I have unanswered and secured three interviews (go me) with fabulous potential candidates for Dave. To thank me, he asked the team not to watch or talk about my YouTube video for the rest of the day. Red light today. Green again tomorrow.

"Don't sweat it Ellie, you'll just be getting your wrists slapped. Some arse wrote in the comments that you worked at Browns recruitment," Benny advises scrolling through the comments. He is the softest of the team. He masks his sensitivity with humour, wearing it like a shield of armour, as do I.

"Respect the work place. Brown's is family, we are representations of our work in and outside the office." Jim bangs his chest, mocking Mr Brown's awful, unmotivating team chats.

"Thanks, I think," I head for meeting room three.

I feel nervous. Nervous as I don't know what to expect, nervous that I can't afford to lose my job and mostly nervous that I may tell Mr Brown to fuck off. He does not know what my divorce has put me through mentally or physically. I feel my night in jail and commitment to six weeks therapy is punishment enough for my birthday night. I am not in the mood to beg for forgiveness to keep my job. However, if I lose my job I may need to move back in with my parents. My life would become best summed up by the 'head in hands' emojis. Dad would be a breeze but my mum. *Ellie you need to lose weight. Ellie watch your language. Ellie you need to be more ladylike. Ellie your biological clock is ticking. Ellie get a man.*

Decision made. I will beg like a dog if required.

"Hellooo." I smile opening the door apprehensively. Mr Brown grunts, he is sitting in between a man and woman looking like extras from the Devil Wears Prada.

"Ellie Benson," a woman greets me with a hug as genuine as Korea welcoming Trump for tea. Her platinum blonde hair, tiny waist and frozen forehead are making me quite envious.

"And you are?" I ask as politely as I can.

Mr Brown shoots me a glare with wide angry eyes. I shrug. I guess I should know who she is. I do recognise her face but can't pinpoint it. I take a seat wishing I had the bank account to tell Mr Brown to go wank the dick dangling from his forehead.

Both blondie and the thin dark-haired man go into fits of laughter. An uncomfortable long drawn out laugh that I join in with. Not because I want to, but because Mr Brown kicked my toe. I'm sure that's illegal. May consider suing. You can sue for anything these days.

"Hilarious - as I expected." She applies some pink lip gloss and pouts. Totally unaware that I really do not have a fucking clue who she is. Barbie is my closest guess. Sorry Rachel, your title has been stolen.

"Cards on the table darh-ling. Your YouTube video has racked up allot of ratings. And to be quite frank, it's fabulous darh-ling." she stands up again pacing back and forth excitedly.

"I want to offer you one thousand pounds. Yes, that's right ONE THOUSAND POUNDS!" she bends down saying the words slowly with intense eye contact. I cough as my breath catches her floral perfume. She slaps a document on the table and a pen.

"For what?" I ask whilst doing a quick subtraction in my mind. Birthday bill £3284 - £1000 = £2284.

"For an interview with me on my show, then it'll be down to our London studios for a live interview there. All expenses paid obviously, luxury hotels, fine dining, fantastic opportunity for someone like you. But we would have rights to your story." She puts the pen in my hand. Ah that's who she is. Queen of prime-time TV.

"Seriously you'd give me £1k just to hear my side of the story?" her words '*like you*' rings in my head. Cheeky bitch. However, I haven't had £1k in my bank, like, ever. I get paid on the last Friday of every month, then when the first of each month rears it's ugly head it turns from pay day into pay away day. Living the dream. And let's not forget my birthday bill.

"People empathised with you in your YouTube video. Your

relatable, funny. There are hundreds of women wronged and divorced every second in the UK. You would get paid time off work, which we will compensate Browns Recruitment generously for," she gave Mr Brown the same wink Jazz uses on the boys when she wants her own way.

"Not sure if I want to share that I spent the night in jail and my ex got me served with a restraining order. I'd rather not give my embarrassing birthday night longevity."

"Fabulous!" Blondie looked like she was about to burst with excitement. The story just got juicier.

"Fuck all fabulous about it," this idiot is beginning to annoy me.

"ELLIE!" my boss apologised on my behalf for the foul language. First time he has said my name ever. Penelope, as I learnt she was called, seemed unfazed by my response and opened up her mobile.

"Girl is crazy! Probs were dating for five minutes…chick is obviously obsessed with her ex…. bet she wishes he would beg her back… Should I go on?" Blondie asks with a sly smile, leaning against the wall. I'm sure if she could move them her eyebrows would be raised.

"Thought you said people like me?" I answer with heavy sarcasm.

"Correct! Majority love you. But a minority think you are a crazy, drunken, Bob obsessed slob." She's now inches from my face. I want to slap her for invading my personal space again. I pull back.

"Wouldn't it be kind of awesome not to play the victim and take control to tell your side of everything?" she stares at me not breaking eye contact and shoves the pen in my hand.

"OK," I sigh. I need the money. Desperation is a dark place to live in.

Before I could sign my name on the dotted line the meeting

rooms phone starts to ring. Relentlessly it rings until Mr Brown nods for me to answer it. “Sorry.” He apologises to Penelope’s impatient face.

I answer it with my politest greeting voice. I doubt Mr Turd realises how awesome I am at my job.

I was not expecting the voice on the other side of the line. “Hi Ruby, I’m kinda in the middle of something.” I was looking at the page contract with the dotted line for me to sign.

“Put me on loudspeaker please Ellie,” Ruby instructs.

“O-K” I am confused. I hit loud speaker.

“Hi Penelope, Ruby, Richardson here. Ellie is my client and she will not be signing or doing anything until we have looked over it.” Ruby spoke with friendly assertiveness.

“Client. Yes, client,” I nod as trying to decipher what Ruby is up to.

Mr Brown rubs both palms over his eyes.

“This has been a long day and it’s not even lunch time. Excuse me.” Mr Brown leaves the room grunting that these minutes will be deducted from my lunch break. How is that fair? I didn’t even ask for this stupid meeting.

“I had no idea Ruby,” Penelope’s face is pink with temper. I guess she is not used to being told NO. She looks like a child, about to throw a diamond encrusted dummy from her pram.

“Leave the contract with Ellie and we will be in touch very soon.” Ruby advises. I can’t see her face, but I can picture her smiling smugly.

Penelope puts back on her pink blazer, grabs her pen from my hand and marches out the room, her nervous side kick flapping behind her like a lap dog.

“Wait…why? How? What on earth is going on Ruby?” I ask, the £1K fluttering away like an admiral on a sunny day.

"I know the HR girl from Penelope's office, turns out your You-Tube video has been the talk of the town..."

I gulp. "Oh, god really?" My face is now pink.

"Ellie, you're going to turn the shit storm that was your birthday into the best worst decision you have ever made!" Ruby sounds excited.

I screw my face up not sharing her optimism. "If you say so."

"Dinner, at mine tonight, I'm making fajitas, Matt's coming too. Heading home now for a sex fest then Jamie's heading out with clients." She giggles. They have been dating two years but are permanently stuck in the lust stage.

I start to laugh. "An afternoon sex sesh..." I think back to the good old days. My sex drive has plummeted.

"Yeah well, can't have both our vaginas drying up," she hangs up. Top of my to do list -buy a vibrator.

11

"Breathe in, into downward dog and hold…" the yoga teacher speaks softly drawing out her words. The soft gush of the sea waves coming in and going out is echoing throughout the bright hall. I can almost smell the sea air as the sounds open my imagination - I am on a beach.

"And up to warrior position," the yoga teacher demonstrates. She glows. I sweat.

Wooden flooring with rows of yoga mats are lined up side by side. Other than body shape, it is very easy to spot the serious yogis. They have their own mats, some with their names embroidered into it, others with stars, bright colours or branded with motivational captions. *Dream. Believe. Achieve.* I have the standard plain blue, collect on your way in mat - but I am not alone. I count another five, out of the seventeen women with a matching blue mat. Also, I am not the fattest in the class. Awful, horrible, bitchy thing to say, but, whilst comparison can be the thief of joy, it can also be an advantage and make you feel better. Given my dress attire - grey joggers, sports bra and a baggy white t-shirt coupled with my makeup free sweaty face and messy bun – I have nothing to be vain about.

Yoga is officially harder than I have ever, ever imagined. My body is stretching (or trying to stretch) in ways I didn't think possible. Jazz is in front of me on her bright yellow mat looking like she's making a yoga tutorial video. Wasted as a secretary, she should be doing this for a living – I make a mental note to tell her when class finishes.

I am praising myself for my first attempt at yoga. Go me. Well done. You are more flexible than you thought. Thank you, Dr

Kendrick, for the suggestion (order) to try new experiences. I may very well make a habit of this yoga.

The yoga teachers voice is soft and buttery, you are drawn to listen. "And downward dog. Remember to focus on the breath. Our beautiful breath, in and out."

Oh, dear God no. I'm in downward dog pose. My stomach rumbles, I knew I shouldn't have eaten the beans before I had to head here. Greedy, greedy bitch. I clench my cheeks together as much as I can, I hope it will pass and be a false alarm.

It's too late. I break wind, pump, fart - whatever you want to call it but I have done it loudly. The noise from my fat arse echoes throughout the hall, momentarily masking the waterfall noise coming from the speakers. A few of the younger girls giggle, so does Jazz – *thank you friend.* The yoga teacher carries on as if nothing had happened. Then the smell hit's me, I feel sick. The girl directly behind me excuses herself for the bathroom wedging the door open on her way there. Then an elderly lady opens a window. OK I am *very* embarrassed. Two of the serious, name on mat, yoga goers gawk at me like I have actually taken a shit on the floor. I check the clock. Fifteen minutes to go. I weigh up my options.

1. Simply get up and leave, but would be rude not to say bye to Jazz and would look like a fool if just lingering around outside waiting for class to finish.
2. Apologise to everyone. But Jazz had said the yoga teacher likes silence. My body functions are rebellious.
3. Do nothing, absolutely nothing. Not everyone may realise it was me.

I decide on doing nothing. We are instructed to lay on our backs for guided meditation. I was really excited about trying the meditation, but now my mind is replaying the fart over and over. I shall have to add 'find a new yoga class' to my to do list.

And remember to never, ever eat before yoga. Ever.

Thankfully the fifteen minutes go fast. My heart rate has slowed down and my face a shade of normal.

Everyone gets up and leaves promptly. It is a little after 7PM. Other than the obvious it feels good to have done something different from my normal routine. Finish work, catch the bus home, pour a glass of wine while turning on the TV and putting a pizza in the oven. Normally by now I'd be on my second glass of vino and have decided what guff I was going to watch while vegetating on my sofa till bed time. Change is good I decide.

"Same time next week?" the yoga teacher smiles warmly. She is a mirror image of Jazz - small, with short brown hair and a warm glow. I guess she is older than she looks.

"Wouldn't miss it, eh Ellie," Jazz looks at me smugly. The pair of them are not actually asking, I am being told to be here next week.

"Yes," I nod wondering if now is the time to apologise for breaking wind.

Jazz links her arm in mine and we head for the door. It is still warm outside with piercing blue skies.

"Mortified!" I say as jazz is doubled over in laughter; she was playing miss mature in front of the yoga teacher.

She stretches. I can feel my legs starting to ache already. "Oh Ellie, I love you, my step brother can drop you at Ruby's, he's picking me up." Jazz checks her mobile.

I feel relieved I do not need to walk. Is it only about a twenty-five-minute walk home, but my legs are wobbling like jelly. "Fab, thanks, is that the one from London?"

"He's just moved back last month. His bitch faced ex, was cheating on him. He moved back when he found out he isn't the father to her baby." Jazz is angry.

"That is a heavy blow to take, poor guy. Why didn't you tell me?"

Jazz sighs and sits on the pavement. I join her. "I was so angry, didn't want to bring my bad vibe into work or stir up old wounds about Bob."

I feel bad she didn't tell me. "You can tell me anything Jazz, anytime."

"The kid was one week old when he found out it wasn't his. He had named him Ben and was totally smitten in every way a father should be," Jazz sighs. I know she is trying for a baby. She would have been so excited to be an Aunt.

"Fuck, who's kid was it?" that's awful. What a bitch.

"That's the double blow. It was his best mate. Sam was working a lot of overtime to bring in money for the materialistic bitch he was, correction, still is, married to. His mate was doing lots of decorating work for their house. Turns out it hadn't been the only thing he was working on." Jazz looked angry. I had rarely seen her look angry.

At that a shiny silver golf pulled up. The windows were tinted. Old house music was booming from the speakers. I have never really been one for music without words. When I had visited dance clubs, I felt really stupid for not getting it. Girls would be like 'YASSS this is amazing' and I was like 'WTFFFF' every song sounds exactly the same. I tried to be cool. I failed.

"Not a word though." Jazz brought her index finger up to her lip.

I motion that I am zipping my lips shut.

Jazz opens the rear door. "Jump in the front Ellie."

"Sam this is my friend Ellie, Ellie this is Sam," Jazz introduces us.

My throat goes dry, my heart starts to race. Nerves, embarrassment, excitement. I honestly can't decide. I truly never expected to see him again.

"Nice to meet you Ellie." Hot police officer holds out a hand. I place my sweaty palm in his cool large paw. God he is so hot.

Sam, I like that name. Once again, he is seeing me at my worst. I look very bad and he looks like absolute perfection in a red football top and white shorts. I cannot for the life of me understand why any woman would cheat on such a fine specimen. I couldn't imagine wanting to have sex with anyone else if his penis was all mine.

"Sugar Honey Ice Tea," I mumble.

Both Jazz and Sam look at me weirdly. Ruby's sister had cleverly turned shit into Sugar, Honey, Iced, Tea for the benefit of her daughter's little ears. I have no clue as to what I am thinking. I am an adult. Lena is five.

"You make me laugh Ellie." Jazz leans forward playfully punching me in the arm. The awkward silence is quickly filled with a smile from Sam and Jazz chattering about her day.

I still can't work out if this is good or bad. But it feels nice being in his company. He has a 'good vibe' as Ruby would say. Matt would just say he's fit as fuck. I will definitely be adding meeting hot policeman and learning his name to my gratitude journal for today.

Sam pulls up outside Ruby's fancy block of flats as Jazz answers her mobile.

"Thanks for the lift." He pulls on the handbrake. I turn to see Jazz deep in conversation, legs crossed on the back seat.

"Anytime," he smiles. He turns the music a little softer. I talk loud enough for Sam to hear me, yet quiet enough for Jazz not to.

"And, once again, embarrassingly you are not seeing me at my best. First drunk, never been my best look, followed by a trip to jail then this fat, sweaty yoga mess, and you look well… hot - like you – god I am mumbling. Good bye, thank you for the lift," I open the car door and climb out wishing I could punch myself in the face. When in doubt of what to say, say nothing. I never learn. One mouth, two ears – for a reason. *I talk too much. Learn when to shut up Ellie!*

"Bye Ellie!" Jazz shouts briefly taking the mobile away from her ear. I give her a wave and shut the car door.

"Hey Ellie..." I turn back around as the window is going down.

"Never, ever apologise for being perfectly imperfect." Sam says with a serious face before smiling and driving off.

I digest his words trying to decide if hot police officer had just paid me a compliment or dropped an insult. *Perfectly Imperfect...* I feel warm and fuzzy at the thought. My stomach does a somersault – I decide to take it as a compliment.

12

A mid-week catch up with Ruby and Matt usually involves eating fajitas, drinking prosecco while reminiscing about the good old days.

However, tonight is a different sort of catch up. When Ruby claimed she would turn the shit-storm that was my birthday (thank you Ruby) into a positive, I did not quite realise the extent of her plans.

Yes, I have eaten fajitas and been allowed one glass of prosecco for Dutch courage, but I am no longer the sweaty mess that rolled out of yoga two hours ago. Matt has my hair and make-up on point. I am contemplating sleeping with my make- up on until my therapy session. But can I take the risk of getting spots as a result of being a vain dirty bitch? I look in the mirror; I look good – thank you Matt. I'll take my chances with the spots.

Ruby is walking about with a clipboard like she's about to direct Vin Diesel parkouring from one high rise to another. I 'star of the circus' am now sitting on Ruby's grey crushed velvet sofa with a mobile on a stand, perfectly positioned to film me.

"You happy sticking with @itismeellieb?" Ruby asks taking a few photos of me on her mobile.

"Sure." I want home to put on my PJ's and finish the half bottle of white wine chilling in my fridge. I can practically hear it calling my name.

"No photo filter." I remind Ruby. If I am going to attempt this Vlogging thing - I want to be me. As real as real can be.

"Eh rudeee. I am the photo filter hen." Matt points his finger and swirls it around my face.

"Keep it casual. Drop in your Vlog, It is me Ellie B, will be live very soon, refer to the YouTube video that has given you this platform and answer some of the Q's from the comments under the assholes Epic fails YouTube video." Ruby spoke assertively, she was in work mode. She had already told me when I'm rich and famous as a client her cut is twenty percent. Which made me perk up. If Ruby was talking money, she did believe in my ability. Although I had no fucking idea how I could make money from this. And I refuse to be called an influencer, every second half naked person on Instagram now adopts the title of influencer. The only thing I influence is the profit my local shop makes from all the overpriced wine I buy. Impulse shopping.

"Emphasis in subscribing to your YouTube channel!" Ruby gives a thumbs up.

"When will this be posted?" I feel fat all of a sudden. Huge, massive, giant whale. Maybe this is a bad idea. My mind darts back to Dr Kendrick - *if you keep doing what you are doing you will keep getting what you are getting. Think outside the box, broaden your skill set, set goals.* I still feel fat but as my mother kindly tells me, no wrinkles in a balloon – every cloud.

"Will take a couple of days to edit. Let's shoot video content then we can add in music, social media tags and so on, we know your brand is going to be Ellie B and on all channels @itismeellieb we just need to brainstorm your opening video, symbol, logo...." Ruby said trailing off into thought.

"A penis, with Ellie B in bold letters busting out the top of it" Matt suggests knocking back a glass of prosecco whilst swirling on Ruby's fancy purple velvet chair.

"Shut up Matt."

"And remember Bob... Bob is a dick, let's make sure you have the last laugh." Ruby winks knowing how to flare me up like a time bomb.

I take a big deep breath. Butterflies in my stomach. *Fuck you Bob.*

"Just as we practised." Ruby gives a thumbs up, pleased her comment had me sitting a little straighter - attitude at the ready.

"Three, two, one...." Matt uses his hands to signal *action.*

I smile at the camera.

"Hi guys, my name is Ellie. Ellie B you may best know me as the fat red head that ..." my mind goes back to my birthday night. I see Bob and Rachel again, him on one knee, I feel the anger churning but it is quickly replaced by sadness. I remember when he went down on one knee as I almost swallowed my circular cut expensive ring. It had been swimming in a glass of champagne. I was so happy that day. When I said yes, I really thought I would have been Ellie Hickinbottom till the day I died.

"So sorry Ruby, sorry but this isn't for me." I grab my bag and plastic bag with my sweaty clothes and call a taxi as I am heading to the door.

"Oh babe." Matt chases me wiping the tears and mascara streaming down my cheek.

Ruby just hugs me tight. "Sorry Ellie, this is my fault. I am a pushy mare."

"No, no, it's just me. I don't feel confident enough." I mumble with watery eyes.

"You'd be a natural Ellie; you love to write - so why not blog at least then? You're real, beautiful, funny. You have more personality than any of those wannabe influencers and bloggers I currently kiss ass too."

I hug her tight. "Biased much."

My mobile beeps. My taxi has arrived and so has a text from my mother.

MUM: Currently digging a hole for myself. Violet just showed me your video. This will haunt my future grandchildren. Stop ignoring my calls Love mum x

My mother's timing is always impeccable. She has a built in 'Ellie's feeling low' radar to give me an extra kick in the fud when I am down. You are a bright light mother.

I say my goodbyes with a heavy load of guilt. Ruby and Matt look disappointed, fake smiling me goodbye, ready to dissect my mood as soon as I leave. I feel like shit. I get home my mind on one thing only. The wine. I asked the taxi driver to stop at Mr Ahmed for an additional bottle of my good friend Chardonnay. I do not feel two glasses will satisfy my thirst.

I walk briskly up the two levels of concrete stairs hearing snips of my neighbours' lives from behind their doors - laughter, music, shouting, then there is mine - silence. I have the best friends, a good family, health, a steady job but I am still consumed by sadness, that deep pit of emptiness at the bottom of my stomach. The feeling that only alcohol seems to temporarily void. I don't love Bob anymore, but I still love the idea of the secure, safe life that I had with him and that makes me feel like a pathetic, weak, fanny.

I am greeted by a council tax final reminder letter, fuck. Coupled with a delightful letter from the bank advising my application for a £3300 loan has been declined. Fuck. Could someone please send me a cheque in the mail!! I should just have taken that £1K offer from whatever her name was. I pour a wine and knock it back. I pour another fully aware that I am drinking for the wrong reason. I fumble through my kitchen junk drawers. Yes! Momentary excitement. I knew there was a cigarette lurking in here. I spark up and take a long deep draw. The crappy mail can hide under my empty fruit bowl until I am ready to address them.

I think about the hot specimen that is Sam, this reminds me to do gratitude journal before I've drunk too much and don't. I set myself up on the sofa with my drink, journal and pen. I hit play on the new season of the Beverly Hill Housewives and write my gratitude's, even though I can't be bothered.

Today I am grateful the day is over. Tired.com

Grateful for wine – although I do plan on a dry spell.

Grateful for the cigarette I found (although I shouldn't be).

To be fair was not a bad day, work was OK.

Had nice lunch, young girl recognised me from YouTube Epic fails and put extra everything on my cheese salad baguette. Felt grateful for her chat and extra everything. Although I fear it may have been offered as from sympathy angle.

Yoga! Yes, I did it. Was harder than I thought.

Biggest gratitude for today – seeing the hot specimen that is SAM. Hot AF police officer, who, sadly, is totally out my league. 10/10 guy.

Grateful for my new black super comfy sports bra. Good purchase that I couldn't afford.

I pause the housewives, change into my black and gold star pyjamas and top up my wine glass. I scroll through Instagram. I haven't posted since I've made my account public and accepted the new followers. Chardonnay is giving me confidence. I set my stage for a selfie - I get a big white bowl and fill it with some balsamic vinegar crisps. My red sofa looks old and shabby so I throw my grey velvet throw over it and plump up my bright, multi-coloured, patterned pillows. I cross my legs. Big bowl of crisps on my lap, big glass of wine held up. I smile clicking my mobile with the other hand. Selfie!

I post the photo with some relevant emoji's and several hashtags including #thisisthirty #winewednesday #whythefuck-not #redhead #redheadsdoitbetter #itismeellieb before hitting play on Kyles angry face.

It is 2AM when I wake up and move from the sofa to my bed.

13

Therapy Session Two – Thursday 14th of May

Birthday Balance - £3010 in the red (made small payment – now living off credit cards till payday)

Instagram Followers – 1459 (account now public)

Happiness Ranking – 3/10

I try to send my mobile a psychic message 'turn off alarm'. It appears I do not have super powers. Must buy an Alexa. I have to get up from my bed and retrieve my mobile from the back of the sofa. I hit alarm off wishing I could sleep for another five hours. Two hours until I will be sitting in Dr Kendrick's therapist chair trying to hide the fact that I am indeed hung over.

I have a large glass of apple juice followed by a bowl of some crunchy chocolate cereal I keep on standby for Lena's visits. I have four messages waiting to be read.

Sorry for being a pushy cow, my bad. I'm sorry. Hope this morning goes ok. Love you. Ruby x

£3,248? Just saying #blogger #vlogger #cashcow Matt x

Have watched the YouTube video again. It wasn't a dream. mum x

Mum AGAIN. Just checked my Instagram account. Drinking wine on a Wednesday is nothing to be proud off. Call me TODAY love mum x

Ruby playing good cop. Matt bad cop and well mum, just being mum.

Mums message prompts me to open Instagram. My usual morning routine. Check social media, emails, social media again before taking shower. Holy shit - 802 people have given me some insta love and double tapped my PJ, crisp eating, wine drinking photo! An array of Ellie loving comments are making me blush-

Beautiful, so real. You inspire me!

Red haired stunner!

Rocky Ba- Ellie, we love you.

Thank you, very much nice people. And then there are the assholes hell bent on making me feel fatter than the size eighteen that I am. Luckily, I have thick – ish skin with comments like;

Harpoon the whale. Fat cow.

Uncanny similarity to the Red Telly Tubby 'PO!'

Ellie the elephant - pack your trunk and fuck off from Instagram...

I like all seventy-three comments, even the fuck wit trolls. Get a life guys, quit with the fat shaming. It Is not cool! I write a comment myself.

Thank you for all the lovely comments, genuinely overwhelmed, THANK YOU!!! And for the assholes, you know who you are – thank you for giving me attention. I feel loved. #sarcasm #sofuck #thankyounicepeople

I shower while my mobile is on charge. Leaving the house without your mobile at one hundred percent is practically like rocking out your front door in your birthday suit. My insta love has given me temporary happiness, taking the edge off my jaded state. I shower and dress in a long black pleated skirt keeping it casual with my yellow converse and a bright mustard coloured top. The sun is shining today. My flat looked dirty before but now thanks to the sunbeams, every inch of glass looks as though it's been smeared with slime. I have clean pants on though, so I feel like a winner.

I wave goodbye to the pigeon peering through my dirty windows, lock my front door and reply to Ruby, Matt and mum with the same message *Happy Thursday, on route to therapy, lucky therapist. speak later, luv Ellie x* I decide today is as good a day to take the first bag of empties to my glass bin before making my way to the bus stop.

“Do you know happiness is an inside job?” Mrs Withering asks, hobbling past with her walking stick and morning paper. She smiles at me with raised white eyebrows and a bony finger pointing to the tenth wine bottle I have just smashed. My 79-year-old neighbour, walks the five minutes every day wind, rain, hail or snow for her morning paper. She trumps walking, sex and Sherry to her youthful appearance. I learnt this last month when she found me crying on the stairs. Took me in for a slice of banana bread and a large nightcap. I can confirm I do not like Sherry but love Mrs Withering.

“I didn’t drink them all on one night,” I say enthusiastically with a thumbs up.

“I should hope not. Your stomach would be getting a pumping!” Mrs Withering laughed. Her eyes sparkled. “When it should be another body part getting pumped. You are in your prime Ellie, find a pumper if you catch my drift.” Mrs Withering continued her journey to our close.

“Oh, my lord,” I mutter face beetroot as I smash the last bottle. You know shit is bad when even the oldest lady in your block is aware you are getting heehaw action.

On the bus thankfully no one recognised me like last week. And I got a nice window seat at the front. I am resisting the urge to check Instagram and my emails again. It’s not even 9AM and already I can tell you what several celebrities have eaten for breakfast, who is dating who and what is the latest fad diet. All from Instagram. Social media literally eats my time like a hungry gremlin. Time is precious and SM munches away until the possibility of achieving anything in my disposable time is impossible because I have no fucking time left.

Bet it would have been cool to live in the old days, before technology, but after the witch burning days; (I fear I would have been burned for my #superpower of saying the wrong thing at the wrong time). If you wanted to visit your bestie across the other side of 'town' you would have to ride for a couple of days praying she hadn't moved or worse, died. Imagine, Wi-Fi ceased to exist? I mean would any millennial person be able to survive without the internet? I observe the young adults, the mums, the suits. All of them engrossed on their mobiles, I think the answer to my question is NO. All millennials brought up with the internet would most definitely, myself included, struggle to live without it. It is no wonder we are encouraged by every self-help guru to meditate. Many successful celebrities (again info learnt while celeb stalking/time wasting on SM) credit meditating to their success. Because, in my words - our minds are so full of shit. Even though it is about shit that doesn't matter, we still churn it over like a conveyor belt. I predict I have had more thoughts going on in my mind in the past two hours than my bestie from the 17th century would have had in two days!

Food for thought. I guiltily eat a chunky Kit Kat, my snack meant for after therapy. I hadn't stopped thinking about its presence in my handbag. A woman walking on the bus looks at me then her Fitbit. Cheeky beanpole judging the fat red head scoffing Kit Kat at this time of day. Well, that's what 'I' think she is thinking. I choose not to say *fuck off and eat a kebab,* even though I really, really want to.

My stop. I dust the chocolate crumbs sticking to my top and thank my smiley bus driver.

"Thanks mate, have a great day." He looks happy. Ear to ear smiling, infectious happy– must have been laid, could not be a lottery win as still at work. Maybe he just likes his work? Would anyone keep working if they won the lottery? Nope. Not me. I'd buy the biggest sofa, hire the hottest Tom Hardy lookalike as my personal butler and vegetate. Only moving from my gigantic bespoke Ellie B made sofa for the toilet and to wash. All other 'stay alive' requirements - eating, drinking and shagging personal butler would take place on the sofa of all sofas, idyllically placed in front of my cinema sized television screen.

With these delightful thoughts in mind reality kicks in. I have not won the lottery – sadly. I am standing back in front of Dr Kendrick's receptionist. Sarah is smiling as wide as my bus driver. I smile too.

"How lovely to see you again Ellie. Can I fetch you a water?" she asked eagerly.

"Please, that would be nice, thank you" I sat down in the corner and picked up a Vogue magazine. I flick it open at a bag. Beautiful bag, bright orange with a gold strap. £4,900 WTF! That is serious dosh for a bag that would not match every outfit. Fear not – it comes in seven other colours. I'll take them all.

"Dr Kendrick is just finishing with her client, she will be with you shortly" Sarah hands me a glass of water, beautifully presented with crushed ice, lemon and one mint leave. I try not to down it in one go, but I am feeling a tad dehydrated. Sarah kindly took my glass unprompted and returned with more.

"Thank you," I blush; she knows I am hungover. Darn it.

I sit up straighter as I hear the door to the 'fix it' office open.

"Thanks, Lacy." Sam shakes her hand gently before turning to look me straight in the eye. He stops in his tracks staring at me. Sarah eyes Sam up unapologetically.

"Oh lord! My drunken antics pushed you to therapy!" I snort laugh inappropriately to fill an awkward silence.

"Miss Ellie Benson." Sam nods before striding out the door.

"Ellie" Dr Kendrick greets me with a warm inviting smile gesturing me to her office. I plonk myself down on the mustard sofa. The soft leather feels warm. Sam's hot sexy arse now being replaced with mine. *Sorry sofa.*

Dr Kendrick takes her seat, crosses her legs, fixes her black rimmed designer glasses and looks at me. I feel like an onion ready to be peeled. My layers are going to be exposed, and there shall be tears.

"Ellie, how have you been?"

"Still a fat, poor, loud mouth with shitty flirting skills" I pull a face.

Why did I not just smile and say hi Sam like a normal human...

Once again, I leave the therapy room feeling lighter. I bared my soul to Dr Kendrick. I know I cried my mascara is halfway down my cheek. I sit for a moment in reception sorting myself and photographing the bag in vogue. May do a funny insta story about it later.

My emotional baggage and negative thoughts are currently inside red balloons floating high in the sky. I'm guessing, doc is a Charlie XCX fan. Red Balloon song? Or maybe not. Maybe her choice of floating things in red balloons is purely coincidental. Either way it is fucking genius. In my hypnotic, meditative state, I skipped effortlessly to the top of a hill where the sun was shining and I was thinner. My subconscious chose to wear a red bikini on my adventure up the lush green hill. My voluptuous size 12 figure was just way too hot to be hiding behind clothes. I placed several images inside Dr Kendrick's magical balloons...

First - Rachel's vagina got shoved inside a red balloon. I held the balloon string tightly in my hand. I experience a whirlwind of emotions – anger, bitterness, jealousy, sadness. Then I let go of the image that killed my marriage. The breeze takes the balloon higher and further away until it is nothing more than a small dot in the blue sky. It feels liberating. Then I start shoving everything and everyone that needs to be floating in the sky with Rachel's vagina.

Next up, my cheating, lying ex-husband, bawbag Bob. My so called one and only true love - I would have popped that balloon but no harm was to be done, sadly, just releasing bad energies. If I had been in charge of the guided meditation Bob would be getting dangled by one foot off the edge of a high rise, Sky Atlantic, Gangs of London style. I'd be watching, obvs, while he pisses himself - and, if I was lucky, it would trickle up to his face. My hunk of a bodyguard wouldn't let him go... I'm not a murderer. But he would let Bob dangle there until he said sorry and begged forgiveness.

As I shoved Bob in the balloon, it felt different from sending Rachel's lady parts to space. I thought it would be an explosive combination of rage and bitterness but I felt nothing but sadness. Sad and empty. I had flashbacks of the good times. The first encounter when he employed me, how he calmed my nerves with his confidence and laughed at my awkward over talking. Don't get me wrong it was not even close to the first encounter with Mr Grey. The fact I am even comparing them is ridiculous but there was something – a spark, a look, humour, his confidence. He was a successful businessman and became the first proper adult I had ever dated. Good bye quick shags with binge drinking, sofa crashing, party people, hello businessman Bob. Without even realising, I strived to please him and I did, until he said 'I do,' which is when he realised in his words *he had won, he had me.* The excitement had been getting me to commit, it seemed like an impossible task, I was - *ok now am (again)* - a loose cannon. His project became to tame and slim down, fat, fun party animal Ellie, his secretary. He did, I lost three stone, joined a gym and was partial to the odd green juice. I fell in love, much quicker than I had ever expected. I moved in with him, signed a prenuptial (which rung alarm bells for Ruby) got married at twenty-nine years of age, on my fucking birthday then divorced five months later. I had no evidence of the affair other than physically seeing them together. Should have taken a photograph.

I shrunk my mother down too. She was the size of a mouse. I could hear her squeaking but was not able to make out her words of disappointment. Into the balloon you go Nancy. I remember waving her off as she floated upwards. I love my mother dearly, but she doesn't half want to make me pull my hair out at times. I also shoved prosecco, fags, chips and chocolate in the same balloon as mumma. Mainly to piss her off, but also because I know they are bad and would love to cut down my intake of all four items.

I say my goodbyes to Sarah after having another glass of water. I feel more empowered than I did when I came in. Dr Kendrick has praised me for my yoga efforts and commitment to writing my daily gratitude. However, she did hit a nerve stating it is NOT Bob's fault I am unhappy now. She said my happiness is MY responsibility no one else's. This adult - ing responsibility sucks. It went down like a led balloon when I added in 'happiness is MY prosecco's responsibility' which led on to talks about detoxing. 'All in good time' I agreed.

14

The sun is shining. A roasty toasty day. I wish I was a few stones lighter to enjoy short floral dresses without getting sweaty. My inner thighs have recently needed talc powder to assist on warm tight-less outings. Chub rub is a bitch.

"Hey Ellie!" I was approached from behind. I turn around to see Sam. God, I hope he did not see me fixing my knickers wedged up my arse. I was discreet. *I think.*

"Sarah told me what time you'd be done," he added casually.

"I'm confident she would have done you too if you'd allowed her." I joke raising my voice for the word 'done'.

"Do you want to grab a coffee?" he asks completely gliding over my sarcastic remark.

"Love coffee, why not."

Third time lucky. Third time I've seen hot AF policeman and yes, I look semi decent today.

"I just wanted to say..." Sam started. God he is so tall, I want to rip his clothes off. Mrs Withering, I have found my chosen pumper. I rein my thoughts in before I have a hot flush.

My mobile phone rings. My mother. Ignore it. She rings again. I ignore it. She rings again.

"Maybe you should get that," Sam suggests nodding to my mobile buzzing 'again'.

"I should." I say my eyes on his arms. He works out as well as football. It is obvious.

I snap out of my trance and hit accept.

You think my mother's maternal instincts would kick in and

she'd know this is seriously bad timing. "Hello mother" I say sternly. She could be jeopardising the future of her future son in law. Lord please let this thought become a reality, I will never drink again… (on a Sunday).

"Ellie, YouTube really? I had to skip bowls darling, Betty and Violet said even Mr Henry, you know the one Violet bonked in her forties was talking about you. And he talks about nobody," mum rambles.

I smile awkwardly at Sam turning the volume down so everyone two streets away can't hear her. He looks amused by my mums opening to the conversation.

"Are you just calling to lecture me Mum? I'm kind of busy." I only have fifty-one minutes before I need to be at my desk. I want to spend that time sipping coffee and attempting to flirt with Sam, not being lectured by my mother.

"I was just calling to say Auntie Patsy has asked if you would make up some speech for her retirement, birthday bash? It can be anything, anything at all as long as it feeds her ego. Just keep it short and sweet. Is that a yes I hear?" mum waits for my response. The room will be jam packed full of Aunt Pasty's acquaintances - work colleagues, old school and university friends, men she bonked over the years, neighbours, relatives. It would be a recipe for disaster should I fuck up a speech – hence my mums *keep it short and sweet* advice.

"Yes, yes OK OK!" I want to wrap the call up quickly.

"Excellent my cherry pudding. Over four weeks to go, so plenty of time to shed some weight. Violet's daughter has lost three stones Ellie. She said to tell you Slimming World are giving the first week free for -"

I stop my mum mid-sentence. "Veronica had a gastric band fitted, so tell Vi to shove that in her pie hole," I hang up. Really mum. Fat shaming me into losing weight. Vi's daughter did get a gastric band on her trip to Latvia. Apparently, she got 'food poisoning' on her most recent holiday. And it was so bad she had to extend her trip. It's amazing the information your local hairdresser can gather. I had not planned to use the information but now the newly skinny bitch is giving *me*, slimming advice, when she's been sliced and diced...

"Sorry about that." I turn my attention back to Sam who seems amused by the whole conversation.

"It'll pass," he smiles.

My fat or my YouTube fame? "Not soon enough." I sulk reaching the coffee shop deciding he meant the latter.

Sam strides ahead to open the door for me. As expected, he is a gentleman. I notice a group of thin, well presented females' glance in his direction. *He's with me bitches.* I walk shoulders back, back straight. The way a woman would walk if a sexy specimen like Sam was behind her.

We find a window seat looking onto the bustling street. Sam gets us both a cappuccino. I resist putting in three sugars. Just in case he thinks I plan to be fat for eternity.

Yes, Sam we can spend time together, yes let's help each other get through the awful infidelities, yes OK I will have sex with you...if I must.

I am in the middle of visualising what our children will look like when he drops the bombshell...

"Jill is moving back to Glasgow next month" he says clearing his throat.

"Jill?" who the fuck is Jill.

"My childhood sweetheart.... My wife."

Sledge hammer to my chest. I have a surge of compassion for his bleak expression.

Jack and Jill went up a hill to fetch a pale of water Jack fell down and broke his crown and Jill came tumbling after... and she didn't stop tumbling until she was far far away somewhere in the bottom of The

Clyde. The End.

“Wife?” I act the best I could. Jazz had already shared the information.

“She had an affair and a child with another man. I thought Jazz would have told you,” he looked ashamed.

“Nope, but she, your unfaithful wife, does sound delightful.” Heavy sarcasm. I sip my cappuccino. Should have put in the three sugars this is not going how I planned.

“Jazz understandably hates her, but we are going to give it another go,” he smiles.

I am rarely lost for words. But I have no words. I slap myself inwardly for thinking this was the start of my fairy-tale ending. Fuck your Walt Disney, my younger self really did believe in Prince charming. Sam would be a perfect Prince Charming.

“Jazz speaks very highly of you.” He starts with a look of desperation. “I had hoped, if you wouldn’t mind, you could help soften the idea to her?” he whispers “please” with raised eyebrows. Seeing the six foot plus, hunk a chunk begging makes me weak.

“Sure, yes OK” I shrug. I am pleased Jazz values my worldly opinion. I’m shocked though - a girl has an affair and a child with another man and she is worthy of a second go. She must be a goddess in the bedroom.

“Appreciate it Ellie.” He breaks eye contact and stirs the spoon around his cup.

“Why though? Just out of curiosity.” I ask as brightly as I can. Don’t want to mimic my actual, hit by a bus like feelings.

“Because I love her,” he said looking like a knight surrendering - ready for execution.

“Love is a bitch.” I joke. He laughs.

The ice is broken. Sam is getting back with his Ex. He doesn’t judge me for being a drunken resident at his work. We are just two friends sharing some banter over a coffee. He is a good listener. I am talking too much as per. Not just small shit, but big life stuff. We exchange numbers and I agree to help with Jazz. He is relaxed and easy going, I decide if I am not going to be bonking him, I would like him as a friend. My friend the policeman. Who would have thought, eh?

My mobile flashes. Twenty-eight more people have followed me on Instagram.

"What's your Instagram page?" I ask, ready to type and search. Secretly hoping for the odd topless selfie. I'm sure it would not disappoint.

"Hate that shit," Sam shakes his head.

"Twitter?"

"Nope"

"Facebook?"

"NOO"

"Are you an alien? If I stab you would your blood spurt out like green gooey slime?"

"No and weird. But I may arrest you for assault."

"Seems fair." I nod.

"Nobody lives in the moment these days. Everyone is so busy trying to get the best photos to make their life look amazing to people that aren't going to be next to them at their death bed. Idiots if you ask me – no offense." He points to my insta page noting my big smile for gaining more followers.

"You are Albert Einstein reincarnated." I gasp.

"Ha I wish; he'd be a billionaire in the twenty first century."

It does seem alien for someone not to have any social media account. Sam is the first person I have ever met under the age of… wait.

"What age are you?" I ask.

He looks at me with a pause.

"Normally I'd look this shit up on your social media but since your Mr No Social Media I'll have to get info the good old-fashioned way..."

"I am 35 years young. Anything else?"

"Favourite food?" I probe.

"Is this common information given on social media?" he asks.

"No, I just love food. I'm curious." My guess is steak and chips.

"Nachos and pineapples."

"On their own or at same time?"

"At the same time, obviously. You put pineapple on a cheese pizza," he pleads his case.

I think about the combo. Nachos and pineapples. I am disgusted and I am rarely disgusted by food. "You – do. Huh, this has thrown me. With or without guacamole?" I want all the nacho info.

"With. Is there any other way?"

"Sorry Sam, but you are the one that needs arrested." I add another sugar to my coffee. Fuck it. He never planned on seeing me naked anyway.

A group of teenage boys pause at the window dressed in shirts and ties. They should be at school. They bang the window, getting our attention. When we used to bunk off class, we were never as brass as the young adults today. We at least had the decency to hide discreetly in graveyards with our joints and bag of junk food. The spotty teenagers point at me and laugh. I can tell from their role play and lips they are talking about the fat red head from Epic Fails.

"The degenerates that shall rule the future," Sam flashes his police badge. They scamper like antelopes being sprung on by a hungry lion.

"That made my day." I laugh loudly. I snort. I get unwanted attention from fellow coffee goers for my snort laughing. I can't stop. I am stuck in a burst of unnecessary laughing.

Sam starts laughing at me laughing. We get caught up laughing at each other forgetting what we are laughing about. Note to self- must try laughing yoga.

It's only when I am at my shitty work desk, I realise Sam made me feel happy this morning. Even though doc said it was no one else's job. It was either Sam or Dr Kendrick's remarkable session. Who cares, happy is happy. It is a nice feeling.

Ben stares at me. "You look like you got laid Benson."

"Just high on life," I smirk. I wish I had been fucking laid.

Ben points to a new employee. "Simon is single." A tall, thin pale male in his late twenties. He looks confident with a head full of brown curly hair.

Bit thin. But fuckable. Would need a haircut and to tone down the shine on the black loafers.

"Not my type," I lie.

I've never really had a type. Pre Bob, I had several types – there was the no alcohol type, then a glass of wine type, then a bottle of wine type, then a disgustingly drunk type. Basically, I went from having high standards to settling for anything with a penis. The past me was a slut. Who would believe it? I AM, correction – 'WAS' a slut. Slut face Ellie must gain some dignity and respect for self. Have not had sex for months and months (dream with Tom Hardy does not count).

Realisation for the day - get laid (sober) before sex drive reappears and I slip back into slutty tendencies. Must buy that vibrator.

15

I love Saturdays. No alarm.

I squint my eyes to read the time on my mobile. It is 1PM. I don't need to open my grey curtains to know that the rain is battering off my window. I'm glad it's raining, helps me feel less guilty about being in bed past lunch time. I stayed up to ridiculous o'clock last night writing an article about being a newly 30-year-old divorcee. Ruby was correct, as per; writing is a good way to release my negative energy. So be it, I was fuelled with prosecco and chain smoking like a Carrie Bradshaw wannabe - banging away at my computer keys into the early hours. But nevertheless, I enjoyed doing something other than bingeing on box sets. I had sent my article to Ruby at exactly, I check my sent items, 3:55AM. Which makes sleeping till 1PM more excusable. I decide not to read what I typed, as I can't remember exactly what I wrote but I do know it was about yoga.

I check my gratitude journal. The writing looks like a five-year old. Wait, sorry – that is an insult to five-year olds. My writing is slopped and large, barely readable. Instead of the gratitude sentences I have become accustomed to doing I have just written a list of words.

Chocolate

Blueberry muffins

Jam doughnuts

Tunnocks Teacakes

Jaffa cakes

Cookies

Fags

Scratch cards

Prosecco

White wine

Red wine

Gin

Mocktails

Spanx

Chips and cheese

I am disgusted with myself. This gratitude list simply highlights that I am a fat, greedy, smoking, alcohol dependent, Spanx wearing loser. And I have written mocktails instead of cocktails. I have never traded a cocktail for a mocktail in my puff. Dr Kendrick you have four sessions left. I hope this is enough to shape a new better me.

Mobile rings. Must change ring tone. Matt keeps changing it to Jessie J's song - It's OK not to be OK!

"Ellie. Ellie. Ellie!"

"Morning Ruby."

"Actually afternoon. But I'll let you off because editor at the Daylight Gazette, not just likes, he bloody loves your article," she squeals. "I toned it down a bit obvs, or more specifically removed the swear words and tidied it up. But minus the horrendous language, they think their readers will really relate to you! It's getting published next Friday, in their newspaper and online. See! Told you not to take Penelope's shit offer."

"Serious?" I perk up opening my laptop. I must re-read what I wrote.

"They want you to write another four columns covering the other new things you will be trying." Ruby's positively buzzing. So am I.

"I can't actually believe it. Go me, columnist for the Daylight

Gazette, the most popular newspaper in Scotland– thanks so bloody much Ruby." I am in shock.

"Obviously they will pay, I have to negotiate your fee, but it will definitely take a chunk away from your birthday bill!"

"Amazing, you are a legend." I have to pinch myself. Yes, I have got a column in a very unorthodox way but I've still got a column.

"I'll see you in an hour."

"An hour?" why am I seeing Ruby in an hour.

"To drop off Le-na..." Ruby speaks slowly.

"You FORGOT!" she snaps with renewed irritation.

"Of course NOT!" I snap back frantically checking my text messages. Can't find anything.

"My sister's away on her anniversary weekend so I am on Auntie duties. I asked you weeks ago to watch Lena for a few hours today. I've got an event I must go to later." Ruby said knowing all well I had totally forgotten. I need to start actually using my diary.

"I better clear the empties," I joke.

"Yes, please do and stop wallowing in self-pity Ellie. It's getting boring."

"OK Doc." I mock her.

Ruby hangs up abruptly.

Only a true friend could be so brutally honest. Even if it is rude. It is deserved. I know my friends are the best cause they are the sort of friends that speak nicely behind my back but then are brutally honest, and rude, if required, to my face.

Speaking of friends. I text Matt for backup.

ME: Watching Lena for a few hours. Pizza and monopoly?

MATT: Ruby asked me first, actually. Mature one ha. Finish work in couple of hours then will be round.

ME: I know I've hit rock bottom when YOU are being considered the responsible one.

MATT: Please F OFF I'm busy trying to turn a hot married man with a double expresso and a Belgian chocolate twist.

ME: Wrong, on every level

MATT: Away watch your YouTube video biatch

ME: I hate you x

MATT: love you too x

It is a blessing Lena is coming around, she is a bundle of sunshine - and motivation to tidy up. But first coffee. The need to pee coupled with the need for caffeine acts as a catalyst to get my lazy arse out my comfy double bed. I boil the kettle then pee and change into my unflattering yet so super comfy black velour tracksuit.

Coffee hits the spot. I check my Instagram. I had posted on Instagram last night - photo of my laptop open, with a white blank word document. I had carefully dressed my photo with a white mug, branded with the slogan 'she believed she could so she did'. If you follow founder of Spanx Sara Blakely you will know the mug. She often poses photos of herself sipping out of motivational crockery. I'd be smiling too if I was a billionaire. Well-deserved billionaire at that, an inspiration. At this very moment I just want to be able to pay my bills comfortably and not have massive anxiety every month on the run up to pay day. Serious fucking stress money is. I think about the 'lack' of it way too much! For my insta post I wrote - *BLANK PAGE, NEW START, NEW BEGINNINGS...* over the photo of my laptop. I used a bold font in white writing and the coffee cup GIF spinning and around with steam from the top and hash tagged it -

#highoncaffiene #writersofinstagram #unfuckingmylife #everystoryhastwosides #itismeellieb #elliebenson #bethebestyou

Even though it was a total lie. The mug was filled with prosecco. A red alert that I need to calm my drinking - the fact I am lying about it to my now 2987 followers confirms this. I HAVE 2987 followers, still can't take this in. I am an idiot, yet random people are still curious to my life. Matt kindly advised they are probably waiting for my next epic fail.

I got close to a thousand likes. 921 to be precise. Lots of clapping hands and love hearts in the comments. Sympathy pouring in from other heartbroken females wronged by their men. My page is becoming a mini hub for women to rant about their dip shit exes. A safe place to support and empower each other. It was starting to get out of hand though -

@gemsthebestx1 - Lets round them all up and let a pack of hungry wolves feed on their flesh

@foxylady13xcx - But first we shoot them in the kneecaps

@gemsthebestx1 - Excellent idea. Ditch the wolves, let's just shoot them in the kneecaps and watch them bleed to death.

@foxylady13xcx - I'll bring the popcorn and vodka

Another several ladies got involved in the popcorn eating, vodka drinking, men bleeding to death chat. I had to quickly intervene when they were trying to confirm a time and place and best site to acquire hit men.

@itismeellieb - After two compulsory therapy sessions I am starting to believe the best form of revenge is becoming the best version of myself (never, ever thought I'd say that). Let's stop giving our cheating, fuggily, mangina, shit for brains men head space. Let's not give a shit about them. Let's give a shit about us. What you guys doing for YOUrselves this weekend? Ex

@notthemusicjazz fucking love you Ellie. I am doing a yoga retreat. Yoga is a great stress relief and great for the mind #womansupportingwoman

@foxylady13xcx I have been thinking about starting yoga. Better than a murder club lol. Fancy it?

@gemsthebestx1 Guess so. Give me quality time to try convince you about the wolves again haha

Before long, it has flipped from negative to positive chat about yoga. They most likely viewed Jazz's page. Her super slinky, firm and toned body would make anyone want to try whatever she does to get in that shape. I'm on my second week of yoga and while I don't look like Jazz, I did manage to touch my toes for the first time in as long as I can remember. Winning at life! Next mission is to eat healthy enough so I can maybe see my toes again. Another comment pops up.

@SamSam2456 Well said Ms Benson. You'd get life for murder.

I quickly click on @SamSam2456 profile request permission to follow. Permission accepted I am following Sam! Hah, he joined.

Bio: A crazy red head made me do it. Will never hashtag. Nachos and pineapple.

Posts - 0

Followers - 2 - Jazz and myself

Following - 10 me, Jazz and some certified accounts, all athletic people and footballers – not one that I recognised.

@SamSam2456 welcome to the world of Instagram!! For the record all the best people are crazy. #fact #youwillhashtagoneday

@SamSam2456 - Never. And yes, crazy is good. If not crossing over the man-eating wolves' lane.

@itismeellieb Cannot confirm. That lane may be present in my future haha #joking

He liked my comment but no reply.

I feel happy. That giddy first date happy. Sam has joined Instagram and mentioned ME in his Bio. This is amazing, maybe after our brief time together (coffee shop not jail) he has thought about me and my exquisite company. I will know more once he posts his first post.

Door knocks.

"Where is the coolest, cutest kid in the whole entire world?" I scream arms wide open.

Lena jumps up hugging me tightly. "Aunty Ellie!" She is cuteness overload, her long brown hair in pigtails, beautiful olive skin and twinkling brown eyes.

"I have serious clothes envy." I point to the coolest multi coloured unicorn top with matching leggings.

Ruby kisses my cheek then Lena's button nose. "ELLIE!!! So happy you are writing again. Genius. Long overdue and don't feed her any sugary treats, swear or watch anything inappropriate for her five-year-old eyes. Even Horrid Henry. My sister HATES Horrid Henry." Ruby wags her manicured nail, mouthing to me that apparently Henry is a didi and a very bad example.

"Horrid Henry?" I thought she was talking more along the line of no American Pie, Bridesmaids, or anything Stephen King.

"For real. Will be a few hours tops. I'll be able to get you two hundred and fifty per column, maybe more depending on how the people respond."

"Awesomeness!" I high five Lena.

Ruby shuts the door hurrying away.

"Auntie El's what's a loose cannon?"

"Eh a train. I think - crazy runaway train. Why'd you ask?"

"Ohh OK. My mom thinks you're a big mouthed train." Lena says innocently, skipping around the living room.

"Oh, does she!" I chase her doing my best choo choo train noises. Beatrice, Ruby's sister, walks around like she has a stick shoved up her arse. Ruby and Beatrice grew up with a lovely family but little money. Ruby has carved a career for herself, Beatrice married some rich guy and now speaks with marbles in her mouth. As Lena's adopted Auntie I see it as my duty to keep her grounded, and normal.

"OK let's drink lemonade, eat chocolate and watch Horrid Henry!" I say hugging her again.

Lena throws herself on the sofa kicking off her tiny trainers. Then starts to jump up and down. "I am SOOO excited!!!"

I pour two glasses of lemonade with ice, dig out my emergency bar of chocolate and settle on the sofa.

The day is far from over and I already have so much to be grateful for on this rainy Saturday. I am a paid writer, columnist - the first positive to come out of Bob leaving me. Sam has joined Instagram, so the chance of a topless selfie is now possible. And I am cuddled up on my sofa with Lena, ready to learn how Henry has earned the title of Horrid.

Dare, I say - I feel happy.

16

Sunday morning. I wake up feeling bright and fresh. My happy bubble pops when I look at my mobile. Text from mum -

MUM: Change of plans now meeting at Princes Square 12 noon.

ME: For what?

MUM: You are joking? Lunch with Auntie Patsy, it has been in the diary for weeks Eleanor.

ME: Mum, my birth certificate says Ellie. Quit with the Eleanor.

MUM: I know it annoys you. See you at 12

ME: Is dad coming?

MUM: Don't be silly Ellie x

My dad will use this Nancy free opportunity to binge smoke and sip Whisky in the garden shed listening to Radio Two in peace.

ME: Tell dad I say hello x

MUM: He says hello back. See you soon x

I'm feeling great after my sober Saturday and I have to waste my energetic enthusiasm on my mother and Aunt. My plan was to put on the tunes, clean my flat then reward myself by watching The Greatest Showman - Ruby, Jazz, Matt and even Lena were all appalled I hadn't yet been swept away in the magic of the inspirational 21st century hit. We had planned on watching it last night but our Monopoly game turned very serious and lasted for over two hours. Matt cheated as per, only it took us longer to bust him for thieving from the banker - Ruby. At the end we crowned Lena the winner, Ruby and I were tied second and Matt was disqualified for cheating. Ruby told Lena that cheating was wrong and made an example of Matt. Matt pretended to cry, so

Lena sung Baby Shark, loudly with all the actions three times. It cheered him up but by the fourth round he was praying for silence, as all adults pretending to like that song do.

At least I will get a good free lunch today. Aunty Patsy always pays, she's pretty well off. She likes to brag about her wealth by gushing over paying restaurant bills, but ask to borrow fifty squid and she'd be spreading your poverty about the town like plague. And technically, I still have time to clean and watch The Greatest Showman later if I don't waste hours mindlessly scrolling through Instagram or playing Word Cookie.

I decide to make an effort for lunch. Probably because I am not hungover and I know it will make my mum feel better witnessing me indulging in some self-care. And it is sunny. Sunshine always helps. I fully expect an MI6 interrogation as mum and Aunt Patsy have sent several YouTube related texts.

MUM: Still in denial - can't believe you are a YouTube star for all the wrong reasons

AUNT P: Your poor mother Ellie. Really, she is mortified. What happened?

MUM: Glad to hear about the therapy, long overdue. proud of you going, want all the details.

AUNT P: Watched your video. Swap Spanx for Slimming World. I say this from a place of love x

I run the straighteners over my hair then follow Matt's step by step process to apply my make-up. Flawless finish, pink shimmering eyes and red lips. I swap my PJ's for a black silk top and comfortable floral print trousers. Spanx on to keep everything in place, of course.

The trip into town was pleasant. I climb off the bus, which was unexpectedly quiet and pop on my dark sunglasses. It feels good having my new MK bag on my arm.

I love the vibe of Princes Square. Should Bravo ever film The Real Housewives of Glasgow I bet Princes Square would be prime location for the rich Glaswegians to splash the cash at Vivienne Westwood or Kurt Keiger. After spending more in a minute than people earn in a month, they could move onto a swanky restaurant and consume enough Champagne for their claws to come out. I can't lie, I love The Real Housewives of... well anything. Guilty pleasure, fabulous escapism from reality.

"Ellie" mum greets me with a hug and kisses both cheeks. Then Aunty Patsy does the same. I feel their eyes on my stomach.

"You look lovely mum." I lie staring at a long leopard print dress - *what the fuck is she wearing?*

Aunt Patsy has always been a classier dresser than my mum, despite poor Nancy's effort. Even weeks away from turning sixty, Patsy is in skinny jeans wedges with a cream camisole top and a navy-blue blazer. Her blonde bobbed hair is sleek and simple.

"Do think she's lost weight?" Aunt Patsy chirps in, staring at her sister.

"You might be right," my mums screws her face up, trying to decide.

"I interrupt throwing my hands in the air. "Eh I am HERE!" I should have played sick. My mum on her own is bad, but teamed with her sister, they would tear through the thickest of skins.

"We love you sugar plum," my Aunt squeezes my cheek. More of a pinch than a squeeze.

"You need to work out your healthy weight Ellie." my mum said.

"Bugger off, I am only a size eighteen. And if you really want to know… my healthy weight would be Tom Hardy on top of me!" I snap and ask the passing waiter for a large white wine A-SAP.

My mum blushes as the table next us tuts. "Ellie!"

"You need sex darling," whispers Auntie Patsy with sympathy.

"Not doing this. Subject change NOW!!!"

"Thank you so much." I take the glass and knock back a few big gulps as the Satan sisters order something from the seafood section.

I order spicy spinach spaghetti with garlic bread and sweet potato fries. I saw someone tag that exact meal on Instagram the other week. Looked delicious. I change the subject to Aunt Patsy's birthday retirement bash.

"So, what's left to do for the party of the year?" I know the venue is in Edinburgh, beautiful location looking up to the Castle. Ruby had used her contacts to help make sure the best event planner was in place with all her contacts. So much details go into event planning. Come to think of it, it is actually like Aunty Patsy's fifth wedding. A sit down three course meal, followed by speeches then a disco in the ballroom.

"The band has confirmed, so glad. It's the amazing brass band from my second wedding. The one with the lesbian lead singer," Patsy joyfully exclaims.

"She's not a lesbian Aunt Patsy. Her husband plays the trumpet in their band." I know this for a fact. A drunk Matt attempted to 'borrow' said husbands trumpet for an after party – for the record, Matt CANNOT play the trumpet so god knows what he was thinking. After security wrestled Matt to the ground she grabbed the trumpet and screamed - "This is my husband's trumpet you bloody idiot!"

"Well she looks like a lesbian."

"Because she has short hair?"

"Yes." Aunt Patsy nods.

"That's so not PC," I shake my head.

"Neither is causing carnage for the world to laugh over on YouTube." My mum adds.

"True." I agree not wanting to elaborate.

"I love the band; I was so disappointed they couldn't play at your third wedding." I say sarcastically diverting the chat away from my rising fame on YouTube.

"I can't actually believe I am going to be sixty, and retire! It is making me quite emotional," she wells up.

"Only as old as the man you feel," my mum rubs her sisters' hand and winks. We all laugh.

Husband number four, is only 51. My cousin Joel, Patsy's only child, is from marriage number one. Husband number two and three were so short lived I can't remember their names.

"Are you done?" I ask, knowing this question will annoy her.

"Done?"

"DONE, done with men, marriage – have you found the one in uncle Brian?" They have been married for nine years, the longest survivor yet.

"You know Ellie. I've realised it's been more me than the men. Apart from number three he was just a total arse," she laughs rolling her eyes.

I tilt my head, to show my ear waiting on a reply.

"Yes, yes, yes!" she repeats herself brightly.

"My relationship advice would be..." Aunt Patsy starts. I resist the urge to say 'I'm not taking advice from a three-time divorcee.'

My mum smiles at me gratefully, as if reading my mind.

"Don't bank on a man to make you happy. Make yourself happy first and the man will follow. Your dad is a rare gem Ellie. Kind and laid back, so much, that he has been able to put up with Nancy for all these years" We all laugh as if it is a joke. But there is an element of truth in what she said. My Aunty may have charged her way up the career ladder, but my mum won hands down when it came to men.

"He knows what side his bread is buttered. Lucky man your

dad."

"He sure is Mum." I smile thinking of my dad no doubt on his third fag and shot of Whisky as we speak.

My mum takes a minute to gather her thoughts - "But, for goodness sake -speed up with the happiness, your biological clock is ticking Ellie."

All she has ever wanted is to be a gran. I think that's why she championed Bob - viewed him as a sperm bank. A walking sperm donor ready to impregnate her daughter.

"Talking about biological clock, exciting news – Joel called this morning…"

Oh, dear god no, Joel is four years younger than me. This will send my mum over the edge.

"Tiffany is pregnant! I am going to be a gran!" Patsy squeals with joy.

My mum starts to cry.

Fuck. My poor mum. Poor me.

17

I have the Monday blues. I grab a takeaway coffee before work - swapping my usual cappuccino with three sugars for an oat milk latte and honey. It tastes unexpectedly good. I have decided to be consciously healthy, as often as possible. I should have remembered summer bodies are made in the winter – but I am not a fan of the winter. One of the crappiest things about winter – the darkness. As if it isn't depressing enough having to go to work, it is dark when I wake up and dark when I get home. Sometimes I wish humans had built in hibernation - ideally, I could stuff myself fat for nine months then sleep for three. But seen as I am not an actual hibernating bear, I really should use winter to ensure I have a half decent summer body.

After the mental battering I took from my dear mother and Aunt, I have decided I want to lose some weight and feel more confident in my own skin. I reckon I have to lose about one to two stones to get to my size sixteen target, so I am aiming to shed three pounds per week. This morning I glued a photo of my head on top of Kelly Brook and pinned it to my fridge. She... CORRECTION...I...AM wearing a yellow bikini and standing on white sand with a back drop of turquoise blue water, I think *I am* in the Maldives. My future figure is to die for. Flatter stomach with curves in all the right places. The future me, may find work as a Kelly Brook body double. Bod Goals.

I have arranged for Matt to weigh me weekly, tonight is my first weigh in night, he is meeting me at mine with his scales after I do a healthy food shop. Can't fucking wait. NOT! I did have a beautiful set of glass scales but when they insisted on lying constantly about how much weight I gained, I threw them down the communal concrete staircase. Turns out avocados, while being healthy, were not sin free. I spent an embarrassing evening with a brush and shovel cleaning up the stairs whilst apologising to my neighbours for my emotional, aggressive outburst. *Fuck you avocado, you tempting little bullshitter.*

I slump down at my desk and switch on my computer. "Morning all." The whole room smells of doughnuts. A box of fresh, warm doughnuts topped with toffee sauce and sprinkles are teasing me from across the room. They smell disgustingly amazing - all nice smelling foods such as these doughnuts, should be barred from our working environment in support of my weight loss. Noticing me gawking at her teams' doughnuts, Hilary holds one up and nods with a smile. I give a thumbs down, pull a sad face and point at my belly. She laughs, points at hers and makes an awkward *I shouldn't be eating these either face.* If I were to eat a doughnut, even just a nibble my brain would respond with its usual mantra;

Well that's it's Ellie, you have totally fucked your diet with the nibble of that doughnut! Green light alert! Please use this moment of weakness to stuff your face with whatever bad food you can get. Start again tomorrow.

WHO WOULD HAVE THOUGHT THE CRUMB OF A DOUGHNUT CAN HAVE THAT MUCH POWER!

Jim, Dave and Benny are arguing like toddlers about football results. It starts off all jokes, then becomes serious. So serious, that Benny once lamped Jim, giving him a sore bleeding lip. They never learn. But at least the football diverts their focus away from me. The three amigos are squeezing every last drop of laughs out of my YouTube fame. I am agitated and beyond over it.

Gemma, the newest recruitment consultant, walks in depressing my Monday even more. She is a walking advert for a Victoria's secret model. Thin - legs to her armpits, glossy blonde hair and a creamy bronzed complexion I thought only achievable by a snapchat filter. She seems invincible to the smell of tempting doughnuts she doesn't even glance in their direction. Admirable willpower.

"Morning Ellie." Gorgeous, nice, doughnut resister. I am green with envy.

"Hi Gemma, hope you had a fab weekend!" I reply as chirpy as I can be.

The football chat has ceased.

"Put your tongues away, or I'll take a photo for your better halves..." I use my fingers to mimic me taking a photo.

"Good morning, our ray of sunshine!" Benny smiles sitting down. I notice he isn't wearing his gold wedding ring.

"Good weekend?" I ask curious.

"It was OK thanks, you?"

"Benny's team got royally humped!" Jim shouted over the desk before I could answer.

"Fucked your maw Jimbo!" Benny replied raising his middle finger.

I shake my head and open my emails. Morons.

Why does it always go back to the mum abuse? I expect such comments from teenagers screaming down headphones while playing some aggressive online game. But married men at their age – seriously? Give it a rest.

"Done yours too Dave, just in case you're feeling left out." Benny added before answering a call in a well-spoken mannerly voice.

Dave shook his head and kidded on he was wanking mid-air.

Benny replied with the same hand gesture.

Mr Brown walks in clearing his throat loudly. His presence sucks banter like a tornado. Unlike gorgeous new girl Gemma, Mr Brown cannot resist the lure of the doughnuts. He makes a beeline straight for them. Watching him shovelling one in his fat pie hole has indeed put me off, chewing with an open mouth, exposing his coffee stained teeth. A bit of the toffee topping trickles down his chin. He wipes it off with his fingers and sticks it in his mouth, not before itching an armpit with the same hand. He takes another doughnut, shouts some orders at a flustered Hilary and thumps up to his desk at the top of the room. I may be sick. Thank you, Mr Brown, for taking away any doughnut temptation I had.

I pull out my mobile to discreetly text Jazz. She is unusually late.

ME: Heads up. Mr Jobby already at his desk x

JAZZ: Urghhh asshole. I better call in. Will be at hell in 5 mins x

ME: Hah. I'll be here – burning with Monday morn BS. C u soon x

Five minutes later Jazz skips into the office all bouncy and smiles, she too resists the doughnuts, and she hadn't witnessed Mr Brown eating one. Ruby and Gemma clearly have more willpower than me when it comes to food. The proof is in the waistline.

I'm in the middle of editing some CVs for Benny when Jazz emails.

JAZZ: Sam said he bumped into you. Then he starts an Instagram account with your influence...spill?

ME: Ah yes, I did indeed share a coffee with your hot AF step bro.

JAZZ: And? Are you going out for another coffee? It's about time he met a decent girl. Oh my, imagine if we were related. I could be your kid's auntie. Holy moly guacamole x

ME: I wish. No tbh Jill is moving to Glasgow, he was nervous to tell you. Thought I could help soften the blow...so to speak.

Given the 'FUCK NO' scream from the back of the room, I take it Jazz is not happy.

JAZZ: Just been given the look of death from Mr Brown. Jill might be moving back but Sam is not stupid enough to associate with her, ever, again.

ME: I am not so sure.

JAZZ: Over my dead body will he go near that cow again, I hope I bump into her to give her a piece of my mind!

Not sure if Sam realises the extent of Jazz's hate for his lying scumbag of an ex. I would say the chance of her ever-forgiving Jill are a solid ZERO. But I did promise Sam I would at least try to help. Will think of a plan before lunch.

ME: Namaste lover. Must go work, will bitch about Jill at lunch. Yayyy! x

JAZZ: It's a date x

18

I am outside the supermarket. I hate food shopping, especially when I am hungry. It is warm but a rain shower has just appeared. Everyone's scrambling for a trolley to get in out the rain - bumping into one and other, screaming *your welcome* sarcastically. The only smile I've seen is from a young child trying to rip open the packaging to a shiny new doll, the rain does not seem to bother her in the slightest – happy as a pig in shit. Her mother, on the other hand, looks demented fumbling for car keys and juggling a million bags.

It rains heavier, I put my bag over my head as a pathetic attempt to stop the frizz and make my way to the entrance. Once inside, I double check my credit card app just in-case I hadn't accounted for any transactions. I still have £249 available. Rich.com. I dig out my shopping list I had composed in work time. I'd titled it for some motivation.

KELLY BROOK'S SHOPPING LIST – DO NOT GO TO THE DARK SIDE

Strawberries

Blueberries

Bananas

Salad

Onions

Garlic

Red peppers

Spinach

Tomatoes

Brown rice

Baked pots

Small sliced seeded brown bread

Brown bagels

Cream cheese

Wholemeal pasta

Quorn mince & bacon

Toilet roll

Deodorant

Orange juice

Dark chocolate (85%)

It is a small but sufficient list, that will see me through to Friday if I stay on plan. I keep my head down and work my way up and down each aisle scoring off each item with a brown eyeliner as I can't find a pen. My bag is like a junk yard, I find sanitary towels, paracetamol, one half-drunk bottle of juice, a million bobbles, lip balm, receipts from a decade ago but NO pen. Call me Mary Poppins.

I am standing in front of the drink's aisle. My favourite dry white wine, with a subtle whiff of peaches is on special offer with 50% off – temptation being thrown in my face. £4.99 instead of £9.99 - the offer ends in three days. But if I buy today, I will drink tonight. Then my mind will keep reminding me of this offer that ends on Wednesday. So, no doubt, if I drink tonight, I will come back tomorrow and the day after. Then if I drink, I will not see the point in eating healthy as the number of calories and sugar in wine is horrific. May have to switch to gin or vodka with soda to eliminate this thought process. I take a photo of the tempting bitch of a bottle and insta story it along with the caption 'When you decide to have a dry week and this is on offer' then a very appropriate GIF of a woman crying her eyes out, with the hashtags–

#it'sismeellieb #myfav #wine #healthyismynewattitude

#prayersneeded

"Why oh, why are you on offer?" I ask the bottle, still undecided if the angelic me shall win, or if I am just delaying the inevitable. Feel like a bit of a dick just staring, as if waiting for an answer.

"Hi Ellie," the tall floppy haired guy picks a bottle up and drops it in his basket without a thought.

"Heyyy..." I shall allow will power to win this week – or today anyway.

"Simon – new guy – Browns Recruitment..." he offers some info, knowing from my blank expression I have no clue.

"Sorry, so rude of me. Yes, I remember – Simon!" I blush slightly remembering Benny insinuating I should offer myself on a platter because we are both single.

He looks more handsome out of his shirt and tie. Casually dressed in dark jeans, boots and a dark green jumper.

"So, how you finding it?" I ask, tilting my head up to meet his blue eyes.

"It's OK." he shrugs.

"Shithole, eh?" I screw my face up.

"Nah, it's OK!" he laughs.

"Good wine huh?"

"My favourite." I almost drool.

"My sister's too."

"She has good taste!" I am jealous she will be enjoying the subtle peachy flavours this evening.

"So, you're a PA for thee K Brook?" he looks at my list. How embarrassing - note to self, don't write shit like this again.

"Haha I wish. I think... no just Monday motivation for my fat arse." I laugh curtseying like an idiot.

"Your arse looks fine to me," he flatters me with confidence. I blush.

"Why thank you - I better get to the checkout before my 'fine' arse picks up the vino." I say honestly. I really did have to go, or I'd pick up the wine.

"See you at work, tell Kelly I say hello." He smiles and walks away.

Cute. Simon is cute. Must remember to check surname so I can have a good dig on all things Simon related on social media.

I score deodorant and toilet roll off my list. Shopping complete. And for the first time ever, I have wasted no money on shit I did not need. On my last trip to the supermarket I came home with car de freeze (I do not own a car) and the newest window cleaning tool kit, if you look at my windows, you'll understand this is laughable – cleaning them is never on my to do list. I pay swiftly grateful that a new checkout opens as I approach the long line of people waiting to pay. Bus or Taxi? I saved money on shopping, did NOT buy wine so yes, I will reward myself.

"£8.20 please love," the taxi driver said looking at the meter. He has parked right outside my block of flats.

"Keep the change." I hand over the £10 reluctantly, I am bitter that that £10 could have bought me not just one, but two bottles of wine. There is no question – I would have preferred the wine.

I give my fridge and food cupboard a much needed clean out before putting my shopping away. I pop a baked potato in the oven, grate some cheese and prepare a salad to go with it. I am so bloody hungry. If there were any sugary delicious snacks in the house, I would eat them all. I remind myself, in my hungry state that preparation is key! If I let myself go hungry, I will 100% go off plan. I wash strawberries and shovel them down but my mind is thinking about the veggie hot dog with steak cut fried chips I had last week. I am sure I dreamt about this particular meal last night. I couldn't decide if it was the food or the hot-dog which was penis shaped. I concluded my dream meant I am a hungry penis deprived divorcee. Something I need to remedy and pronto!

"Helloooo paid columnist." Matt shouts using his key to let himself in.

"Matty, how's your day been?" I hug him. I'm catching a whiff of pizza mixed in coffee. *Pizza, pizza, pizza. I love pizza*

Matt steps back. I am sniffing him like a dog. "You ok?"

My belly rumbles loudly. "Oh hen, your starving!"

"Hardly" I suddenly feel very selfish. The TV is playing an advert to help end hunger across the globe. The child looks so hungry. Matt changes the channel before I cry. Once the birthday balance is paid off, I will donate.

"So how is the birthday balance going? I made £50 tips over the weekend; thought I would contribute. I still feel a little guilty for enjoying the show, then having sex with Leo in your bed." Once the words came out, he slapped his hand over his mouth.

"I knew it!!!" Raging.

"Jealous much!" Matt whispers, eye rolling.

"Ahh please. There is more to happiness than sex... I do not require penis to feel happy. Even if I am dreaming about penis shaped vegan hotdogs... Shit Matt you are right!" I flop down on the sofa.

"Well lucky for you, friend of the year. That will be me – who has organised that blind date you promised I could arrange?" Matt smirks reciting my one a week to do list –

1. Go to a yoga class - tick
2. Go on a blind date – to do, Tuesday at 7PM
3. Get a spray tan – to do
4. ......

"Tomorrow seriously, who first dates on a Tuesday? Is he gay?"

"Gay? Why would you ask that?" Matt jumps back appalled.

"Remember Richard. Yes, Richard the guy you set me up with, unbeknown to me it was actually to see what he thought about YOU!" I remind him of the rotten situation he put me in.

Matt is buckled over in laughter remembering the time he used me as bait because his gaydar wasn't working. Turns out Richard was not bisexual; he was very straight and didn't like Matt or red heads – so we both didn't stand a chance.

"What does Mr. blind date do? What's his name?"

"No social media stalking shall be done. I will tell you exactly what I told him. Tuesday 7PM Table 13 – it's a new place in Merchant City, I'll text the address. I will confirm he is sadly straight, very fuckable and loves red heads."

"OK then, that's the dry week out the window!" I say grateful. Even if the blind date is a total disaster at least I will enjoy a guilt free glass/bottle of wine. I mean who would go on a blind date without a glass of Dutch courage. *Mature person maybe.*

"First blind date. Ever!" OK I shall do this. Normally I'd be googling the shit out of his name just to make sure he's not some married psychopathic drug taker. OMG what if blind date guy is? I mean it is Matt that has arranged it.

"Does Ruby know him?" If Ruby has gave the seal of approval, I know I am safe.

"Hen, I only met him yesterday. So nope."

"Matt, come on. He's a twat, isn't he?"

"He is fuckable – and you only have weeks to complete Dr Kendrick's list - not months!" he adds with sarcasm.

"How did the blind date subject even come up?" I wonder.

"Well...." Matt rubs his chin.

"Doesn't matter, less I know the better, saves me cringing. Guess it gives me content for next week's column. I submit my work on a Monday to go to print on the Friday!" I remember I am a columnist - I feel a whoosh of excitement.

Matt laughs, pulling a set of scales from his bag. "You're welcome. Call me cupid!"

"We will see." I highly doubt I am going to meet husband number two, call it a hunch.

"Do not be afraid precious ones. Cupid will not leave you here with the scale killer." Matt hugs his white digital scales.

"Fuck off..."

My baked potato was plain and boring. I need to learn how to make an exciting salad. Matt had set up the Greatest Showman ready to hit play once my weight had been noted.

I have stripped down to my bra and pants, as I'm confident my clothes weigh at least two pounds.

"Hurry up jump on, Hugh Jackman is waiting." Matt points impatiently for me to step onto the scale reading 0:00lb

OK here goes. I suck in silently chanting, 'think thin, think thin!'

16 Stone and 11 Lbs.

"See not so bad. 11 is my lucky number!" Matt rejoices.

I have instant regret for not buying that wine. I pull on my onesie, make a coffee for us and dig out the emergency fags and ashtray. My mum's radar is on form. I show Matt the text.

MUM: *I can't stop crying, can't believe my sister is going to be a gran before me. Hope your Monday was better than mine. Love you, mum x*

Matt grabs my mobile and switches it off. "Not tonight Maw." He takes a draw of my cigarette and throws his feet over my legs.

Friends. Friends that become family.

19

Work was, - well work. Nothing exciting happened, other than the new coffee machine that got installed. By noon I had consumed three cappuccinos compared to my normal one (with half a teaspoon of sugar opposed to my normal three). The caffeine high was good at the time, then I crashed and burned by 3PM. I am home now, it's 5:30PM. I have one hour to beautify myself before heading back to the bus. I have to be in Merchant City by 7PM to meet my blind date. I know I should be feeling excited, but I'd much rather be going for a long soak in my bath. I am treating it as work though, this blind date is the content I need for my next article. I am more nervous about what I am going to write than the actual date. Oh god, I so hope people like my first column. Ruby's confident if this five-week slot is successful I may get something more permanent. Would be a dream come true.

"Hi Matty!" I answer my mobile, half hoping Mr blind date had cancelled.

"Are you super hyped?" he probes.

"More like super anxious. He better not be a fucking weirdo Matt." I wish Ruby had met him.

"Oh, take a chill, he is hot and funny Ellie, guarantee you will click!" Matt assures me.

I notice Matt's voice is flatter than normal. "You OK Matt? you don't sound yourself."

"Leo's got a boyfriend."

I can hear Matt choking back the tears.

"Aw, I'm so sorry. But you know deep down he is bad news. You are way better than his loser ass." I try to be kind. Leo is a total prick, that uses and abuses Matt whenever he can't get anyone else. Leo has Matt on speed dial if he doesn't pull on a night out. Matt's willpower is shit, purely because he actually likes Leo.

"I know, I just thought I'd be the one to tame him. It's not the best living with my mum."

"Thought you loved living with your mum?"

"I means she's awesome, I love her like crazy. Still does my washing like I am a teenager but as soon as I meet a guy and we get serious. It's like, *hey keep your voice down,* I can't wake my mum. Total cock block."

"We should flat share!" we shout at exactly the same time.

"Pause that thought, a group of prams have just barged in. The maws look harassed and in dire need of caffeine," Matt's mood picks up. He loves a chin wag with his coffee posse.

"Bye roomie. If we don't talk again, I'm prob buried at the bottom of Mr blind dates garden!" I hang up. There are so many pros and cons about sharing with Matt. There are so many pros and cons about living with me. Match made. I will need to dig out my tenancy contract. I am sure my lease is up in December.

I insta story two outfit choices - I have no clue which is best. I write in bold writing - Blind Date, please help! I leave my fate in the hands of my stylists aka my now 3021 followers and go shower. Twenty minutes later I am showered, I have added some loose waves in my hair and applied my makeup as shown by the amazing Justine Jenkins on insta. If you don't follow her you should, she shows it's possible to apply beautiful make up using cruelty free products.

I check my insta results.

70% voted for the black Jumpsuit, 30% thought my black skinny Jeans and red sparkly top shirt top. Following my dilemma with what to wear I have many DM's wishing me good luck on my blind date. Several more asking if it is my first date since Bob, my first blind date and am I bisexual? But the main questions circulate around my weight. Did your marriage fail because you were fat? What weight are you? Are you on a diet? You seem bigger than most vegetarians... There is a lot of curiosity from my new follower 'friends', some of it insulting. I will reply to them all on the bus, even the twats.

I team the sleeveless jumpsuit with my fav black faux fur jacket, big gold hooped earrings and black ankle boots – not the ones from my birthday night, they got what they deserved - BINNED. I take a rare full-length photograph of myself posing at my full-length bedroom mirror. I screenshot all the weight related DM's cropping it down to fit in an insta post.

I like my photograph. I am a long way from loving what I see in the mirror but I like it enough to post the photo, along with the DM screenshots about my weight. I write a caption -

All 235 LBS of me scrubs up not too bad. Do I want to be slimmer? YES! Did my weight cause my marriage to fail? NO – Bobs wandering dick did. Anyways, out with the old & in with the new. (laughing emoji) OFF ON A BLIND DATE!!! Please disregard yesterday's insta story advising I was having a dry week. I will resume the dry week, next week. #it'sismeellieb #dontjudge #confidence #is #beautiful #sizeeighteen #plussize #womansupportingwoman #goingona #blinddate #shitting-myself #notliterallyhahaha

As always, I used several appropriate emojis. My regular one being the glasses clinking.

I take a big breath in. I would NEVER, EVER, EVER normally announce my weight to anyone, let alone complete strangers. I am hugely embarrassed about my stretch marks, hanging stomach and bingo wings! But I have been getting so many lovely messages of support from women, I feel a peculiar, overwhelming duty to be honest with them. No filter, no lies - just straight up Ellie Benson.

I hit POST and head out the door.

A tall happy girl greets me as I enter the restaurant and passes my coat to a girl not sharing the same work enthusiasm.

"Ellie Benson, Table 13 please," I prompt the girl scanning the reservations.

"Of course, mam right this way."

I follow her through the tables to the back of the room. I can only see him from behind as she points in my table's direction. He has a thick head of brown curly hair. And, I can tell from his sitting stance his is quite tall.

It has been over four years since I have been on any date. I have lifted cash. As a 'strong independent woman' I do not expect the man to pay for my food. Although my bank balance and birthday bill would be grateful if he did. I got such a mixed response when asking the dating etiquette on paying –

Ruby: "Always pay your own way, it shows strength, we do not live in the Victorian days."

Jazz: "He should pay, end of."

Matt: "So, because he has the dick he's expected to pay. Women are messed up."

Mum: "Darling, set off the way you intend to go on. Let him cover the bill."

I decide to go with Ruby's approach. I do not want to look like a damsel in distress, although I may want a man to pay the bill (due to lack of money), I do not need him to. I am stalling getting to my designation of table thirteen. I am walking super slow; it's annoying the waitress who spied at my feet for issues. I feel full blown flustered. A blind date. What the fuck was I thinking? At least on Tinder I would know what I was visually up against, and I would have some basic foundations to start a conversation. Shit, I hope this guy can talk or I am going to nervously ramble my way through dinner. Wine. I need wine.

"Thank you." I say to the girl as we *finally* approach the table.

Candlelit, no less.

I start to laugh as my eyes lock on his. He laughs too. We both laugh. A slow R and B tune is playing in the background. I have an unexpected desire to twerk Beyoncé style, but I manage to contain myself.

"Well this is most definitely a surprise." Simon smiles and orders a bottle of white. He stands up as I sit down. Gentleman.

"Fate," I joke. Then blush, thinking he might be thinking, I am thinking wedding bells. Fuck I think too much. Stop. Over. Thinking. Everything.

"Time will tell, eh?" he winks. I have never been one to find a wink sexy. But my lack of sex or any male attention finds me tingling at the wink. And he looks so fine in fitted dark denim jeans and a casual cream shirt, loose at the collar. He is going for the relaxed look, but you can tell he has spent more time in the bathroom than me. He is perfectly groomed.

"So, you met Matt?" I ask the obvious question, but don't want to push for too much information in case Matt has not sold me in a great light. I gulp down some courage.

"Nice guy. I went in for a strong coffee and came out with the coffee, plus a blind date. Bonus!" he smiles again. Keeping his eyes locked on mine. He oozes confidence. I like it.

Conversation flows easily. I find myself laughing at jokes about Mr Brown and other idiots from Browns recruitment. I learn he is actually twenty-eight, so an acceptable two years my junior. He is a freelance consultant for businesses and is contracted to Browns for two days per week. He shares a flat with his sister, which explains the wine buying. He is very complimentary, flirty and attractive. Yes, Matt you have done good. Simon is very fuckable.

20

Therapy Session Three – Thursday 21st of May

Birthday Balance - £2920

Instagram Followers – 3029

Happiness Ranking – 4/10

"I HAD SEX!" I announce triumphantly before flopping down on the sofa of confessions. I am excited to share my good news with Dr Kendrick. Matt is beside himself with self-praise. He's wanting to pitch a new reality show to ITV with him as the star host– 'Marvellous Matt, *matchmaker king.* I was delighted though, I had serious doubts about ever getting laid again.

Ruby was happy I had been, *serviced.* She hopes now I have been *serviced,* I can focus on making myself happy. I pull out my gratitude journal. Last night's excerpt was centred around praise for Simon's large penis and excellent love making skills. Do people still call it love making?

It was alarming how comfortable I felt sharing my secrets with Dr Kendrick. She is sitting perfectly poised in a long lime green satin wrap over dress, her hair in a high bun. She tilts her head to the side with a smile, staring at me fumbling in my bag to turn off my mobile. Missed call from mum. Text from Ruby.

RUBY: Coffee after therapy? x

ME: Yes, sounds good. x

"Sorry, sorry." I turn my mobile off and give my full attention to Dr Kendrick.

"So, Ellie, how are you?" she asks gently with that intense hypnotic stare.

"I had sex!" I say again, except this time not as loud. I wasn't bragging, ok - LIE. I am bragging. Simon is the first person I have slept with since Bob. And it was good. Good for me at least.

"Congratulations. With whom may I ask?" she asks politely. No doubt thinking big fucking deal, I have it twice a day biatch. Minimum. She has that confident sex glow beaming from the perfection that is her face and body.

"Blind date which, hilariously, turned out to be a new guy at my work, can you believe it?" I smile reminiscing about my orgasmic state.

"Will there be a second date?"

"Don't know, I haven't seen him since I was a shameless slut and got a taxi home at 1AM." I laugh and wink like some gushy teenager.

"Isn't Tuesday your yoga night?" she asks looking at her notes. Yes, I had said I was committing to Tuesday night yoga. Zero praise for the sex.

"Fear not, Jazz made me go last night instead, which put me in healthy state of mind so I didn't drink." The Doc dives into a fury of note taking.

"How do you feel about a second date?"

"Eh, don't know. Would be good – I think. Simon is confident, attentive, hot. I wouldn't say no to a few more rounds in his bed sheets. It has given me confidence again. I am back in the saddle. Fat, divorcee can still get laid. YAYYY! Winning at life!"

"So, where would you say you are in level of happiness right now?" the Doc asks flicking back through her Ellie notes.

"Eh a four, I guess. Maybe a five – no it's a four." It came out before I could over think it. If I had thought about it more, I may have been swayed towards a seven.

"OK four is good," she smiles.

"I had sex, I am getting a paid article published on a five-week contract. I still owe shitloads of money but thanks to writing it's not so bad. I still feel and look fatter than I have ever been..." I ramble rationalising why I am a four.

"How exciting. Paid work. Do you enjoy writing?"

"Yes."

"Amazing. Does writing make you feel happy?"

"Yes."

"What else makes you feel happy?"

"Prosecco and ice-cream." I shrug.

"Temporarily makes you feel happier, than what you were prior to consumption."

"They do, YES, I consume them together. Large spoonsful of ice cream in between large mouthfuls of - anything alcoholic actually." I answer abruptly. Easy for Doc to give advice when she looks amazing, has a massive sparkler on her wedding finger and giving the designer clothes, bag, pen, journal...I doubt she gets daily debt reminder letters.

"Everything we have in our life, is a result of our choices, actions, standards. This is an exciting concept Ellie. You have the power within you to be, do and have anything you want."

"Bob signing up for the move to Mars would make me happy. My mum backing the fuck off would make me happy, losing weight would make me happy, winning the lottery would make me happy, not being a fat divorcee that lives month to month, barely making ends meet would make me happy..." I am now spitting out my words through tears.

Gold star to Dr Kendrick who has successfully made me shout and cry, AGAIN. Five minutes ago, I was on a sex high now I am a blubbering mess.

"I'm so sorry. I am a mess, aren't I?" I drop my head embarrassed at my outburst.

"Ellie, you can shape your future with the choices you make. You control your state of mind. You can choose your thoughts and decide how you perceive the world around you. Today we will work on some hypnotherapy for self-esteem and raising your standards. Then I want to do a goal setting session before we finish. Sound OK?" She smiles handing me a box of tissues.

"What have I got to lose." I drop my heads in my hands, wiping my tears away.

"Absolutely nothing to lose. But everything to gain. Let's begin." Dr Kendrick speaks in an optimistic tone.

I partake in an emotional rollercoaster when I step into this room. Once again, I am leaving more positive and focused than when I went arrived. I have a new theory. Happy Sarah, the eager to please receptionist, drugs the satisfying glass of water prior to each session. Either that or Dr Kendrick is the real deal - magic.

I walk briskly towards the coffee shop, wishing I hadn't cried. My eye make-up was now non-existent and I looked like I had been crying with puffy red eyes. A cheerful lady opens the door for me. Ruby is already there, comfy in the corner with her latte and laptop. She gives me a big wave and makes gestures to suggest she has ordered my drink.

"Heyy. Excuse the puffy eyes. Doc likes to reduce me to tears at least once." I take off my sunglasses and sit on the comfy sofa. It feels like being in your living room with a few dozen more people.

"Hey back, Miss Columnist Extraordinaire. I've read over article number two and pinged it to the editor. Bloody brilliant Ellie!" Ruby shrieks.

"Bias friend," my face beams. I was doing somersaults inside. The worst word Ruby ever used was *bloody*. This time it is a positive, a couple of weeks ago, on my birthday evening, it was – "Bloody awful state of affair to be in Ellie." If Ruby thinks it's bloody brilliant, then the editor will no doubt agree.

"So excited for your first piece to come out tomorrow, it's going to be the same photo of you as your Instagram profile and it will print your social media tag to drive up your followers. As my client, I really have to admit this is the time to jump on vlogging. Whether it's setting up a YouTube channel or starting to do IGTVs."

"You say jump on vlogging like it's riding a bike. What would I vlog about? Everything I have and want to say is going to be in my articles and my Instagram stories oh and I have re-opened my Twitter – as recommended." I throw in the 'recommended' to highlight I am taking her advice seriously.

"Yeah OK, it just excites me. So many of my clients, lovely clients may I add, but other than being *lovely* and visually stunning, they haven't a brain cell between them." Ruby shook her head frustrated.

"Lucky they have you and your bulging brains then, eh?!" I tease.

"Obviously," we laugh in unison.

We sip our coffee, eat two scones (me) and a banana (Ruby) and brain storm ideas for me to make some money out of my insta platform and promoting my upcoming columns. Ruby has more ideas than I can keep up with. I agree to go over it all in more detail once my first article goes to print and I get some feedback.

In truth I am nervous about how my writing will be received. But as the Doc reminded me,

"You can't be everyone's cup of tea and you shouldn't want to be. Good vibes will be attracted like a magnet!"

21

The magical half-moon has my full attention. It is peaceful sitting under a blanket of stars. I am kitted out for dropping temperature; hat, thermal underwear and a flask of coffee. I should have brought a pillow for the parks bench. Arse is now sore. Sore arse aside, it is nice to be here, in the park, at night, star gazing. I hadn't planned on staying long, it's already been over an hour and I'm not ready to leave.

I have been having more good days than bad days lately. Dr Kendrick is educating me that bad moments do not mean I am going to have a bad day, I can change my state of mind with happy thoughts and movement. My whole life I thought if I stubbed my toe before having my morning shower my day was over. That painful stubbed toe has caused me to scream *FUCK* on some memorable occasions. It has been blamed as the catalyst for many shitty moments too - spilt coffee on my new blouse, the bus getting a puncture, forgetting to rub in my concealer. Seemingly all that blame was in vain. It was not the stub of toe that rippled on to be a bad day; it was because I didn't change my state of mind after the toe stubbing.

Today has been a bad day. Period. I have struggled to change my mindset since I got 'the news' via text at 6AM from my darling mother. However, credit to me, I have not reached for my crutch – alcohol. Welcome to adulthood Ellie Benson. I sip my coffee. Probably not the best drink of choice when I am hoping the late-night park excursion will help me sleep.

Bob is pregnant. Or to be specific Rachel is carrying his baby in her womb. Once again, I have been angry, sad, and asking myself the million-dollar question I still don't have the answer to - WHY? Why did Bob marry me when he was having an affair?

Why did he choose Rachel over me? WHY WHY FUCKING WHY!

I stop myself from crying and blow my nose loudly. A tall silhouette is walking down the path towards me. I panic – I am alone in the park, it's almost midnight, my screams for help would not be heard. Oh, please don't let this be some drunk crazy asshole. I could not take any more shit today. I am going to buy some pepper spray.

As he appears under the light of the street lamp I see a friendly face in police uniform.

"Mind if I join you?" Sam points to the bench.

"Heyy, yeah – yeah of course, please do." I am so surprised to see him.

"How are you?" he asks sitting relaxed unfazed about the time or location.

"OK I guess, you?" I don't make eye contact. The tiniest bit of empathy will have me crying. And I do not want to ugly cry in front of Sam, again.

"Jazz told me about your ex."

"It shouldn't have been such a shock, but it hit me like a train. I had planned to be pregnant by my 30th birthday."

"But instead you were banged up in the jail with a sick bucket and a pending restraining order," he jokes.

"Not cool!" I find myself laughing for the first time today.

"If you hadn't ended up in jail – I wouldn't be sitting here now," he raises his eyebrows with a wide smile.

"True, every cloud," I smile back. Is Sam flirting with me?

"How did you know I was here?"

"Instagram…" he pulls out his mobile.

"Insta stalker?" I smirk.

"I stalk all my followers" Sam holds up his phone to prove he only follows five people. He points to a sign in the background of my video, clearly stating exactly where I am. Wouldn't take a police officer to figure it out.

"Jazz told me about Bob, so when I finished shift and saw your depressing insta story I thought I'd swing by, make sure you weren't thinking of doing anything stupid."

"Like drinking Buckfast, stripping to my birthday suit and running around the park naked pretending to be Eve looking for my Adam." I think back to the summer of 2014.

There is a moment of silence as he digests my words. "That really, really, didn't come close to what I was thinking," Sam shakes his head slowly.

"I would never do that again, not till I shed a few stones anyway!" I admitted. Sam was processing what I'd just told him with a curious expression. He couldn't work out if I was being serious or sarcastic.

"And a heads-up Ellie, safety first, post your insta stories once you've left the place you are at, especially if you're on your own. You don't know what nut job could turn up." Sam spoke assertively.

I slide further away from him on the bench.

"I'm serious," he said very intensely. It was nice. He was looking out for me. It is true though, another social media red alert. People could easily track your whereabouts just by stalking your pages. Maybe I will start the planned posts that Ruby encouraged me to do.

I check my insta story. What was I thinking? A video of me in a dark, empty park looking like a depressed moron. I had included a crying GIF for a representation of my mood with #lifesucks (just in case people couldn't work it out). I posted on impulse. Embarrased.com. I've had lots of genuine concerned DM's; I must reply back to them all tomorrow. I feel shameful. It looks like I have posted for the sympathy vote and attention.

I feel embarrassed, I am in the same category as the people on social media, that post shit like – 'OMG the most amazing news ever!!' Then they receive outpourings of comments asking what the good news is, only to read… 'can't say yet, sorry!' *If you can't say, just don't fucking post.* This is my pet hate of social media and the main reason I deleted my Facebook page years ago. Tonight, I was a dick on social media, appearing to open floodgates for grief thieves sharing their shitty lives. Your vibe attracts your tribe – meme of the year. I open up my story and delete it. Tomorrow I will do a post explaining my miserableness like a responsible adult.

"Right enough wallowing." Sam stood up and held out his hand.

I let him pull me to my feet. He is strong.

"My mates run the best late-night takeaway, time to try the legendary Nacho's with pineapple."

"Food! You don't have to ask me twice. But seriously fucking pineapples on nachos? I still can't get my head around it."

"You'll see," he grins quietly confident.

We talk easily as we stroll to his car. I ask about Jill. She moves back in a few weeks. He agrees that the chances of Jazz developing a renewed sisterly bond is slim to none. Less than that actually. I think even if Jill and Jazz were the last humans on the planet Jazz still would rather suffer in silence, and she loves the chat.

"Can't blame her, really, she just loves you." I say climbing into the front seat of his car. I put my hands over the warm air blasting out the heaters.

"Would you get back with Bob?" Sam pings the focus back to me. Sneaky. No one has ever asked me this question.

"Sorry, if you don't mind me asking?" he adds interrupting my silent thoughts.

"Mm in truth I don't know. I would say HELL NO, to anyone

else that asked, but that's because I know he doesn't want me. He wants some skinny blonde bitch with a bun in the oven. But maybe if he came crawling back on all fours begging for forgiveness and pledged to be the best husband for the rest of eternity, things might have been different. Maybe. It would make me feel better having the power back, the power to choose whether I want him again or not. With him choosing *her,* I feel powerless. It's like the world pulled a carpet from under my feet and I'm just tumbling down and down with no one to catch me…" oh crap, I am crying. I manage a sob and hold my breath for a few seconds to stop the horrendous noise that is me wailing.

"I couldn't have put it better myself. You must be a writer – eh. Columnist, read it on my lunch break. Must say I was impressed with your honesty. YOGA & BEANS!" he laughs a genuine laugh. We pull up outside a takeaway in the west end. There are several drunks falling about aiming chips at their pieholes and hitting their cheeks. My normal Friday night appearance.

"Thanks Sam."

"It really was good, even made my sergeant laugh and he's a hard egg to crack. No pun intended."

"That's bad. So bad."

"Sorry," he shrugs laughing at his own awful joke.

"But thank you, for this. For taking my mind of everything. For making me laugh, I appreciate it more than you will ever know."

"I've been exactly where you are. It is horrible. I used to have this recurring nightmare, I had it so much I used to panic it was a premonition. I was on a beach, then the sand started to sink and it never stopped. It kept sinking until I disappeared. Thankfully Lacy sorted out whatever crazy shit was going on in my subconscious, cause for a while I thought I was going mad."

"The doc sure is magical" I agree. Lacy Kendrick is a legend.

"Let's make a pact"? I decide.

"Never to repeat what each other has just said?" he gives a thumbs up.

"Yeah that too... obvs. From this day on there shall be no more tumbling or sinking. We will take back the power, no more wallowing – *guilty*. We shall swim not sink." I sit up straighter, shoulders back and take a deep breath.

Sam holds his hand out locking eyes on mine. I shake his hand; my hand disappears in his. His touch has me tingling inappropriately.

"Here's to swimming not sinking," he agrees, holding my gaze longer than needed.

"Let's go eat some fucked up nachos." I step out the car to see a girl vomiting by the side of the road. Poor thing, we have all been there. And if you haven't - I salute you!

"Pleased to take your pineapple and nacho, virginity," he winks stepping out the car too.

I laugh loud. *I wish you had taken my actual virginity Sam. I'm sure it would have been a much better memory than the fumble in a closet with some spotty, sweaty little weasel, Ryan the Rat, as I named him. He told the whole high school I took it up the arse. For the record I DID NOT.*

22

I have not thought this through. But the pain will distract my mind from the little person growing inside Rachel. I blame Dr Kendrick – *try new things, it will be fun*. 'Without change there can be no change.' I love the idea of having a tattoo but the 'getting' part less than excites me. In fact, I would rather sign up to walk the West Highland Way. With that said, the length of time to get a tattoo would be far less than the time it would take to hike the famous Scottish walk. Tattoo wins! I have spent the entire morning googling painless places to get a tattoo. Turns out painless and tattoo are a rare combination of words. I'm thinking a ladybird on my arse would be the best solution if I am making a decision based on pain– but then I would have the worry of over-drinking, gaining confidence and showing it off to - well - everyone. The best advice Google could offer was that -

"Pain is subjective – what hurts more for one person doesn't for another."

In theory I just have to pray I have a high pain threshold. It can't be that bad, surely? Otherwise why would people go get multiple. A bit like children. Given my mother's in-depth recollection of my arrival in the world, labour is no rollercoaster. However, it doesn't deter women going on to produce siblings. The question I ask myself is– *do I have a high pain threshold?*

My first memorable experience of pain, quickly made better with Calpol and candy floss. Ten years old - fell off my bike when my lace got caught in tyre. Skint knees, hands and a stone in my head that needed removed with small tweezers unplugging squirting blood. Fainted. I remember the humiliation more than the pain.

Fifteen years old - Adam, the hottest boy in school was having a sixteenth party and I wanted to look hot. I agreed with Matt that I needed a make-over. Hot wax almost removing my skin let alone my leg hair. Followed by burning my forehead with an iron (on the same night) trying to tame my frizz. Resulted in a trip to A & E and Nancy banning Matt from our house for three months.

Broke my ankle at sixteen when fell off gigantic chestnut horse. Was grateful that I had missed the steaming pile of horse shit that was inches away from my face as I landed. I hadn't even wanted to go horse riding, but Ronda a popular girl, had invited me to her horsey birthday and despite warnings from Ruby, I went. In hindsight I think breaking my ankle was actually a god send. I learnt the real reason for my invite was to play 'pin the tail on the donkey' …the donkey being me. Last time I searched for Ronda on SM she of course fell in the 2.4 children, happily married, successful skinny bitch category. Another example of how I question karma.

The time I fell on Aunt Patsy's cactus plant display. My sadistic Aunt loves the spine covered plants; she still has a display of them as you walk into her conservatory. To her they represent survival and strength, that was until I showed them no mercy. I tripped (may I add whilst sober) and flattened many of the angry prickly beasts. Aunty Patsy was quite displeased. It took, cousin Joel (pre-med student at the time) one full hour to remove the spines from my derriere. He was bright red for the full hour. It was the first naked female arse he had ever seen.

OK – this trip down memory lane isn't working. STOP mind trailing off NOW. This is just to get a feel for what I want, to find out costs and book appointment. No pain shall be had today!

"Hi love" the warm, light voice did not match his tall, rugged tattooed physique. He wore a leather waistcoat, his arms a masterpiece of pictures and words. He had sleeves on both arms, they told so many stories.

"Eh, see something you like?" he asked I lift my head; his nostrils have more hair than necessary.

"OH sorry, bit close eh!" I laugh pulling back cheeks now pink. I was holding and breathing on his biceps trying to work out if it was an eagle or a flying pig. I resisted the urge to ask, just in case it is neither.

"No – well – yes. Obviously, your tattoos are fantastic but I'm just looking. I want one, but am worried about the pain, have no idea what to get or…." I ramble.

"Take a look around, the photos on walls are the work of me and my team. There is more in the folders over there. Or if you're looking for something totally different, we could draw something up. My Mrs has an eye for tailoring art, she can design something unique for everyone at a small extra cost."

"Maybe a tiny ladybird on my buttocks!" I say trailing off staring at the walls. Some of these tattoos were unbelievably amazing. True art.

A group of girls come in rocking the goth look quite successfully. I listen in to their conversation. It's impossible not to.

"I want a skull…"

"Nah. His bitch ex has one…"

"Rose, maybe…"

"If you want me to poke out my eyes."

What a charming bunch, throwing out insults like bullets. I manage to squeeze past them huddling round. *Its ok girls do not move; I will just get friction burns on my arse as I scrape against the wall.* They continue to bitch about some poor girl called Sadie. I hope Sadie has a thick skin; they are brutal.

"How about three monkeys ladies?" the tattoo man winks at me then looks more sternly at them. I keep my ear to the conversation but eyes on a folder of art. I do not want to become their target.

"Monkeys?"

"You know...see, hear and speak no evil," he points to a drawing above the door. Three monkeys, one covering their ears, eyes and mouth.

"Dick." The ring leader spits venomously. They all glare from under their long black hair and heavy black eyeliner, slamming the door on their exit. I try so hard not to laugh.

"Turns out the monkeys are bad for business." I squint my face.

He nods uncaringly, "seems so". A tattoo artist is at work in the background. He is younger and bulkier than the guy on the desk. I hear him tell her two minutes. I go on my tip toes to sneak a peek.

"Looks fab." I give the woman two thumbs up as she eagerly watches my expression. Given the size of her biceps I am too scared to say anything but *Yay!* Even if the cartoon bunny rabbit looked better suited for a toddler's bedroom mural.

"What you getting doll?" she asks.

"I like the see, hear and speak no evil but I'm not a monkey fan," I say honestly. I want a tattoo with meaning but not words.

The door to the tattoo parlour swings open. In walks Matt dressed to impress, like the captain of a multimillion-pound yacht all blue and white stripes. This is embarrassing.

"Well here's the fat red head I love. Column number two, all about tattoos!" Matt slaps my arse.

"Less of the fat PLEASE! And it's column number three Matt!" he looks so out of place in this setting.

"Yes darling, but three doesn't rhyme with tattoo, DUH!" Matt skips over to the folders flicking through. He has a suspicious spring in his step. No apology for calling me fat. As per.

"Hey, are you Ellie. Ellie B from the mail column?" the bulging, bicep lady asks before I could call Matt out on having sex.

“Eh yip that’s me Ellie” I say cautiously. Is being me a good or a bad thing? It depends which perspective you have read my article from. I am finding most women are team Ellie. Except one extremist, who thought my bad behaviour on YouTube gave men the power and women a bad name.

“Fucking loved it, you, hilarious hot mess.” She comes out from behind the counter admiring her new tat in the mirror then throws her arms around me. She hugs me tight. Matt sees the hug and comes to join in. Just a random stranger giving me the best bear hug I have ever had.

“Thank you, thank you very much!” I will take it. *Hilarious hot mess*. I have been called worse.

“Watched your epic fail vid. Little prick that filmed that deserves a tattoo on his baw sac,” she says angrily.

“Love that idea, the more pain the better! Don’t have a clue who it is though, sadly.”

“Seeing your ex proposing on your birthday and what should have been your first anniversary. Babe you done what every woman on the planet would have done. I would have smashed her face in too though.” She was getting angrier. Time for a subject change. This woman had been wronged in the past by a man too, it was easy to spot. It starts with the sympathy as they can relate, then the anger comes.

“Thank you, in a fucked-up way it’s been a blessing - without that YouTube video, I wouldn’t have gained friends on Instagram and be getting paid to write a column for the Daylight Gazette.” I think of my pact with Sam, no more sinking into the ‘poor me’ vibes. Positive fucking vibes only.

“Good for you doll. Good for you. I’m Eleanor by the way.” Eleanor hugs me again. I get her insta tag and follow her. Her posts are mainly of her dogs and beer.

“So nice to meet you Eleanor!”

“Can’t wait to see what tat you go for…I’ll be insta stalking…”

she paid £370 for her cartoon bunny and left.

A woman comes out from the office behind the desk.

“My Mrs” the guy nods. His wife had more muscle than him, deep set wrinkles, white bleached hair. More tattoos and piercings than I thought possible

“Ellie Benson @itismeellieb?” she asks.

“Guilty,” I say sheepishly. She scares me. Matt takes a step to hide behind my back.

“I am Michelle,” she stoats out to the floor and shakes my hand. “Come on through, I have an idea for your tattoo.” Michelle walks in front. We follow.

“She is going to kill us!” Matt whispers in my ear.

“Well you first.” I whisper back with a chuckle following her through to a brightly lit room.

“Grab a seat please.” Michelle points to the black leather seats behind her desk. The office is covered with wall art, an incense stick is burning, creating a lingering vanilla smell. She sits down at her desk.

“You have beautiful features,” she states no smile just staring at my eyes then lips.

Matt squeezes my hand. “Why thank you…” I say slowly.

“Can you open your mouth slightly?” she asks. I oblige.

She’s going to stick a cock in your mouth I am confident this will be the exact thought running through Matt’s mind. He is trying so hard not to laugh.

She starts to draw with pencils. Looking at me then the paper. Her face is a picture of concentration.

“Wow!” I say as a pair of lips are starting to form. My lips - exaggerated and in rouge red. After five minutes, my eye is sketched inside my lips, she colours it an emerald green with beautiful shading down to the pupil. She is working so quickly but with so much detail. Then behind the lips she starts to draw a simple outline of an ear in black.

“Fuck me you are good!” Matt holds up the paper.

“Thank you,” she smiles pleased with Matt’s compliment.

“Awesome!” I agree. I love it.

“I heard you say you liked the monkeys meaning, but don’t like the monkeys. Gave me this idea of overlapping your ear with your lips and your eye. Like a bespoke personalised - pictorial maxim, embodying the proverbial principle see no evil, hear no evil, speak no evil.”

“This is sheer genius!” I am welling up. It is better than I ever hoped for or imagined - I love it.

“I saw your YouTube video; I followed you on Instagram after my son talked about your Epic Fail.” I pull out my phone and follow her back. “You see people past their exterior, you listen and connect with your followers so I presume you are kind in real life, and while your words are colourful, you speak truthfully with enthusiasm, whether you are sad or happy.” Michelle says. Deep, meaningful words. I may cry.

“Oh my god. I love you!” I stand up and move round to embrace this woman. A tear rolls down my cheek. This is the second hug from a stranger I have had today. I am now a hugger.

Matt starts to sniffle too. Not one to be outdone.

“So glad you like it” Michelle looks very pleased.

“Like it. I love it! When is your availability and how much would it cost roughly?” I ask praying it no more than my new credit card limit of £500.

“We have a two-month waiting list, but could you come in tomorrow, morning about 10AM? Sunday is my day off but I would open the shop. No charge if you agree to promote it on social media and feature us in your column? What do you think?” Michelle looks at me. She really thinks I am ‘thinking’ about this.

Matt and I look at each other a combination of shock and excitement.

“Holy shit it’s a big fat yes. Thanks so much, I was planning to write about it in my column anyway! And I’ll defo be shouting from the rooftops about getting my first ink done.” I am jumping up and down.

“Brilliant, I am looking forward to creating it. Think about where on your body you want it. Me personally, I would go for the inside of your wrist or maybe a thigh?”

“Wrist so people see it. You only expose the tree trunks to half naked drunk men.” Matt chirps in.

“Thank you, Matt,” I glare. But I agree, inside of my left wrist it is.

“And take a couple of paracetamols before you come.” Michelle laughs showing us to the door.

“Forgot the pain element of it!” I gulp. I can’t believe I am getting my own bespoke tattoo for free. So much to write in my gratitude journal tonight.

Gratitude is the attitude.

23

I feel like a bad-ass. I have a raw, fresh tattoo on my wrist and it is fricking awesome. I am popping pain killers like skittles but as I said – I am a bad-ass. My personalised art work will serve as a daily reminder to see, hear and speak no evil. If I cannot abide by these rules, I shall only ever be seen in long sleeved tops. I have one on today, a loose fitted black silk shirt. I will expose my masterpiece to the office when it has begun to heal.

It's Monday, again, and I am still a greedy bitch. For the twenty millionth time, I am using this Monday as a chance for me and my food addiction to start over. They come around so fricking fast. I'm back at the coffee machine, preparing my team's dose of caffeine. This Monday is different though - I am a tad excited about life. I woke up earlier, did my hair and make-up nicer than my normal Monday 'can't be fucked' bun, I already started writing my column about my tattoo - (while the hour of pain is still fresh in my head) and I replied to several DM's on Instagram.

I don't credit Simon with all the points for my unfamiliar Monday morning happiness, although the fact I shall see him in approximately fifteen minutes is the reason my hair looks nicer than norm. I am happier than I have been in a while. Reasons for happiness –

1. I got a shag. Thanks Simon
2. I have made a new hot, kind, caring friend. Thanks Sam
3. I have a column.
4. I am getting good feedback about my column.
5. No one has yet called me a fat red head today, however the day is young.

6. I have not thought about Bob, not once. Until now.
7. I think I have maybe lost a little weight.

"Good weekend Ellie?" Benny strolls into the open plan kitchen eating an apple. He is nowhere near as happy and cocky as his normal self. I clock his wedding ring is still absent. He looks vulnerable.

"Yeah OK actually tried nachos and pineapple for the first time and got a tattoo!" I say proudly rolling up my sleeve. Benny had to see it. We've had in-depth chats about tattoos over the past few years – it has been on my bucket list since I met him.

"I like...didn't think you had the balls Ellie..." Benny nods in approval.

"You've not been yourself lately. What's going on with you mate?" I ask while it is just the pair of us. Over the years we have had frequent moments of confiding in each other. I drew the line when he asked my thoughts on ribbed condoms and pink trousers.

"Not great Ellie. I'm getting divorced," he is visibly shaken, biting his bottom lip.

"Aw Benny, I'm so sorry." I put my hand on his shoulder. I just keep it there. I want to go in for the hug but Dave and Jim are making motions like they are humping the air. Maturity of teenage boys.

"Cheers Ellie," he bites his lip again, like a child trying not to cry. He didn't retaliate to Dave and Jim, confirming his sadness.

"I'm always here to chat it over Benny - I will kid on I am listening while silently day dreaming about something else." I offer support, he laughs then comes the smell of burning. Smoke is streaming from the toaster.

"WHAT FUCKER KEEPS TURNING UP THE TOASTER?" I scream across the office like a woman possessed. It should stay at three for the perfect toast, who keeps changing the dial to ten!!! A few months ago, my cremated toast (due to some idiot turning up the toaster) made the fire alarm go off. The unrequired evacuation of the whole building (seven floors to be precise) while the fire department pin pointed the toaster, got me a written warning from office manager Wanda. Negligence she said.

Benny laughs loudly, taking some joy in my madness.

"Are you coping OK?" I ask waving the smoke away from the fire alarm with a shabby grey dish towel.

"I'm OK I guess," he shrugs. Benny looks so vulnerable without the bravado of his cocky attitude.

"What happened? You don't have to tell me." I quickly add as he drops his head lower. I pray he has not cheated. I couldn't cope. I may hit him with the smoky toaster.

"Nothing much, we just realised we don't like each other's company."

I really can't decide if he is for or against this change in circumstance. His posture and chat say he is not, but a sparkle in his eye speaks differently.

"Ouch." I empathise.

"Seven years together and it took less than seven minutes for us to agree to separate." Benny chuckles rubbing the finger where a gold thick wedding band used to be.

"Well take it from a divorcee – better to be on your own than be with the wrong person. Has taken me months to believe that. But it's true." I recited the Doc's poetic advice.

"Might do an Epic Fail video, something totally mortifying that makes me popular overnight," he mocks.

"Dick," and just like that Benny's usual, stupid sarcastic grin was slapped back across his face.

I feel my attention leave Benny and his misfortune. Simon is striding into the office with Gemma by his side. They are giggling and whispering like teenagers. I feel a pang of jealousy.

“Ah young Simon,” Benny perked up. He stood by my side watching what I am watching.

They are coming our way.

Gemma could roll about in a field full of cow shit and still look better than what I do and I made an effort – this is the first Monday I have made an effort in as long as I can remember.

“Morning Ellie!” Gemma smiles kindly. God, I hate her. And Simon – Simon gives Benny the throw back of the head ‘what’s - up bro’ I get a wink!

“A wink – huh?” Benny nudges surprised noticing my pink cheeks.

“SOO what!” I bark buttering freshly toasted bread.

“I’ll get to the bottom of that wink.” Benny grabs my toast and takes a large bite.

“DICK!!!” I scream, again too loudly.

Wanda is marching over in what looks to be black Croc wedges. Steam sprouting from her ears.

“Ellie, if I hear your voice, shouting unappreciated language, once more, while calls are going on -” she took a deep breath and continued. I ate my Benny bitten toast while nodding. I was day dreaming about Simon while agreeing with whatever she is saying.

“You will get your final written warning. Do you understand Ellie?” Wanda spoke with scary assertiveness. However, I can’t take her seriously - my eyes keep darting to the unflattering footwear. If Monday was a shoe…Wanda is wearing it!

“Sorry Wanda, one shall not use foul language in the workplace again, promise!” I say sarcastically. I suck in my belly to squeeze past the door way she is blocking. I am not willing to let this draw into a conversation. *You are a dick Wanda, with the shittest choice in footwear I have ever seen. Fuck off.*

I get to my desk delighted to have unread email from Simon – he sits too far away to make eye contact.

SIMON: Hi Ellie, you look radiant today. S x

ME: Why thank you, not too shabby yourself. E x

I am actually bursting with joy that he is flirting with me. I followed his account on Instagram with no follow back and the only text I got was to say 'thanks for the fun S x'. Bedroom antics must have been good. I always thought I was good in bed; he must want round two.

SIMON: Hah, same place, same time tomorrow? S x

I am correct, I am a sex goddess! Shit, yoga again tomorrow night. I will need to join Wednesday's class. Knowing I am going to have sex, again is great for my waistline so I cannot refuse. Being naked in front of another human being will keep me away from the.... CAKES that Jazz has just stridden in with. Oh, shit they are bright, sprinkle, delicious, unicorn cupcakes. I shall resist.

ME: Yes, yes, yes. Repeat of last week would be delightful. E x

SIMON: Let's make it two rounds S x

ELLIE: Yes, let's do. E x

I stand up and pull a blue popper. BANG!!! Confetti shoots in Jazz's direction. Wanda looks like she's about to have a heart attack with anger. Mr Turd Face Brown is off this week so I don't give a shit. I start to sing. People join in...

"Happy Birthday to you, happy birthday to you, happy birthday dear JAZZZZZ... the cutest, sexiest twenty-nine-year-old with a super tiny waist, Happy birthday to you!" I sing loudly, Jazz twirls round with the tray of inviting multi-coloured cupcakes.

Everyone sings over my remix of happy birthday. I catch Simon looking at me with a big smile. I smile back knowing his well-proportioned penis shall have me screaming in less than forty-eight hours.

"Cupcake?" Jazz offers me one before she takes the tray to her table. It's tradition, everyone brings cake in for their team on his or her birthday.

"Absolutely not" I shake my head and take two from the tray. Simon is practically in the bag so what difference will a couple of cakes make. Monday – ELLIE 0, FOOD 1. I pledge to be healthy for the rest of the day.

"Happy birthday my favourite yogi." I stand up and hug her tightly. She is so tiny.

"Love you Ellie!"

"Love you more!" I hand my friend a yellow and pink butterfly gift bag containing some pink gin, lavender scented bath bombs and an Essence of Harris candle that smells so good I could eat it.

"Ellie you shouldn't have." Jazz is about to open her gifts when Wanda stares and points to her desk.

I resist the urge to show Wanda my middle finger.

"Tomorrow night we are going out for a meal and a few drinks, just all been arranged last minute. Me, Tom and a couple of friends. Would be so good if you could come? Jazz brought her hands to Namaste.

"Sam going?" I ask curiously.

"Ohhh laaa laaaa" Jazz dances.

"Bugger off." I turn my attention to the screen.

"He may, or may not be, you will need to come to find out." Jazz blows me a kiss and twirls.

"LADIES!" screams Wanda with enough force to hurry Jazz to her desk.

"I'll email you," I whisper rolling up my sleeve to show my tattoo.

"Loveeee!" whispers Jazz back before apologising to Wanda and whizzing up to her desk.

24

Jazz's birthday dinner. Apparently, Jazz's rules. As soon as I gave birthday girl the low down about Simon, Jazz had skipped to his desk with a make shift invite to her birthday dinner the following night. I sat at my desk blushing so bright my face matched my hair. I sat beaming like a tomato trying to block Benny from photographing it.

So here we are, at the cosiest Italian restaurant I have ever been in. I feel like I am actually in Italy. I have arrived early for once. I sit up on the bar stool and bring out my mobile, Simon has sent a sweet text saying he can't stop thinking about dessert. I'm more prepared this week. Waxed, moisturised with matching underwear. I went for my lacy red number. SEXY AF.

I've been catching up on WhatsApp with Matt and Ruby on the way here. Matt has ditched me as a future roomie before we have even discussed it. I am being dumped for a special someone he wants us to meet next weekend. For once he is not over sharing, we are meeting at his coffee shop so he must be serious. If alcohol is absent then whoever this person is, has Matt's full attention. Ruby is back in London; she too has exciting news to share, I quote, 'in person'. She has voice noted in between meetings feeding my ego on how amazing my article has been received and speaking about fabulous, cash building, opportunities in the pipeline. I voice note her back stating she is fucking awesome in every way and if I was a lesbian, she would be my go-to, number one, lover.

"Yes please," tall dark and handsome barman has offered a shot of tequila. Thank you kindly. I wonder what opportunities are in the pipeline. I make £1471.74 each month. On the last Friday of each month this exact amount is paid into my bank account.

Within a few days, after rents, rates, credit cards, store cards, catalogue is paid off, I have a pitiful amount to live off till the last Friday of the following month. If I dropped dead right now, and went straight to hell, it would take me at least a week to realise I was not at work!

“Cheers love,” he pours himself one also. I guess his age around the same as mine, I notice he has on no wedding ring. I’ve developed a bad habit since Bob left me. I meet people, guess their age then check for a wedding ring.

“On three,” I say, ready to lick the salt off my hand.

“One, two, three,” we lick, down and suck in unison.

Turns out hot barman’s wife had an affair. He found out two months ago, got rip roaring drunk at a family BBQ, screamed details of her infidelity to all, then vomited over her elderly grandparents waiting in the toilet Q. I could see the shame in his eyes as he shared his drunken tale. I smile in empathy open my YouTube app and type in Red Head Epic Fails. Five minutes later Greg can hardly move for laughing.

“Fan – bloody – tastic,” he pours us another tequila and uses his shirt sleeve to wipe the laughter tears on his cheeks.

“Not at the time. Cheers,” we clink shot glasses; the doors open. In bursts Jazz in the arms of her loving, wish we could multiply him, husband Tom and her two-school friends, whose names I cannot remember with yes, their husbands. Yuk.

A waitress greets Jazz pointing to a reserved table beautifully decorated with all the birthday trimmings, poppers, party hats. Four yellow helium balloons are on the table, a J, A, Z and another Z. Happy Birthday banners all over the wall. I thank the, still laughing, barman for the shots and congratulate him on his very own ‘epic fail’.

Jazz screams hello waving her hand off at me. I jump off the bar stool as the door opens again.

Ah Simon. There he is, skinny jeans white t-shirt and black

blazer. My stomach flips. He strides up to me with confidence. His cool fingers run over my shoulder to massage the base of my neck. *Would it be rude to call a taxi already*? He kisses my lips gently.

“You look beautiful,” he takes my hand to walk to the table. The barman gives me two thumbs up and a wink.

“Thank you. You too are beautiful… I mean handsome.” *Fuck shut up Ellie.*

“Ellie!” Jazz throws her arms around me. She is her usual hyper-active self, times ten.

“Stunning, as per” Jazz is in a shimmering rose gold dress.

“You remember Sally and Anna, their husbands Duncan and Ronan, right?” Jazz points at them as she reminds me of their names.

“Of course, Sally. Glowing, so nice to see you again. How far on are you?” I ask manoeuvring my hug around a big baby bump. Her first child.

“Thirty-two weeks, she gushed. And you?” she asked looking at my stomach. Bitch. Unless a woman had a very fucking obvious baby bump you never ask that. I mean I guess I have the fat of first trimester pregnancy. But again, you would never ask that. Full stop. One shall never leave the house again without Spanx. The chattering stops as everyone awaits my answer. Simon excuses himself to order drinks. Jazz looks horrified. I’m sure Sally is smirking.

“Oh I. Am…” she begins rubbing her belly. I presume she is going to apologise.

“With all due respect -” I interrupt, which annoys her. “Thankfully I am NOT pregnant, just fat.” I smile shrugging my shoulders. I look at Jazz warmly and smile. She is mortified. *It’s OK,* I mouth silently.

Sally scoffs, forgetting she was the one that launched an insult. "Why would you not want to be pregnant Ellie?"

"Can't drink for starters!" I take a sip of the cocktail Simon has produced. *Listen Cruella Devil you were the one that insulted me. Bitch.*

"Heard your ex-husbands fiancée is pregnant. Really hope your OK," Sally adds with sarcasm. Sally and I have never gelled. Sally has been Jazz's friend since primary school. Jazz is too kind to tell stuck up Sally they have outgrown each other and to fuck off. If she keeps up this shit I may pass on this info.

"Ah well, at least I can take peace in knowing her fanny will stretch to look like a flappy sleeping bag with the zip opened. Bob's tiny cock will bring satisfaction to the widened man hole. It will be dildos from dusk to dawn for mother Rachel." I wink at Sally's husband on his mobile, most likely Googling what happens to vaginas after childbirth.

The conversation comes to an abrupt end. Sally tugs at her husband's pressed to perfection pink shirt. They take the seat furthest away from me. Result. The chatting continues. Awkwardness over. Well I thought it was over until Sally casually mentioned funny YouTube videos after our starters. Thankfully Simon swooned in and saved the day talking about some video he just watched. He kept his hand firmly on my inner thigh as he had everyone laughing.

I see the door open again. In walks Sam. Jazz jumps up. My heart beats faster.

"Sorry I am late," he kisses her on the cheek then shakes his brother in laws hand. Everyone greets Sam, with hugs and air kisses.

"Ellie Benson, are you out on a school night?" he jokes giving me a gentle squeeze on the shoulder.

"Sam this is Simon, Simon Sam," I introduce the men. A part of me wishing it was Sam that would be treating me to dessert.

"Nice to meet you mate," Sam shakes Simon's hand. Simon's cool calm stiffening. Testosterone – he is no longer the best looking male in the room.

"Oh sorry," Jazz apologises moving her bag and coat for Sam to sit down. She had slumped them on the chair to my left. I think this may have been deliberate. I scowl across at her with my perfectly waxed and tinted eyebrows. Her shrug and tight-lipped smile tell me I was correct. *If only she knew Sam was driving down to collect Jill and her son next week.* Sam had promised to tell Jazz the truth soon.

I began to feel uncomfortable with Simons PDA, kissing my neck like a dog in heat in between drinks and mouthfuls. I head to the toilet with Jazz. She was in her element seeing me uncomfortable.

We take the obligatory toilet selfie. Caption it as it 'BIRTHDAY TOILET SELFIE' And insta story it with a dancing emoji #livingourbestlifes #friendsthatdrinktogetherstay-together #partyingonaschoolnight I tag Jazz and Sam as the 'schoolnight' hashtag was aimed at him.

"You are one hundred percent getting action tonight sexy red head. What is the deal though? Is it just sex or do you see the B word?" Jazz asks applying some pink lipstick and perfume.

"B?"

"Boyfriend," Jazz giggles. She jumps up to sit on the bathroom unit. I would join her but my derriere would crack the wood like a paper box.

"He seems a bit full on tonight. Not that I am complaining I mean my vagina was exceptionally grateful last Tuesday, and I am sure it won't complain tonight." I can't kid on I will not sleep with him. It is all I have been thinking about since yesterday morning when he instigated it to happen again. And, I am on my fifth alcoholic beverage so any resistance has gone to shit. Thinking of willpower, I really need. Not need, I really want a cigarette. Now I have thought about it I will not stop thinking about it until I get one.

"Have you spoken with him since last Tuesday?"

"No, just two text messages. He has a few different clients."

Jazz looks suspicious. "And that means he can't call?"

"Heard Mr Shithead Brown is pleased with the social media campaign he is fronting up." I add more non relevant info about Simon, which has nothing to do with us as a couple, if that is ever to be.

"So – who cares?" Jazz jumps down and hugs me.

"Sam talks about you more than necessary," Jazz nudges me having a final glance in the mirror.

I open the bathroom door. "Sam has made it very clear; we are, and only ever will be friends."

"Time will tell" Jazz floats past me with a wide grin. I feel a pang of guilt not telling Jazz about Jill. But it would ruin her birthday night.

The lights are dimmed. A beautiful Alice in Wonderland themed cake is being carried in our direction by my tequila drinking.

We start to sing happy birthday to Jazz – fellow diners join in. All eyes on Jazz. Simon passes me another cocktail and a shot of something.

"To Jazz," we all raise our glasses and take a drink. Pregnant

Sally looks bored out her skull and fuming with her husband – he is getting louder with every whisky he knocks back.

On my right-hand side Simon is rubbing my thigh, again. Whispering in my ear to leave now.

On my left Sam is texting someone. Simon is overpowering with the vanilla aftershave. The smell trails behind him like a skunk. Sam has just a subtle smell of cool spice. I glance over and catch his eye.

My mobile vibrates in my pocket. I take it out as Simon turns to discuss stock shares with Sally's intoxicated better half.

SAM: Toilet selfie? Are you 18? ...With lots of laughing emojis.

ME: In the waist line. Sadly, not in years. What do you think of Simon?

SAM: Not sure.

ME: What's there not to be sure about?

SAM: Not sure.

I do not reply. Sam's wife had an affair and a child with another man and he forgave her. So, if he is 'not sure' about Simon, I don't really give a crap.

It is 11PM by the time we settle the bill. It has been an odd but enjoyable evening. Jazz has had the best night, which is all that really matters. The collision of some different characters has been challenging but I must say, my social skills have been on point. And I have stopped drinking at precisely the right time. One more would have been too much.

Simon is caressing my lower back as I watch Sam jump in his car. Jazz and her husband climb in the back.

"Wanker doesn't drink," Simon snorts as our Uber arrives.

"Remarkable self-discipline." I wave to Sam staring at me from his car. He gives me a one finger wave without eye contact.

But who cares, Ellie Benson is on route to have drunk sex. With a detour to the twenty-four-hour garage to buy fags.

25

Therapy Session Four – Thursday 28th May

Birthday Balance - £2740 (But £250 per my 6 columns, still to be paid so technically I 'only' have to come up with £1240)

Instagram Followers – 4137

Happiness Ranking – 6/10

Yoga on Wednesday night is good for me - I feel fresh as a daisy. For the first time I am excited about my therapy session. My gratitude journal is bursting at the seams. My tattoo is healing nicely, I have upped my intake of H2O and decided to lower my intake of alcohol. And I *know,* I have lost weight; my black skinny trousers are no longer popping at the waist when I sit down. Since last Thursday the only night I have binge drunk and ate was Tuesday night, which really isn't my fault – it was Jazz's birthday dinner and to be fair, you cannot have 'drunk sex' without the alcohol.

"Thank you, Sarah." I take a sip of my water. *See Sarah, just a sip. I am not hung over.*

"Pleasure Ellie," she smiles, a genuine smile before answering a call. I love non-judgemental Sarah.

I flick through the luxury magazines, teasing me with an expensive lifestyle I cannot afford. The reading material is a long way off from the three-year-old Take a Break magazine I have read several times at my local doctors.

"Good morning Ellie, please come in." Dr Lacy Kendrick opens her office door like an angel. She is radiant in a crisp snow-white suit, black Jimmy Choo's and her hair poker straight past her shoulders. She welcomes me into her safe haven and sits elegantly on her seat.

I try to mimic the Doc, graciously sitting down. I fail. I slump, dropping my overstuffed bag - out tumbles my banana, peanut butter sandwich wrapped in tin foil, journal and a few sanitary towels.

"Stand up with me, arms stretched out" the Doc instructs springing up on her thousand-pound shoes, then slipping them off. Her feet are so small with her perfectly polished toe nails.

"Take off your socks and shoes," she orders. I gulp.

I sit back down; it is not an easy task for me to take off my shoes standing up. I take off my unattractive yet practical, comfy black memory foam trainers, embarrassed by my uncared-for smelly trotters. My hamstrings, calves and inner thighs are very tender from the last forty-eight hours exercise. Hamstring and calves curtsey of yoga. Inner thigh pain - from straddling Simon!

"Close your eyes. Bring your hands slowly up above your head. Deep breath in. Clear your mind. Go to the forest, filled with bluebells and the stream running through."

Her voice is soft and magical drawing me in like a magnet. "Roots are emerging from the soles of your bare feet. You can feel the moist of the lush green grass, the roots are sprouting down deep into the soil. You feel steady, strong." Doc speaks with a tranquil sense of knowing that you willingly follow her instructions.

"What makes you happy Ellie Benson? Don't think just say images or words that spring into your mind."

The first image is a red heart rising from the stream. Like a butterfly it floats. "Love." I say,

"and writing," words are flying past me like a train. I feel excited by their presence.

Then it all goes to shit. Call it my subconscious or my self-sabotaging mind playing tricks on me, not allowing me to get to the root of happiness. I see myself falling about drunk on my birthday night all the words of disappointment from everyone over the years. And yes, once again Rachel's vagina is there haunting my dreams. This time when I look up to her face, she has a baby bump, huge, big baby bump. I feel worse than before.

The Doc continues to talk, her echoing voice now seems far away. I am lying on the sofa bed comfortably; I follow her instructions to put everything I don't like into one big circle. Along with anything bad anyone has said; about me or to me - anything that has hurt me no matter how big or small. My bad thoughts are now motionless and in black and white, just being still inside an imaginary wheel of pink light. The light surrounding them gets bigger and brighter, my worries, problems and fears get smaller and smaller until they are gone. A bubble of pink light is there. A light filled with love. Then it disappears.

Now it's just me. I don't feel lonely, or sad as before. I feel – I don't know what I feel.

"Ellie, Ellie, open your eyes when you are ready." I open my eyes to see she is handing me a tissue.

I sit up wiping tears streaming down my cheeks. "You have to be shitting me. I came in here happy."

She just smiles like a sadist. If I had been paying for this therapy I would be asking for a refund.

"Sorry." I apologise for my shitty tone.

"I agree you are happier; I'd say a six – sound, about, right?" she asks smiling.

Yes, a six is good I will take that. Best so far. Going up on the happiness scale. "Sure, yes, yeah."

I look at the clock. It is 11AM already. Fastest ninety minutes of my life.

We stand up together. Doc opens the door and places a reassuring hand on mine.

"Ellie, you should be so proud of you. You are a beautiful person, inside and out."

I am about to reply 'if you saw me naked you would retract that sentence,' but she raises her finger to shush me before I can speak.

"Just simply say, thank you." Doc crosses her arms giving me a stern look.

"Thank you," I say with a pathetic giggle, I have never been one for receiving compliments. But thank you Doc, very kind of you to say.

I say my goodbyes to the lovely Sarah and make my way to the city salon recommended by work colleague, Hilda. It is time to book my spray tan appointment. If they can give me that slimming goddess glow that Hilda has, I am all in. It's a crisp bright morning, but the sun is shining so I don't complain. I power walk to burn calories. After congratulating myself on definite weight loss this morning, I ate not one, not two, but two and a half bagels with cream cheese and veggie bacon, topped with cherry tomatoes for breakfast. The proof will be in the pudding, or more specifically the scales on Monday when Matt weighs me. While a spray tan will help you appear slimmer apparently it doesn't melt away any fat (sadly). Hilda looked at me like I was a dead corpse when I ask 'how' it made you slimmer, questioning, 'where did the fat go?' In all fairness I asked the question before my morning coffee.

I march off the bagels, fighting through the aches of my leg muscles. Next time with Simon, I will fully encourage doggy style as the main position, less effort, and kinder on my inner thighs.

I drop Simon a casual text as I arrive at the salon. I haven't heard from him since I kissed him goodbye late Tuesday night. I had thought it would be easier to bring work clothes to his to save going home, but I thought he may freak out. I think next time, I'll make a discreet overnight bag with essentials toothbrush, clean pants, change of clothes so I can go from his to work, instead of his, taxi home, barely any sleep, then work.

ME: Hey you, thinking of you x

I hit send then panic about being too cheesy 'thinking of you' – Ruby would kick my lady parts for sending such a text. I drop my mobile in my bag as I arrive outside the salon. Two girls are going in chatting and laughing, care free. Big white smiles, designer bags, hair extensions down to their buttocks and waists so tiny I could wrap my hands around them. I hope the tan therapist is used to seeing woman of real proportions. I gulp.

I open the door and a little bell chimes. It is a cool shabby chic salon, off white walls, grey velvet seating, and lots of pretty love heart shaped lights. Lady gaga is playing on the radio. The girl behind the glass reception desk is in a grey tunic too. Her smile is warm and friendly.

Fake it don't bake it! I'm drawn to stare at the gigantic poster behind their glass reception desk. The dark-haired goddess lookalike is in warrior pose with an orange bikini and a stunning tan. Must be photoshopped, no way one human could be so flawless.

"Good morning welcome to Bootiful Boutique!" the small blonde-haired girl greets me.

"Morning, If I could make an appointment to look like her please" I point to the poster. I guess my thigh would weigh the same as poster girl's entire body.

The young girl giggles.

"I would like to book an appointment for my first ever spray tan please. Do you have any availability for tomorrow night?" I was just about to delve into body shaming myself and pre apologising to the therapist that was going to see me naked when another beauty therapist appears from a treatment room.

"Ellie Benson, yes?" she looks very happy to see me. She darts around from the desk and offers a hand shake.

“Lisa, I am the salon manager, senior therapist,” she dismisses the hand shake and goes in for a hug.

“Hi, hey, hi, yes I am Ellie for all my sins!” I hug back. I did not recognise this girl at all. I am in the process of racking my brain through drunken toilet chats… or maybe she follows me on Instagram.

“Your agent called and said you’d be coming in.” Lisa went back behind the desk.

“Agent?” the young blonde was still confused. As was I.

“Ruby Richardson, the lady that called this morning. Remember?” Lisa said checking her diary.

“Good old Ruby,” I mumble.

“Shannon, this is Ellie, she has a column in the Daylight Gazette. A strong genuine following on social media, a rising influencer,” she introduces me to the girl gawking at my with wide eyes.

“Oh, don’t know about influencer… I got this platform due to my ‘Epic Fail’ YouTube video going viral.” I fill Shannon in on the facts.

“Awww you are….” Shannon has dotted the I’s and crossed the T’s.

“Yes, I am the ‘Fat Red Head.’ Sorry in advance for the unlucky therapist that gets to see me naked,” I laugh.

“Not at all!” Shannon and Lisa say at the same time. Wide eyes, shaking of their heads.

Turns out Ruby told them everything. My therapy and list to try new things (one of them being spray tan). For a free tan I will give the salon a mention in my column. Lisa was hyperactive at the exposure, she agreed with Shannon it would be great advertisement to drive ‘plus size’ clients their way.

I got a patch test and was all booked in for tomorrow after work. They ask if I had time to get my nails done also. For free. Craziness. First, I get a free tattoo then this. It is bitter sweet – I hate the term influencer, but I must say it sure does have perks.

I pull out my mobile and photograph the salon. I Insta story and tag them. FIRST SPRAY TAN BOOKED!! I use a YASSSS twirling Gif along with an apprehensive emoji.

I scroll through who has watched my earlier insta story. Hundreds of people have sent love and DM's. Sarah had photographed me sitting with my thumbs up on the reception chair before seeing the doc. I had told my followers THERPAY SESSION 4 – DOC WORK YOUR MAGIC #healingfromthinside-out #noshameingettinghelp #it'sismeellieb #actionshavecon-sequences

Keeping up with social media is a full-time job on its own. I feel rude not replying to everyone and liking every comment. I will go back to everyone on the bus home.

I check my text to Simon. He has read it but no reply. Yet. Dick.

I check my mobile another trillion times before I get to my work. Still no reply from Simon. He must be busy.

I question my excuse for him. Are you really ever too busy just to send back an emoji? Or one X?

I have been out of the dating game for so many years, I do not have a bloody clue what is acceptable dating etiquette.

My phone beeps. *Simon?*

SAM: Good seeing you Tuesday, have you plans tomorrow night?

ME: I could clear my schedule.

SAM: Pick you up at 7PM? Dinner on me. Need advice.

ME: I charge by the hour…

SAM: I think you have misinterpreted my intention… 'pretty woman'

ME: HA, my ADVICE is charged by the hour. If I was a hooker, I would be too expensive for you mate.

SAM: Hahaha see you tomorrow.

Shit. I'm getting a spray tan. Ah well, will need to just make sure we find somewhere quiet and dark to eat.

I am no longer thinking about Simon.

26

"Ready!" I call. Let's get this over with as quickly as possible. I have used the treatment room shower to scrub and exfoliate with a sweet-smelling passion fruit exfoliator.

I am naked admiring my new gel nails – gradient blend of orange to pink, looks like sunset on my fingertips. I am standing in a pair of paper pants, waiting on Lisa returning to the treatment room. I think dental floss would have covered more. I am modelling an unflattering black hairnet and my feet are stuck to disposable flip flops. Sticky feet, I am told they are called – seems appropriate. I feel like a total dip shit.

"Nice shower?" Lisa asks with a wide smile paying no attention to my body.

"Pleasant, thank you," I say although I did feel odd showering in a room at 6PM on a Friday. Lisa does not look even a tad fazed by my hanging DD boobs and large nipples. I clock a few straggling ginger nipple hairs. Gutter, I wonder if Simon spotted them too, he paid my breasts ample quality time. I figured it's because he normally goes for bean polls with fried eggs instead of water melons. I start mumbling my boob concerns to Lisa, but she is busy plugging in a machine and brushes over my nipple hair panic. She unrolls a plaster resembling a bandage cuts it to shape and places it over my tattoo. Apparently, it's a bad idea to spray over a fresh tattoo or body piercing.

"I will spray your whole body first then your feet, hands and face last. You ready?" she asks turning on the machine. It sounds like we are about to launch into space.

"NO!!! Can't believe I am naked!" I squeal, now cupping my breasts like precious jewels.

"Ah nonsense, we really don't look at the body. It's just like colouring in," she laughs popping on some gloves and squirting moisturiser on her hands.

"Normally when I am naked, I am under the influence."

"You are too funny Ellie. Now jump in and face me, I am going to put some moisturiser on your feet, knees, hands and elbows," she points to the space ship like booth with several spotlights.

Oh my god she is touching my feet. Rubbing cream in while blabbing on about how her ex fiancée had cheated on her. When she discovered his infidelity, she prepared him one last 'loving' meal - which they ate together. Best beef stew he had ever tasted. The main ingredient of his stew was a carefully selected ingredient – dog food.

"I fucking love that, good for you." I like Lisa. I am impressed by Lisa's restraint to sit and eat a whole meal without going apeshit about her findings. I listened as she cheerfully told me the pleasure she took watching him chewing and swallowing piece after piece. Then how joyful she was seeing him run to the toilet when she slammed the tin of dog food down, ten minutes after he had devoured two plates.

"And look to the left and right chin up," Lisa takes a step back and smiles. She was married now, to a nice man. I wish I had caught Bob when I was his fiancée. Ex fiancée doesn't seem as relationship damaging as divorcee. Women generally empathise when they meet me for the first time. Men, just wonder what's wrong with me. Apart from Simon, he didn't judge. Neither did Sam, he could relate. My male work colleagues didn't either, they just got a photo of Bob blown up for the staff room and threw darts at him. Kind, in their own fucked up way.

"Perfection!" Lisa said blowing warm air from the machine under my chin.

Between Lisa's chatting and the coldness, which I hadn't expected, I completely forget I am naked. I have been turning, doing the running pose. The only time I have done this pose this year. I even squatted to tan the smile lines under my arse. I have manoeuvred in a full circle without embarrassment, I was too focused on Lisa's revenge story. Best I have heard to date.

"So just take about five minutes to dry, then put on your loose baggy dark clothing, ideally no bra, or loosen the straps. Remember, the guide colour develops over four to six hours, but you could just sleep with it on. No rush out Ellie. You look stunning, by the way." Lisa drops her gloves in the bin and leaves the room.

"Ideally, the guide colour would melt away twenty-eight pounds of fat – wow." I step out the booth and look in the mirror. A five-minute treatment and I look the best naked me I have seen. Ever. Why oh, why have I never tanned before?

I take a photo of my tan line, tag the salon and add a bright flame next to my tan line #fakeitdontbakeit

Tanning really is slimming, I will post a before and after picture tomorrow when guide colour is off. I look in the mirror again and no longer feel the repulsion that normally hits me on a daily basis. I look, well - not repulsive. I am excited for my next bedroom antics with Simon. Giving his short but sweet text late last night. *'Sorry Ellie, been snowed under with work. Can't wait till it's you that's under me. Speak soon S x'* I am taking it he does want a piece of this fine ass again.

I dress in my black joggers, black baggy top and flip flops before making my way out to reception. Lisa is waiting for me with a bag of goodies. I am so pleased and pleasantly surprised to hear that since my previous Instagram story, yesterday, the salon had received several tan bookings quoting, they seen 'FAT RED HEAD'S insta story.' If I needed inspiration to stay on clean eating plan, it just came right out of Shannon's mouth. We swapped healthy eating tips agreeing that no sin should be wasted on an avocado. Although more nutritional, a freddo beats the avocado hands down. Every time.

I step out into the warm summer evening feeling like dare devil - I have on no bra. Most likely one of the worst decisions of my life. I'm so happy it is Friday or *#Friyay*, as I have become accustomed to calling it on Instagram and twitter. The streets are bustling with crowds heading out for cocktails and beer to unwind after a hectic week. So many poor souls, including me, living for a glimpse of freedom from Friday to Sunday night.

I have been instructed - to avoid all water contact. It is a life and death scenario for my tan results. I didn't tell Lisa I was meeting Sam, I agreed I was going right home to veg out, watch movies and sleep before washing off the guide colour to reveal a perfect tan. I get my mobile out.

ME: In town already. Will just meet you somewhere, prepare to be scared.

SAM: I'm scared that you are telling me to be scared. Where will I get you?

ME: That new place near central, that Jazz spoke about? Can't think of the name but know where it is.

SAM: I know the one, Jazz got me a takeaway from their last week. I'll leave mine in 10 mins

ME: KK, I'll be hiding in a dark corner with a large glass of white.

SAM: You are weird, you know that right?

ME: I'm told weird is cool. Look at Billie Eilish.

SAM: Who is Billie Eilish?

ME: Shit you need me more than I realised.

In no time at all a very tanned, casually dressed me is hiding in the back of the restaurant under dim lighting with a glass of white. I use this moment to catch up on my messages.

ME: I got a spray tan!!! Fucking love it!! X

MATT: Yasss!!! Qween, bet you are sexy AF x

RUBY: Amazing Ellie, so proud of you getting one. You have

talked about it for years x

ME: Thanks, been missing you guys. Excited to meet tomorrow? 1PM still? Matt who is the fresh meat?

MATT: Yes 1PM and all shall be revealed. So excited, I could cry.

RUBY: I have a meeting at 5PM in Edinburgh but coming for couple of hours. Matt the suspense is killing me, Ellie I need 30 mins with your business head on. We need to pounce on opportunities NOW, while your column is trending.

MATT: Its crazy girls were talking about you today in the coffee shop, obvs I showed them all our drunken selfies I have saved from like 2010...

ME: Trending?! Slight exaggeration. Thanks Matt, sure I look like a fucking tank. Delete them!!!

RUBY: Trending in Scotland, Scottish banter! Girls are sharing their stories of cheating partners and their embarrassing stories of how they reacted. They use these hashtags. #itismeellieb #fatredhead #epicfails #scottishbanter

MATT: All feels sexist, men get cheated on too. FYI bitches

RUBY: Fair point.

ME: Whatever Matty – I'm scared to take a shit now in case it's not PC.

RUBY: Again, fair point.

ME: Ok I am away. Will see you tomorrow. I will be the red head that looks like she's just come back from the Bahamas.

MATT: Coconut shells on your tits and a Ra Ra skirt? #BOAK

ME: Ha fucking ha. Sorry Ruby I keep meaning to star out the c in fu*king.

MATT: Why?

ME: Respect asshole. Cause she doesn't swear.

MATT: But she's not stupid she will know what FU*KING means

– dip SH*T

ME: GOODBYE!!!!!!!

RUBY: You guys keep me grounded. Haha, see you tomorrow xx

MATT: Can't wait to hear about Simon's cock.

ME: Too far as per. Bye. Bye.

I didn't mention I was out, sipping chardonnay waiting for Sam. I knew they wouldn't ask. One, I am normally at home on Friday night, lone drinking and two, I have just had a spray tan. I'm not sure if anyone gets a spray tan and then goes out. Must Google and check with bronzed Hilary.

Just at that in walks Sam, tall, casually dressed staring at me with those velvety warm hazelnut eyes. He walks toward me, single girls blatantly glance, girls with men steal a sly peak and I – wave like a hyperactive child.

"I saw your teeth the minute I opened the door!" Sam laughs, eyes wide.

Awesome. Spray tan equals instant teeth whitening. Who knew?

"You do know you are paying dinner for my Jazz related advice?"

"Would be rude not too. Choose whatever you like," he smiles passing me a menu.

27

It's Saturday. I have made the decision to have a productive day, as opposed to my normal – stay in PJS, and watch box sets.

It is not even 10AM and I have already taken out my recycling, where I was greeted with an image of Mrs Withering I'd rather forget - dry humping the air in her floral nighty, from her living room window. I am no lip reader, but I would put money on it that she was shouting "ARE YOU GETTING PUMPED YET?"

Back in my flat, I have hoovered, stripped my bed and put away the mountain of clothes hibernating on the ironing board in the hallway - it has lived in the hall for around five months. I just didn't see the need to take it down, to put it back up again. A bit like making my bed. What is the bloody point? One lonely night the bed making thought sprung to my mind. In a moment of wine fuelled boredom, I worked out it would take me an average of three minutes to make my bed each morning, (I set a timer and made my bed – sad cow). Therefore, by *no*t making my bed, I am saving myself 1095 minutes per year. 18 hours a year to spend on my appropriate things. Like an extra three-minute snooze every morning. Result. With that said, today I made my bed.

Why? Simon sent a text message last night. We are doing brunch at a lovely little place a walk from my flat, then he is joining me to meet Matt and Ruby. I am hoping, assuming, that after brunch, and laughs with my friends, we will come back to mine for unapologetically great sex.

I make my way to the shower, after looking out my outfit - dark denim skinny jeans, sandals and a yellow top with white hearts splashed across the front. The warm water runs away dark brown. Off with my spray tan guide colour. I have a thin white line from where my paper pants covered a small part of dignity. My lady parts are hair free, and vampire white.

I dry off and stand in front of the mirror, naked. I wipe away the steam to see my soft reflection. This is bloody awesome – I look slimer. I dress, straighten my hair, apply subtle but enough make-up and dangly star earrings. Now my hall is clean, I snap a full-length photo of me in the hall mirror and post it thanking the salon for my golden glow. Followed by a photo of the quote - *The past is your lesson, the present your gift, the future your motivation!* I include lots of hashtags, some relevant #writersofinstagram and some not #freddooveravo

Sam is first to like and comment - Happy Saturday Red.

I push back the feeling growing inside, like Jack's bean sprouting at super speed to the clouds above. *Remember Ellie* Last night was all about Jill and Jazz and my role in uniting them. I have agreed to soften the blow to Jazz and help try and get Jazz and Jill in the same room. I pull my mind back to Simon. He has texted to meet on a Saturday, looks like this may be more than a mid-week romp. Happy days.

My credit card treated me to a long faux fur baby pink jacket a few months back. It was on sale with twenty percent off. A bargain at £50. I am having second thoughts on my *bargain*. Whilst walking briskly up the street, I can't decide if I look more EastEnders, Pat Butcher, than the sophisticated goddess that I was going for. I catch my reflection in a shop window and pause for a moment posing. *Goddess.*

“Heyyy!” I wave energetically to Simon as I open the glass door. He is sitting looking every inch a gentleman in blue cord trousers, a casual white linen shirt and a pale blue scarf. The smell of coffee and warm bread is making my stomach rumble. I weave in and out of the tables, it is busy, then plonk myself down with a wide smile. This is the first time I have done breakfast with any man other than Matt, Bob or my dad in years. It feels unfamiliar but pleasant.

"New?" Simon nods to my Pat Butcher/Goddess coat.

"You don't like it?" I ask deciphering the look on his face.

"Eh yeah, don't want other men ogling my posh bird," he jokes. "Posh Ellie." He chuckles. This annoys me a tad. I could act posh.

"I will say thank you, even though I am unsure if that was a sarcastic back handed compliment." I let it go and order a coffee and the veggie breakfast bagel.

He laughs but doesn't correct me. "Damn, sorry babe, I have to pop to a meeting before I join you, Matt and Roxy," he is reading a text that has pinged on his mobile.

Oh lord, don't get her name wrong; she will hate you instantly for lack of listening. "Ruby not Roxy," I correct.

"Sorry, Ruby, Roxy, same thing," he ignores and continues texting. I try not to call him a twat but it is on the tip of my tongue. I will need Matt's honest opinion on the coat. Now wishing I spent £50 more appropriately on a case of wine. The extra dry, extra expensive shit I love. It is 11AM and I am thinking about alcohol, Dr Lacy Kendrick, I may need to commit to that detox.

Simon reaches over to hold my hand, glaring at me lustfully. All is forgiven, *call her Roxy if you want.* I'm so glad I tidied up. I am sure we could run back to my flat and have a quick fumble before meeting Matt and Ruby.

"Ellie, you are a kind hearted person so I have to be honest with you," Simon drops his head.

WTF he thinks I am fat. He hates fat red heads. He doesn't like my jokes…oh god what now. What is wrong with me now? I shall not cry.

He bursts into fits of laughter. Taking pleasure in my blank expression. "I fucking hate your new pink coat!"

I relax and smile. "Rude," a wave of relief washes over me.

We eat, finish our beverages, flirt shamelessly, then call an Uber.

We have an hour before I am to meet Matt and Ruby. An hour of sexual bliss.

I need him. Now. Inside me. We jump out the taxi, snogging the face off each other, uncaring that it is now raining. My poor faux fur looking like a soggy cushion. Mrs Withering is at the window, she spits the tea from her china cup and punches the air, before doing the one finger through the hole gesture ferociously with her hands. "ON YERSEL ELLIE!" I cringe pleased Simon did not notice.

As I turn the keys in my front door, I can feel him pressed against me. Hard and ready. His warm breath and soft lips kissing my neck sends tingles down my spine. We fall in the door kissing.

I slam the door shut and drag Simon to my bedroom, I am about to have sober sex – go me.

28

"BENNY!!!" I scream and fall into the bistro sofa. The same sofa where I viewed my embarrassing Epic Fails, for the first time. I was just about to brag about my Saturday morning. But this - this blows my sober sex out the water. What the hell is going on? I expect Ashton Kutcher to run out and scream PUNKED in my face. My best friend Matt and work colleague Benny are, HOLDING HANDS.

"Spill the fucking tea!" I demand in a firm assertive tone. I don't know who to focus my attention on, Matt, Benny or Ruby. Ruby is settled into the cosy bucket chair sipping her latte, observing my reaction from the side-line.

"Gal you golden!" Matt gives me a once over and claps his hands. He keeps touching Benny's hand, bright with triumph.

My spray tan is the last thing on my mind - it is so strange seeing cocksure Benny so shy. Matt squeezes his hand lovingly.

"So, turns out I managed to turn a married man!" Matt makes a joke. A bad joke. Nobody laughs. Benny looks mortified – yet another emotion I have rarely seen.

"So not funny Matt. You twat.," I snap. I pray they didn't have an affair. Benny's poor wife, I only met Linda once. She was dull as dishwater, but kind and loving, she didn't deserve this.

Benny cleared his throat and spoke up. "Linda knew I was gay," he admits. Matt pats him on the back.

"In truth we have been sleeping in separate rooms for almost a year..."

"Thank you lovely," Jilly sits down my usual cappuccino and a warm chocolate muffin.

"No muffin for her Jilly and it better be semi skim -" Matt begins.

"Ignore him." I smile at Jilly warmly, then tight lipped at Matt.

"Little pickers bigger knickers. Weigh in day, in two days, in case you have forgotten? Another thing I do completely at my own free will Benny, the kind generous friend that I am. Do you think I want to see your fat arse on a pair of buckling scales every Monday night?" Matt glares at me with a grim expression.

I flick up my middle finger.

"Back to your corners. Please go on Benny," Ruby encourages him to talk over our bickering.

"I liked guys as a teenager but continued to live a lie for decades. It just spiralled and before I knew it, I was walking down the aisle saying 'I do' to the wrong sex" Benny drops his head. "Then the silver fox came out, I decided it was time for me to grow a pair too," he chuckles at his own joke. "Couldn't have done this without you." Benny faces Matt with a wide smile.

Ruby pushes my jaw back up. "And the Grammy goes to.... I had no idea Benny. The love for pink clothing should have been a hint…But many muscular wannabes prance about in fuchsia and they're straight. I mean, I have always known you are kinder and more sensitive than Jim and Dave, but they are a law into their own." I throw a cushion over with a big grin. Benny catches it and smiles back.

"So proud of you babe." Matt gushes.

"Love Phil Schofield. Inspirational." Ruby adds.

"He is," we all agree.

"When did you meet Matt?" I ask, curiously.

"Let me paint the full picture," Matt perks up flapping his hands. "One early wet morning, this ruggedly handsome specimen came in from the rain to get a coffee. His sad, gay vibes collided with my aura gaining my undivided attention. We chatted at ease and that one coffee turned into another and another.

It wasn't long before we developed feelings for each other and Benny plucked up the courage to tell his wife it was over." Matt smiles victoriously.

"Do Dave and Jim know?"

"They maybe have a small inclination."

"You have just made Monday morning so much more exciting."

Benny laughs. "Fuck off Benson."

"And Matt, I actually like Benny so try not to be a dick, OK?" I grin, going over to and give them both a hug.

"Welcome to team Loserville" I greet Benny into our tripod friendship.

"Not so fast 'Loser'. Let's talk business." Ruby shakes a grey folder marked *Client – Ellie Benson.*

"First I really need to share something, it's all a bit fucked up," I look at everyone. I need to get this off my chest.

"You are pregnant?" Ruby asks.

"Would explain…" Matt points to my stomach.

"NO, god no, and piss off Matt."

"I just shagged Simon."

"Wait, what this morning?" Matt gasps.

"Sober?" Ruby gawks.

"Yes and yes, try not to look so surprised! Simon is charming, witty and leaves me fully satisfied if you catch my drift!" I start to snort laugh.

"Yes, Ellie we catch your drift we are not prudish twats," interrupts Matt.

"What's wrong then Ellie?" Ruby asks, seeing the disappointment still in my face.

"I think I am falling for Sam."

Matt is giddy, drama gives him joy.

“The hot Policeman that arrested you?”

“Jazz’s stepbrother,” Ruby adds nodding at Benny. A soap drama was unfolding.

Benny beams leaning forward. “Wait, Jazz’s step-brother arrested you? Now you are falling for him?”

“YES, YES, and YES! I’ve met him a few times and we talk on the phone. I am helping his wife and Jazz reconnect when she moves here. I am doing it all for Sam but I think I’m falling for him. There I said it. Phew - feels good to off load some truth. I feel lighter already” I stuff the muffin in my mouth.

“Once again, Ellie Benson swoops in and steals my thunder!” Matt tilts his head pouting at Benny then scowling at me.

“Don’t know this Sam guy, but while we are immerged in a circle of honesty, I think Simon is a dick!” Benny advises honestly.

“Now we are going to have our first lover spat. I set them up on a blind date!”

“How did you manage to set Ellie up on a blind date with Simon?” Benny asks curiously.

“Eh excuse me, you’re not the only hot guy that comes in to enjoy my expert barista skills!” Matt shouts ‘hello’ to some regulars hot men walking in.

“At least you’re not obsessing over Bob and his tart, I think this is a win to my favourite red head. And you’re looking good. Real good Ellie Benson.” Ruby said genuinely.

Above everyone she endured endless nights of drink fuelled snot and tears about Bob. She has always been in my corner. Ruby is right – Sam, Simon and Doc are all playing a crucial part in keeping me occupied and off the self-destruct track. It may be a slow process but I feel like my life is just beginning. I have shed my divorcee skin like a snake, casting it off and leaving it behind. Where it should stay. The future is bright.

It is almost 2PM on a Saturday. I feel it is now socially acceptable time for cocktails. I stare at Ruby.

"Cocktails?" she smiles reading my mind.

"You have a Saturday off?" I jump up and squeal.

"James is in London with work and one of my clients just cancelled, so I just have to go over some details with my *last client* then I am free." She smiles waving my named folder in front of her face.

My mobile beeps.

SIMON: Sorry Ellie going to need to take a rain check, work fuck up need to travel to Edinburgh.

"Simon can't make it either," I sulk, showing the text to Ruby. I really wanted to introduce him to my friends.

"Don't like the guy Ellie," Benny said again refusing to budge.

Matt looks irritated. "Why don't you like him?"

"Don't know, just don't. Bad vibe I guess."

I shrug. "Well, I like his penis so he'll have to do for now."

Matt goes quiet then starts to laugh. "Sorry to change the subject. But I have a question." He stares around making sure he has our undivided attention. "Imagine if the pink panther was to breed with a long-haired shaggy dog, a really ugly one. What do you think it would look like?" He asks us. We don't need to answer, our screwed up, *what on earth are you talking about faces* speak volumes.

He bursts into a fit of hysteria pointing at my coat.

29

Hello Monday I am not as miserable as usual.

Oh, weekend how I have loved you!

The sun is shining.

I have lost weight (weigh in tonight shall prove so).

My tattoo is healing. I am trying so hard not to scratch it.

My tan is on point.

I have had Saturday sober sex.

I have mastered a French plait over the top of my head to look like a hairband. Yes - I was up that early. I take a bow inside my head and walk into the office shoulders back, head held high.

My manager aka Ruby has arranged for me to do a radio interview this week.

“Ellie, you are golden gal! Stunning!” Hilary gives a thumbs up from the coffee machine.

“Thank you” I take a twirl in my black strappy maxi dress.

Wanda greets me with her usual scowl. Her venomous stare could paralyse any prey.

“Good morning Benjamin, Dave, Jimbo.... I know what your all thinking? Hot AF?” I joke attempting a twerk. It always seems sexier when I do it in my head.

“Thinking, I’m glad I *didn’t* go to Specsavers!” Jim covers his eyes.

“KNOWING NOT THINKING that you are FIVE MIUNTES LATE and should take your seat, NOW!” Wanda preaches marching past to shout at the new secretary. She’s jammed the printer already.

“Thinking, never, ever twerk again!” Dave screams. I twerk again. I can’t decide if he is pretending or if he has actually thrown up in his mouth. Rude.

“Any news from the weekend boys? What did we all do? Did we have quality bonding time with our partners? Were we gay with joy?” I turn around, positioning myself in front of Benny.

“Jealous Benny doesn’t want to shove it up your ass?” Jimbo asks laughing before answering a call.

Too far. Far too far as always...“I’ll inform Wanda your arsehole wants her pecker. Creep!” I throw back an insult. I also took it ‘too far.’

“We know Benny bats for the other team Ell’s. Insulted he didn’t fancy us actually.” Dave flexes his poor muscles.

“WHATTTTTT! HOW? WHY?” I expected more dramatics.

“Member the Christmas Party when I got so drunk, I barfed all over the toilets?” Benny took my hand.

“How could *I* forget. I cleaned the barf.” I shudder, having a flash-back.

“Turns out I told them both then. Although I can’t remember a thing.”

“You told them! And I was the one armed with yellow rubber gloves, Flash, a face mask and a peg on my nose?”

“I did Ellie, I’m sorry. But do you know what gets me through everything?” he opens his mobile.

“What?” I lean forward. Expecting a meditative app, or a perhaps a motivational video.

He hits play on his phone. There I am the drunk raging version of myself. Red Head Epic Fails.

“YOU and Matt deserve each other!” I punch his leg and turn around to answer my phone.

And just like that Benny had come out. Officially to everyone. Some knew, some didn't, no one cared, or judged. But best of all Benny looked happy. For the first Monday in as long as I can remember he can't wipe the smile off his chubby face.

Neither can I. Simon has walked in all smiles too. Making no effort to divert his lusting eyes from my breasts. The well fitted push up bra is doing its job perfectly. Wanda notices Simons eyes and shakes her head so violently I fear she may sue me for whiplash. This encourages me to lean forward and squeeze them a bit more together. Wanda is fuming.

"Total babe..." Simon whispers striding past my desk.

"Why thank you," I whisper back. Face beaming, feeling like a champion.

"Don't like him." Benny whispers mocking me.

"Don't give a fuck." I hold my hand out, and snap it shut, insinuating he should do the same.

As working Mondays go, it has not been a bad Monday, I have one hour left till home time. Lunch with Jazz went well. I ate three of my five a day in one sitting. Tomatoes, onions and lettuce were all present in my jacket potato. I tried to slide casually into the conversation about Jill coming back to Glasgow. Jazz said she would rather shag Mr Brown than speak to Jill again, which makes me know I am fighting a losing battle. I just don't know how to break it to Sam.

I head to the coffee machine to acquire a shot of caffeine. It will help speed up the last working hour.

"Well if it isn't the sexiest lady in my life." Simon gently runs a hand down my back.

I blush. We move into the staff room for privacy.

"I try -" I joke composing myself.

"Was thinking let's get some wine tomorrow or Wednesday after work and go back to mine, get pissed and have some fun."

Simon runs his hand over my bare shoulder and down to my chest.

I catch his hand, holding it motionless. "Can't tomorrow, I'm doing a radio interview after work, then have yoga on Wednesday. Trying the Sober Sally thing during the week. What about Friday night? We could maybe go out for dinner and drinks?"

"Interview for what?" Simon snubs.

"Not sure really, my friend set it up for me, radio this week," I say excitedly. "Then next week, I am doing a Podcast with Glasglow Girls Club, which I am buzzing about. My insta followers are shooting up and my column is going well – mercifully, don't think I would have been strong enough to handle a backlash of haters from my writing." I answer honestly. I think it may have been the tipping point for my sanity.

"Wouldn't say your Instagram is a great platform Ell's. Would you?" Simon pulls a look of disgust. "Lonely old women who blame men for ruining their lives. You think you're an influencer now you have almost five thousand followers? And does anyone still read the Daylight Gazette?" Simon sniggers.

"HARDLY! Don't particularly like the term influencer and I have no desire to be one! And for the record, yes lots and lots of people still read it." I snap back licking my wounds. I have no clue, statistically, how many people will be reading my column. Must double check figures.

"That's good, would *hate* for you to get your hopes up, I'm away to Edinburgh Thursday for a few days, the joys of work." Simon sighs.

"What about tonight? I could do dinner but no drinks, fancy it?" I suggest thinking I can postpone weigh in if required. Having sex or standing on a scale? There is no comparison, really. And, I could choose wisely from the menu, making sure to not ruin my mindset for the whole week by eating pizza and pasta.

"Boo hoo Sober Sally. Where's the fun in that though?" Simon teases trailing his finger down from my neck to my chest, again. I can see him stiffening.

My heart beat quickens. “I can be fun sober!” I fight my case. I can be.

The staff room door flies open. Wanda has removed her jacket. She looks like she belongs on a Christmas tree. I can’t take her seriously in the golden patterned print dress, I would have expected to see on a great, great, great grandparent. I stare for a moment deciding if I am being an over critical stylist. I ask myself - does Wanda pull off the vintage look she was aiming for? ... Nope. If Wanda was a celebrity, right now, she would be getting papped to appear in the worst dressed column.

“YOU’RE PHONE KEEPS RINGING ELLIE, ANSWER IT!!!!!!!” screams Wanda pulling me out of my stylist day dream.

“Let’s skip tonight.” Simon decides brushing past me.

Cheers Wanda.

30

I lost 4lb. I had hoped to shed more but, if I am being truthful 4lb is a win. Afterall, I did eat a tub of ice cream at 1AM on Saturday and had one takeaway mid-week – which I told *nobody* about. Therefore, technically, it *did not* actually happen. That's the perk of living on your own; you can do what you want, then blatantly lie about it once you step outside the comfort of your four walls. Willpower is a powerful skill, especially for the single people with no one to catch them ordering that kebab three hours after dinner. However, my eating was vastly better than normal (gratitude is attitude) though I do need to up my game with exercise, if I am serious about becoming a Kelly Brook stunt double. Other than Wednesday's yoga class I have not taken part in any form of cardiovascular activity. Several of my Instagram followers are encouraging me to watch Britany Runs a Marathon. They want me to watch it then meet them at the park every morning from 6AM. I went back with a thumbs up and running emojis. Obvs they have never seen me run – a fully grown Dumbo springs to mind. I shall not be running, but I shall watch the movie. Love a women empowering comedy.

Today has been a shitty day at work - at least I'm finishing an hour early. Boring, crappy clients, crappy work colleagues, crappy atmosphere, topped off with a text from Matt every fifteen minutes to send him a photo of Benny. He had praised me last night for my 4lb loss while jumping around like a hyperactive bunny. I haven't seen him as gushy and giddy since his first kiss at high school with a French exchange student. Turned out the French student thought Matt was a girl with his Hanson wannabe long hair. It was thirty seconds of joy for Matt – that was not repeated. Xavier returned home the following week saying he was violated by a thirteen-year-old. Matt said it was love.

My mobile rings.

"Heyy Ruby. I am on route to the radio station! Topped up my make-up and just jumped in an Uber. I'm so nervous but excited!"

"Aw Ellie you will be fantastic! Just be yourself. You are amazing. Speak about your column and don't be embarrassed to give your insta tag for a follow. So proud of you. Also, I have called and paid £500 towards your Birthday Balance as a gift."

"NOOO, please Ruby, that's not your responsibility." I feel happy but pathetic at the same time.

"I'll get it back on all the commission I am going to make from your fine ass."

"You have more faith in me than I have in myself." I snort accidently. The plump, red-cheeked, taxi driver is gawking at me through his rear-view mirror - presumably checking I am not a warthog. My snort is so fantastic I could be commissioned to play Pumbaa in The Lion King theatre. *Goals.* Would be slightly more dignifying than the time I was hidden under a warm costume playing the donkey's arse at ten years old. My teacher said I made the Christmas play memorable so not to be embarrassed. I fell off the stage.

"I'm heading into a quick meeting now. But I will be tuning in! You will love Amber, she is the sweetest!"

"Thank you, Ruby. Bloody love you." I hang up, excitement turning into nerves.

I snort again opening a msg from Matt. His rudest meme to date. I do not apologise for my snorting. The scowling drivers Uber stinks of cigars. I'll be interviewed live on drive time smelling like a rotten ashtray. Thank you, Uber. I shall not leave a bad review though, cause then I'd have guilt that I cost you money. *You are welcome unfriendly man.*

"I won't be tuning in," he remarks arrogantly as I half-heartedly thank him and slam the door shut. Fud.

Tuning in. I can't believe I am going on the radio. Never in my wildest dreams did I think any human would listen to my loud droning voice while driving home from work.

I wonder 'who' will listen, obviously not grumpy Uber guy. Perhaps Sam, Simon, Bob.... I hate when my mind darts back to Bob. I wonder if he has any regrets? Or does he miss me? Is he excited about being a dad? Did he ever fantasise about having kids with me?

I take a big deep breath in. Hold it for a few seconds then let go. It is a beautiful summer evening. The sun is bright and warm. I look at my reflection before pressing the buzzer. Pushing Bob, Sam and Simon out of my mind. I am not doing this for them, for anyone. This is for me. My goal is to be kept on as a columnist. Without any profile and likeability, the chances of the editor extending my five-week contract is slim.

I look good. Could be thinner but I could also be fatter. I'm happy with good. My hair is down with a slight curl at the ends, it looks a lively red with the sun hitting it. I have on a black short jumpsuit teamed with my very favourite, purple and white star cardigan. My cardigan adds a splash of colour to my outfit and the long sleeves hide my scabby (healing) tattoo. My legs are still tanned and complement my gladiator sandals with black painted toenails. I have in Ellie B terms made a big effort.

I take a photo of myself, using the glass door to snap my reflection. Although my thighs resemble tree trunks, I think it's cool. The flashlight bounces off the reflection putting an orb above my head. I have gained a halo for all my good behaviour. *Dear lord, I am trying.*

I open up my Instagram and post it to my 4798 followers.

Yikes! Nervous but excited! Will be live on the radio with Amber in 30 mins! Tune in to hear my fave songs.... Some fun facts and a Q & A…. #noswearingallowed #it'sismeellieb #ellieb #redhead #girlboss #radio #grateful #blessed #swimmingnot-sinking

I hit post, tagging the radio station, hoping Sam scrolls down to my hashtags #swimmingnotsinking was for his amusement. My mobile rings. Mum.

"Hi Mum."

"Hi darling, me and your father..."

"Hi Ellie!" my dad shouts.

"We are ready! I bought the ginger and chocolate biscuits I love, the posh ones from M & S. Poured a G & T to celebrate. I've spread the word wide and far - I made a WhatsApp group with all my bowling colleagues to let them know. Bumped into your old Primary teacher today, Mrs Smith, remember her? The one that got caught bonking the other teacher, Mr Branson, I think he was called. And, I saw that boy you dated at seventeen, the one that called you ugly…huh he certainly hasn't worn well… I tell you…"

"OK OK really must dash mum. Thanks for your support. I'll call you after on the way home. Need to go in now, love you both."

"Aww Ellie Bellie break a leg," my mum gushes.

"Not literally!" shouts my dad.

I hang up. Turn off my mobile and press the buzzer.

31

Therapy Session Five – Thursday 4th of June

Birthday Balance - £990 – (Thanks to £500 gifted by Ruby and the £1250 for my columns – which is being paid directly to the establishment where it all began.)

Instagram Followers – 4998

Happiness Ranking – 6/10

"Oh, my oh my!" Sarah is flapping towards me in her black and white striped dress. She reminds me of a penguin doing a happy dance – Happy Feet.

"Thanks Sarah," I squeeze back she is hugging me tight.

She holds both my hands. "Imagine my surprise, when I am heading home and hear your cheerful optimism blasting out my car radio. Your laugh is infectious, I was actually crying at one point. And may I say you look beautiful today." Sarah gushes.

"You may, thank you," I laugh. Nobody else feeding my ego. This is my second last session; I will miss Sarah.

The phone rings. Sarah walks briskly back to her perfectly organised white desk to answer it. I sit down and pull out my mobile. I am feeling very blessed to have lots of likes and comments congratulating me on my thirty minutes of radio fame. And my followers have jumped up a few hundred. I have a meeting with Ruby and the editor next week to review my columns longevity. *Pray for me.*

"Ellie, hi, please come in." Dr Kendrick opens her door looking her usual lush self. This week she's modelling a plain understated black suit with black patent Louboutin's. I've got on my faithful, pleated black skirt a vest top and the same purple and white star cardigan as I had on yesterday (sprayed with hefty amount of deodorant) and my red converse.

"Sit please," she smiles giving me that deep intense look. Zero blinking.

I take a seat noticing a new smell in the room. A Jo Malone Reed diffuser has replaced the other one that smelt like musty vanilla. Good choice Doc.

"How are you Ellie?"

Doc asks her usual question. Ready to dissect the shit out of my answer.

"I think I'm fine, I should be fine. I have so much positive things going on in my life that I am beginning to get annoyed with myself for feeling anything but fine…if that makes any sense" I scrunch up my face and whisper sorry.

"Makes total sense Ellie."

Doc seems unfazed with my answer. Phew.

"You're not really *fine*, but you don't know why?" she draws out the word fine.

"Yeah, I guess so."

"And have you been doing your gratitude journal?"

"Every night, without fail." I answer truthfully. I have been enjoying scribbling my gratitude. Sometimes it is one word (normally when been on the vino) other times it is full pages of gratefulness.

"Amazing Ellie. And what about the new man in your life?"

"Actually, not sure where it is going." I really don't, he is so hot and cold.

"Question. How did you imagine your life being at thirty?"

This question stings. "I suppose, I assumed I'd be married by thirty and trying for a family." I nod and take a breath, "and have a mortgage, not be renting. Maybe a bit thinner too." I shrug and chuckle defeated.

“OK good Ellie.” Doc smiles scribbling down something. “I have no doubt you will achieve all of the above, but you must change your belief system to know that you are *enough.* Right now. Just as you are.” Doc stands up and motions for me to do the same. “Repeat after me. I am Ellie Benson, I AM enough.” Doc points at me with her fresh long acrylics.

“I am Ellie Benson, I am enough…” I mutter feeling like a dick. I have tried affirmations in the past but it has always been in private.

“Louder! I AM enough!” Doc raises her voice.

“I am enough!” I turn my volume up a little.

“LOUDER!” she commands.

“I AM ENOUGH. I AM ENOUGH. I AM ENOUGH!” I practically scream. “Wow,” It feels good to say that out loud.

“Yes, you are,” Doc replies with a wide grin. “Now lay down, let’s get that drilled into your subconscious.”

I am lying on the mustard sofa with a cream blanket covering me. Eyes closed.

“Now follow my voice Ellie.” My mind trails off to my safe place, the bluebell field with the stream.

I leave therapy deciding I am still a 6 on the happiness scale of 1 – 10. For the first time I did not cry. Not that I can remember. It’s weirdly comforting offloading to a non – judgmental stranger, who is, without a doubt helping positively rewire my brain. Next Thursday is my last session. I would never admit it – but I will miss Dr Kendrick and Sarah. If I’m ever flush enough to have a spare £200, I may invest it in her. At my first session, I angrily wished they’d used *my* therapy money to cover *my* birthday bill, then Ruby did a bit of investigating. Turns out the restaurant owner’s son, is engaged to the Doc, so my therapy cost them nothing. It helped ensure they look good supporting mental health and making sure I pay up.

I step outside and take a deep breath trying to pump myself up for my tedious eight-hour shift.

Mobile rings.

"Hey Ellie, think you're going to be my first famous friend..." Sam speaks chirpily.

"Offft... more chance of pigs actually flying." I redden. I'm so happy to hear his voice.

"You were amazing on the radio! I was on shift in middle of a case so couldn't text."

"Aw didn't expect you to listen. Thank you." I start to jump up and down – he listened! An elderly couple turn away as my boobs almost jump out my vest top. I pull myself together.

Sam praises me. "Honestly, you really are swimming Ellie, you should be proud of yourself."

"More like a doggy paddle really. One more therapy session left, £990 outstanding on my birthday balance and I have to write a speech for my Aunt's retirement bash a week on Saturday. Everybody I know, plus their dog and granny is going to be there" I really do need to work on a speech. My Aunt Patsy had inherited several asshole friends along her sixty years of life. My mother kindly booted my confidence by reminding me they will most likely film my speech for their 'twatter and instadram page'. I have given up telling her it is Twitter and Instagram.

"You'll be great Ellie," he assures.

"So, why did you really call?"

"To hear your beautiful voice?"

"Whatever, why did you really call?" I ask again. I wish he had just called to hear my voice.

"Ok, ok so Jill is on her way to Glasgow, she's coming earlier than expected. I have broken it to Jazz and she called me a fucking, stupid, twat faced, step brother. And that was mild in comparison to what she called Jill."

"Yikes!" *Go Jazz, could not have put it better myself.*

"Thing is, Jazz and Tom have been so good to me. I enjoy their company; I want to be able to do stuff with them as a couple." Sam sulks.

"I really don't know what I can do to help?" I picture his sulking face and feel guilty not being more persuasive with Jazz.

"On Saturday night Jill's parents are having the baby for a sleep-over. We are going to the cinema...I wondered if I could persuade, beg, even pay you to get Jazz out too and we could 'accidently' bump into each other. I'll pay your cinema ticket!" Sam pleads.

"I also have a large popcorn, a large tango blast and a packet of chocolate buttons." I add mulling it over. I am going dress shopping with Ruby on Saturday then Sunday lunch with my mum and dad – but I have no plans on Saturday night.

"Popcorn and slush obviously part of the deal. Would owe you big time. Is that a yes I hear churning over in your head?" Sam holds his breath waiting for an answer.

"You already owe me big time. OK. I'll check what's on and get it's sorted with Jazz," my voice is flat. I am trying so hard not to judge his stupidity.

"Yes, thank you Ellie. You are a legend!!!"

"This Legend needs to get to work. See you Saturday."

I hang up and ask myself… *what the fuck am I doing?*

32

Today is all about Ruby – It is dress shopping day! Six months until her winter wonderland wedding. I am hoping by then I will have mustered up a date to take a plus one. Perhaps Simon...perhaps not. I got another spray tan last night. I followed Lisa's instructions and scrubbed off the remains of the previous. Once again, Lisa, very kindly made me a golden goddess, for free. *How lucky am I?* She said they had floods of bookings after being featured in my column.

It's 10:30AM. I am perched on a wooden bench at George Square, basking in the morning sunshine. Sipping a coffee, while demolishing an overpriced breakfast roll. The pigeons are eagerly pacing around, hoping I drop a crumb. *Sorry dudes this human does not leave crumbs.* Their beady little eyes are staring at me as I take a bite – *yes, yes rodents I know I do not need this.* Feeling guilty, I rip a piece of my roll and throw it behind me.

Oh shit. "Sorry!" I shout as it bounces off a man's leg. I am super early so not to give snotty Beatrice any ammunition on my time keeping. When Ruby announced I was chief bridesmaid, her sister complained it was a ludicrous choice and I would be late to her wedding. *Jealousy makes you nasty.*

We have five appointments booked at high end boutiques across Glasgow. First one at 11AM, last one at 4PM. I am hoping by 4PM or maybe earlier, she has found her dream dress. For as long as I can remember, my high school friend has fantasised about a winter wonderland themed wedding. Christmas is her favourite time of year. She has always intended on combining the two. I have never shared her enthusiasm for December, I am more of a May, June, July person – the time the sun is 'most likely' to shine in Scotland. However, as my fellow Scots know, the weather in

Scotland is never guaranteed.

"Hello, hello, hello" Vivienne is running towards me. Arms open.

"Gorgeous Vivienne!" I stand up and embrace her hug. I love tall, skinny, outspoken Vivienne.

"How are ya hun? Eh weather here is so shite compared to London. Should have packed my thermals," she starts to do her morning stretches. Viv lives in London, Ruby stays with her a few times a month when she's down for business. They met on a course in London years ago and clicked. I can see why Ruby likes Viv. She's cool, funny and uplifting.

"I'm good thanks Viv."

"Happy to hear it, saw your video. You throw a good punch Ellie! And you know what they say, No PR is bad PR!" she winks.

"Thanks, I guess – how's life treating you?" I change the subject and walk to the bin to throw my rubbish away. Passers-by are looking at Viv in her tight leather leggings and white vest top. Her feet modelling stunning Balenciaga trainers. If I was to steal her trainers and flog them, it would cover half my remaining *birthday balance*. However, because I am not a thief, I have applied for a new credit card with a £1000 limit. Fingers crossed.

"Life's good thanks Ellie, got promoted at work. Sales manager of the year last year, smashed it – huge fucking bonus. YASS!" she screams punching the air. Much to my amusement, passers-by jump back in fright. "Bought a big Louis Vuitton bag for £2500 then sold it on eBay when the novelty wore off. Ruby loves herself a designer bag, she encouraged me to get it. And I have run a marathon this year." She brings both arms up to show her muscles.

"Wow, go you! Amazing Viv - any man?" I ask curiously.

"Fuck that, me first, man second. The right one will come along when he's brave enough" she laughs, flicking her high mousey blonde ponytail out of her face. Move over Arianne Grande.

Ruby, her mum and sister are walking towards us. I smile at Viv's statement 'me first, man second' – my new motto. Working on *me*, for *me*. Viv is two years older than me and seems in no panic about her biological clock. But then again, she hasn't met my mother.

"See Louis Vuitton Queen" Viv mutters under her breath, giving me a wink – Ruby is carrying her signature designer tote.

"Hi girls" Mrs Richardson smiles, as they approach the bench. I pray to be as visually striking in my late sixties. Her hair is in a high bun and she has on a pretty blue floral dress with navy sandals. Her dark skin is perfect with beautiful laughter lines. My hair is piled in a bun too, more the messy shabby chic image not a neat hair sprayed masterpiece like Mrs Richardson's.

"Beautiful as always." I hug the mother of the bride – retired English teacher Mrs Richardson. She played a big part in my childhood. From soothing skint knees with her homemade antiseptic cream and toasting marshmallows in her garden, to helping with my English studies and offering a shoulder to cry on when I got dumped by Carlton, the fifteen-year-old chubby blonde I wanted to marry.

"And you my darling, are looking pretty as always. Love the yellow cardi." She rubs her hands over my shoulders and gives them a gentle squeeze followed by a loving motherly smile. I've opted for the same black short jumpsuit to show off my tan, but instead matched it with my yellow cardi and flat yellow shoes.

"Heyyy..." I smile at Ruby and her sister. Beatrice dismisses me with a soft grunt. I can't take my eyes off her white blouse, buttoned up to her chin. Queen Victoria someone has stolen your blouse! Wanda - you have competition on the OAP style contest. Beatrice makes a bee line for Viv, gushing over her success and wealth. Turns out B had thoroughly researched all things Viv on LinkedIn. Viv met her approval with several impressionable career highlights to date.

"Where is Tiana?" I ask, rubbing Ruby's back, it feels satisfying touching the fabric. A nice plum coloured velvet shift dress.

“She’ll be here soon. Poor Tiana, she’s been up half the night with the twins. They have chicken pox.”

“Shame, what age are they now?” I met them twice when they were new-borns. Took gifts. Was raging because they kept it a secret, she was having twins, I bought one baby gift in the sales. Then surprise, out pops baby number two, so had to buy another gift. We should have known really – she looked like she was carrying a baby hippo.

Ruby pauses counting the months in her head. “Almost a year old.”

“Wow time flies.”

“Talking about children. Lena said you let her watch Horrid Henry Ellie?” Beatrice raises her voice, in disgust.

Everyone went silent. Ruby bites her lip not to laugh. Viv put her hands round her throat shaking her head at me.

“Kids these days. Exaggerating little monsters. Let’s go!” I link my arm in Ruby’s for moral support and we walk toward dress shop number one. Beatrice tuts loudly following behind us.

It is a warm welcoming boutique not far from George Square. Posh and expensive. Exactly what Ruby deserves. I remember my wedding dress shopping day; I was the thinnest I have ever been – I felt like a princess. I pull the brakes on memory lane – it is Ruby’s turn to feel like a princess. If I ever get married ‘for the second time’ I’m going to fuck off to Vegas and spurt out my vows intoxicated under the voice of Elvis #rockandroll.

“Ladies, welcome please come in. Bubbly?” A manager greets us in a cream suit with a blonde bun and a pretty face that didn’t move – a walking advert for botox and fillers. Soft classical music was playing. I am not a big fan of classical but the violins on this upbeat tune are somewhat enchanting.

Rails and rails of beautiful wedding dresses are displayed, every style, shade of white, cream, ivory.

"Sorry I am late!" The little bell chimes, Tiana practically falls in the doorway. If this is what having kids does to you, count me out. Her tired, bloodshot eyes and dark circles under them scream sleep deprivation. She has on nice black jeans and a black top that is inside out – no one has the heart to tell her.

We all hug Tiana trying to miss the small milk stain on her shoulder. Maybe it's yoghurt, or actual baby sick… Tiana confirms she is definitely going back to work part time. When the girls were born Tiana was adamant, she would not work again till the kids started school. Turns out taking a lunch break and actually getting to eat your lunch in peace is far to enticing. Administration duties it is.

The shop attendants gush over Ruby. We all sit on a very long suede sofa and sip our bubbly. Tiana finishes hers in seconds and asks for the glass that Beatrice didn't take.

"Stunning, gorgeous, ohh you will be to die for in this one." They presented Ruby dress after dress. Thankfully my bestie is an assertive person, so she knew instantly if she would want to try it on. She just said YES or NO. My mind takes a flashback to when I was dress shopping, *poor Ruby and Matt.* I tried on eleven dresses in the first shop, even though I knew half of them were not 'the one' – what an indecisive mess. *Note to self: Ask doc to code in some more assertiveness on my last session.* Despite the sales attendant's efforts, neither of the two dresses Ruby tried on gave her the wow factor. The second boutique she tried on none, I felt marginally sorry for the sales assistant, she was going to bawl her bloody eyes out as we left the store.

We stop for lunch and a cocktail to refuel. Tiana, hell bent on refuelling for us all. She is overjoyed to be child free and is knocking back the bubbly like her life depends on it. It feels odd being the observer and not the binge drinker. Beatrice almost choked on her orange juice when Tiana called her angelic looking girls 'cock blocking little energy suckers'. I told her she should be lucky she has a cock at all. I changed the subject quickly by talking about the hen 'parties' when Ruby went to the toilet.

We agree the first one will be an elegant, beautiful afternoon tea, with appropriate entertainment organised by Beatrice and her mum. And the second one was all down to me! YAS. I'm thinking long weekend, flights, shots and strippers. So excited to start planning, wherever it is, one thing I know for sure – it will be a hen party that Ruby will never forget. Will get Matt on eBay looking up penis accessories for the party bags. May have to apply for yet another credit card to fund a no expense spared hen party.

Third wedding boutique was a disaster. Bad service, average dresses, extortionate prices. We were in and out in twenty minutes. The last boutique was magical – it all boiled down to two dresses. Much to the annoyance of Beatrice, Ruby called Matt via FaceTime.

"You are letting that little idiot choose between these two completely different styles?" Beatrice gasps horrified.

Ruby laughs hugging her sister playfully. "I am."

Beatrice still has not forgiven Matt for his loud remark at the engagement party. Matt accidently smashed a plate and when they couldn't find a broom, he recommended pulling the one out Beatrice's rectum. You could have heard a pin drop. Beatrice is delighted Matt is not joining us today. Instead he is being an usher and is saying a speech. *God help us all.*

"One trillion, billion percent the first one," Matt confirms, then starts to cry.

"Thank you. I love you." Ruby hangs up before he wails louder.

One of Matt's qualities, or downfalls, depending on the situation, is his honesty. It can be brutal. I am buzzing he has voted for wedding dress number one, as did I! Beatrice voted number two. I try so hard not to smirk.

"Total babe gurl!" Viv hugs Ruby.

“To be fair, you could wear a bin bag and still look a million dollars.” I declare.

“Finally, something me and Ellie agree on!” Beatrice gives a little smile.

“My baby girl. I can’t believe you are getting married. Jamie is one lucky man.” Mrs Richardson, cuddles her youngest daughter. A tear slides down her cheek.

“Thank you so much everyone. I have had the perfect day.” Ruby swoons, admiring her vintage masterpiece, tiara and floor length veil.

I rush out the boutique and take a photo of Ruby leaving and upload to my Instagram. I caption it -

“Five shops later… after friendly debates, laughs and tears. A very excited beautiful bride to be said ‘YES TO THE DRESS’ #mybestieisbetterthanyours #winterwedding #december2020 #planningthehenparty #it’sgoingtobemessy

33

I am sunk in my sofa munching on a cheese pizza, zapped of motivation. I am so pleased Ruby chose her dress. The way she glided from the fitting rooms I knew it was perfect, she looked fit to play a Disney Princess. And, bonus, we have made a collective decision that the bridesmaid colour will be jade green. Suit's me as matches my eyes. I look decent in green – *at least I think I do.* Bridesmaid dress shopping is next month. This is music to my ears as 'I shall' be losing 14lb of fat before then. Now for part two of my busy Saturday – cinema with Jazz to accidently, 'deliberately' bump into Sam and Jill. Although I adore Jazz's company, I would be content with a PJ's, Pizza and Prosecco Saturday in. I still have to tick off going to the cinema on my own for my final column, which will be published the week after my last therapy session. I contemplate asking Jazz to sit a few seats away from me. Two birds, one stone. I text Jazz.
ME: Hi Jazz, I'll just meet you inside? Ruby chose her dress it's lush. Thanks to Tom for sparing you tonight! He is a good man lol x

I text Jazz with mixed emotions. I have butterflies that I am going to be seeing Sam, but then I feel sick knowing he is going to be with Jill. And on top of it all I am hoping Jazz doesn't kill me (or Jill) when she finds out I knew they would be there.

JAZZ: Hah Tom is secretly delighted. He has beer chilling and a movie sorted. See you soon luver!!!

Jazz's fun happy text makes me feel guilty – like the time I said I had a doctor's appointment instead of going to my Aunt's charity coffee morning. I text back a few love hearts and take my consumed guilt and sweaty everything for a shower. I hate getting myself into silly predicaments. Must learn the power of saying NO.

"HEYYYYY!" Jazz skips in and out of the crowds waving her hands in the air. I've already bought the tickets which Sam said he will reimburse. I had planned on saying no – but the cinema is no cheap excursion and let's face it, I am in no position to knock back money. I have seven days to pay the outstanding £990 or it will be going to a debt collecting agency.

"Hey you," I hug Jazz and hand her a cinema ticket.

"It's on me…well that's a lie. It's on…" I can feel my cheeks going pink and I start to waffle on about me re-enacting the Bridget Jones scene where she's singing 'All by myself'. *Yes, I have done this.*

"Ellie, I have known you long enough. Spit out whatever it is that you are worried about. Is Simon here? Did you ask me because he cancelled on you and now he has shown up?" Jazz smirks with a twinkle in her eye.

"No. God no, he's in Edinburgh, but we are going out for dinner and drinks on Tuesday."

"Thought you weren't drinking during the week? You are doing so well!" Jazz encourages.

"Yeah, I know, peer pressured at thirty. Who would have thought?"

"Sure, you OK?" Jazz asks squeezing my arm.

We head to the escalators. Our screen for the fast action comedy is on level seven.

"Can I start by saying I love you." I look at Jazz and take a gulp.

"This is serious chat. Did you blame me for something you did at work? Cause I wouldn't mind. Wanda hates you. Me she can tolerate. Spit it out?" Jazz giggles.

"Sam and Jill are here. They are in a movie just now and plan to bump into us when we come out…" I blurt out the words fast and furious.

Jazz takes her eyes off mine. Her cheeks go pink with temper then drain to a ghastly white.

“And Sam asked you to orchestrate this?” Jazz asks coldly.

“I guess, aw Jazz I am so sorry, he said he’d pay for tickets and snacks and I really did want to see this movie with you” I pleaded, saying sorry another five times.

“OK, OK, it’s ok Ellie, I am not angry with you. Sam on the other hand, he should know better. Stupid idiot, you know a leopard never changes its spots, she’s cheated once, she will cheat again. It’s not a case of *if,* it’s a case of *when!*” Jazz rambles out her words in frustration.

“I know Jazz, I’m sorry he’s been good listening to my shit and we can empathise with each other...”

“Difference is Ellie, you weren’t stupid enough to take Bob back!” Jazz continues clenching her fists.

“Bob never wanted me back though, so it was never an option.” I look at my feet ashamed. I went on Rachel’s Instagram account earlier. The photo of her, Bob and the baby scan caused me to throw up. I had to run to the bathroom and hurl my emotions down the pan.

“OK, plan. Eat as much snacks as we can, on him. Then I’ll have whatever I am going to say to that slut ready for when we bump into them.”

We high five getting off the escalator. The teenagers in front stare like we are actors from a soap set. They had heard our whole conversation on the way up.

The movie is good, great actually, Ryan Reynolds took his top off a couple of times, so it is Sam’s money well spent for that alone. I feel sick with all the overpriced snacks we have consumed - Nachos, popcorn, slushes, pick n’ mix and another slushy – each. I have a receipt for Sam, treble what he was expecting. I have that need to sleep food coma coming on, like the obligatory siesta on Christmas Day from stuffing your face three times more than normal.

The credits roll up.

“I don’t know if I can stand up Ellie!”

I laugh at Jazz rubbing her tiny bloated stomach. Jazz springs to her feet and offers me a hand. “Good movie, good food. Now let’s go and consult a biatch!”

My mobile beeps.

SAM: Just heading down to exit. I need to speak with you on your own Ellie, nothing to do with Jill or Jazz.

I don’t even reply. I link my arm in Jazz’s, we head to the escalators. I have no intention of getting involved, but I have no intention of quieting Jazz either. She loves her step brother very much. Her anger is through love.

I see them as the escalators travel down. I feel like everything is in slow motion, my heart races seeing Sam. Then I see Jill, she is a small slim pretty red head, dressed in a tight LBD, thigh boots and hooped earnings that could be used in a circus. She fits the image of the female I’d expect to be hanging off Sam’s arm. I take a breath wishing I hadn’t chosen my comfy grey tracksuit from M & S. I just don’t see the point in being uncomfortable at the cinema, and the lights are out half of the bloody time. Compared to Jill, I look like I am in my pyjamas.

Sam locks eyes with Jazz. He shoots her a pathetic look of desperation. If he were a dog he would be begging right now.

“Oh god, look at him Jazz?” I mutter empathically.

“He is a disaster; and her smug face is giving me a new tactic.” Jazz mutters back waving her hands excitedly.

Jill looks so self-assured, the corner of her lip sniggering her hand firmly on Sam’s thigh. She knows if push comes to shove, Sam will choose her.

We walk towards them. I expect fireworks but Jazz goes in for a hug.

What the fuck is going on? I am so bloody confused right now. From the look on Jill and Sam’s face they are equally as confused.

“Welcome back to Glasgow Jilly. Happy to be home?” Jazz gushes.

“Jill.” She corrects straightening up. Jazz’s warmth is unnerving her. Sam sighs with relief.

“Good movie?” I ask filling an awkward silence.

"Yip, good, you?" Sam asks.

"Amazing. PayPal will do," Jazz replies slapping the receipts in his hand.

I gulp. Sam knows that Jazz knew. Now Jill knows that Sam knew that we were going to be there.

"Dinner next week at ours, a catch up is long overdue?" Jazz looks directly at Jill.

"Sur-ree. Why not, sounds good. Eh Sam, baby next week?" Jill spits back uneasily firming her grip on Sam.

"Dinner would be great. Ellie can I have a quick word?" Sam pulls me to one side away from prying ears. I gather it is to say thank you.

"Ellie, I am so sorry to be the one to tell you this. I have done a bit of digging. Long story short – Simon is the person that filmed you on your birthday night, he then sold it to Epic Fails. I have footage and emails to back it up. I am so sorry. Thought you should know before you get in too deep." Sam attempts to put his hand on my shoulder. I jump back my eyes welling up.

I try to hold back the tears; I try to catch my breath.

"Well – I think YOU should know -" I am now crying and shouting.

"Know that it is fucked up getting back with that tramp!" I point at Jill.

The bustling crowd follows my finger to Jill who is now beetroot. I'm unsure if it is embarrassment or anger. Jazz shrugs her shoulders when Jill glances at her for back up.

"After everything she has done to you, you are a bloody idiot taking her back."

"Ellie, I thought you'd be grateful?" Sam looks shocked. He wasn't expecting this reaction. What did he want? A fist bump, high five. *Cheers mate.*

"You thought NOW, in the middle of a room full of strangers, was an appropriate time to casually inform me, the guy I have been *shagging*, is responsible for making me a laughing stock to millions of people? The award for Mr Insensitive goes to…Well fuck you and your cheating wife – never contact me again!"

I turn and march out the cinema. Worst cinema trip, ever.

34

"Cheers Dad." I hand back the silver worn hip flask filled with whisky; my mum is baking in the kitchen while we watch Still Game. My dad takes a gulp and stuffs it in his body warmers pocket. I smile as he winks.

There is nothing quite like home. The smell of my mums baking still delights me, she is the best baker in the town. She takes pride whipping up trays of deliciousness for every community gathering. My childhood home hasn't changed much in the past thirty years. The red brick bungalow, just outside Glasgow is bright and very floral inside, lots of pinks and net curtains. My mum is a fan of antiques and collects every item imaginable. She still has to find an antique that is worth any value. The display cabinets are full of coins, spoons, postcards and other things that look odd and old would seem better placed in a car boot sale. The whole lot would probably get a fiver.

It is cluttered, cosy and safe. I forget how much I like being home, until I come home. I've sent Simon an abusive text, blocked Sam's number and notified Jazz, Ruby and Matt that I really am OK, but shall be phoneless till Monday evening. My dad hid my mobile in his shed with strict instructions not to give it back to me until I leave. The moment Sam broke the gut-wrenching news I knew I'd be 'sick' on Monday. I need to compose myself before I see Simon, the manipulating, arrogant, wanking piece of shit. I need to rack my brains and remember what lie I fobbed Wanda off with the last time I was 'sick'. I once said there had been a death in the family – truthfully, I had a hangover from hell. Imagine my horror when my dad's great cousin died the same day. I felt guilty for weeks, even though he was ninety-nine - I feared my lie was the karma-tic BS that stopped William getting birthday wishes from her majesty the queen. God bless him.

"You figured out what you'll be saying on Saturday?" my dad gently pushes, knowing I'd rather be swallowing bleach than speaking to two hundred people.

"Rough idea, going to write it tonight while I'm home. Let mum give it the seal of approval."

"Jolly good, that will keep her happy, and if she's happy, I'm happy, makes my life easier," he reaches over from his reclining chair and squeezes my hand.

"Did you hear about Tiffany?" dad asks sitting up, taking off his glasses.

I slouch. "Yes, she's pregnant, mum has been reminding me frequently."

"No no not that."

"She's pregnant with twins, one boy, one girl…" I joke then panic. This would send my mother into overdrive. A granddaughter and a grandson in one round. My life would be over.

"Hah Aunty Patsy wishes. Turns out mum's bowling friend, the nosy one, with the round arse and a husband half her age…" my dad searched his mind for a name.

"I know who you mean Dad. Can picture her face but can't member her name."

"Aye that one, she bumped into Aunt Patsy at the Co-op while she was having an argument with Tiffany. Tiffany called her an old over-bearing mother in law that needs to back the fuck off!" my dad laughed.

"NOOO in front of people, Aunt Patsy would have been horrified?" I joined in with the laughter.

"Your mother is acting outraged, but secretly she's jumping for joy it isn't as perfect as the picture is painted," he taps his nose.

"What are you two gossiping about?" Mum appears with coffee and a tray of freshly made scones, including little pots of jam and cream. She pops them down on the side table.

"Just talking about your awesomeness mother." I smile sarcastically and reach for a scone.

"Mm…well that is a good subject, isn't it!" my mum frowns taking off her pink apron to sit down. She sips her coffee and works on a half-finished crossword. My dad closes his eyes while my mums susses out what is tall, sturdy and has the bark of a dog? You have to admire my mum's willpower; I tell her to look up the clues on Google but she never does. If there was a prize for the longest time to finish a crossword, Nancy Benson would win first place.

"I'm going to my room. Want to work on my speech for Saturday, will let you check it before I say something I might later regret." I stand up and stretch both hands to the sky.

"Sure, you're OK Ellie?" my mum takes off her black rectangular glasses and puts down her pen.

"I'm fine mum, really." I go over and hug her.

"That's what worries me Ellie, normally when you say you are *fine* it is usually the calm before a very stormy storm," my mum looks at me with empathy and love, but mostly panic. Her shattered nerves could not take the YouTube humiliation again. I have redeemed myself, slightly, by being a writer for her favourite newspaper. My Daylight Gazette columns have been cut out and framed for all to see in the hall (where my wedding photo once hung) – displayed proudly, next to the grandfather clock that chimes loudly every hour, on the hour. The one antique that I wanted to smash as a teenager, I now am talented, to tune out its dulcet tone.

"Not this time mum, I promise." I sit down and hug her again. "Promise" I say both hands on the side of her face.

"It's a tree mum – Four letters starting with T!" I point to the T and jump back before she can hit me with her newspaper. She hates being told the answers.

"ELLIE!!!! Yes, you'd better run. Dinner will be ready at 6PM." I hear her and my dad laughing. This makes me happy.

If I jumped into a time capsule and zapped myself back to 2005, my room would look exactly as it does now, minus the American pie posters. I had a fascination with Jim Levens. At fifteen, I pinned a poster of his face on my ceiling. Then my mum watched American Pie, took down all the posters and refused

to make her scrumptious apple pie ever again – *cheers Jimbo*. My room is like a security blanket, I step into it and feel tucked away from the world. The cream wall with blobs of blue – tac everywhere, my double bed with navy star bed sheets and the side cabinet with my globe is just perfect. I lie down on my bed and look at my world globe covered in small yellow stickers. My Aunt Patsy got me this pretty globe light with an engraved brass base for my twenty – first birthday. It reads -
"Happy 21st Ellie. The world is your oyster!"
I spin it around remembering Aunt Patsy's kind words at my twenty-first family lunch –
"You are young, healthy, no commitments, you can achieve anything Ellie, go anywhere – you have the ability to be great". She urged me to strive for greatness. I have always been fascinated looking at the size of the UK in comparison with the world. I remember having butterflies in my stomach when I placed the yellow stickers on all the countries I wanted to see first.

New Zealand
Canada
Japan
Netherlands
Portugal
Italy
Spain
Los Angeles
New York
Iceland
South Africa

Fifteen years later, I have ticked off Italy, Spain and New York. I ask myself why have I not seen the Northern Lights, walked Table Top Mountain, hiked to the Hollywood sign or smoked a joint in Amsterdam? I have had years to plan, organise and work towards expanding my knowledge of culture through travel, but I haven't, why? Life took over, paying bills took over, Bob took over, somewhere along the days, weeks, months, years I have lost sight of what I want to do. Where I want to see, what lights a fire in my soul – cheesy right? But the only fire my soul has come close to igniting with is the flames from a sambuca.

Bob loved Italy, so we went there every year, twice a year – to the same place, to eat at the same restaurants, to shag in the same hotel. Not that I'm complaining, the pizza and wine were out of this world. Then again so were the females, which made me feel guilty for scoffing all the pizza and wine. Been to Spain a few times too, cheap all-inclusive deals, memorable for all the wrong reasons – I am pretty sure Matt and I are barred from several bars in Alicante. NYC was my honeymoon week, so technically it does not count, as I am trying to erase happy Bob memories from my mind.

I spin the globe with a heavy heart and lie in the foetal position cuddling my pillow. A tear streams down my cheek as I mull over ideas for my speech. I push Bob, Sam and Simon's betrayal to the back of my mind and close my eyes. Aunt Patsy is reaching sixty years on planet earth… she deserves a heartfelt spectacular speech. And I am going to deliver just that.

35

Tuesday morning. I feel recharged and ready for this week ahead. I have not binged on booze, or eaten my feelings, after the crappiest Saturday night since my birthday. I wrote like a ninja at my parents.

Speech for Aunt Patsy completed (approved by mum). Column on my spray tan complete. Gratitude journal bursting at the seams. I have consciously chosen to focus on the positives in my life – I feel empowered.

My empowered persona has been thinking up ways to deal with Simon, I must have the last word, my sanity depends on it. I have a mature idea and a spectacularly immature idea...... spectacularly immature it is.

I take my mobile out on the bus and double check my Instagram and twitter for the fourth time. It is 8:30AM. I am secretly buzzing about my growing followers, despite playing it cool. Ruby said my goal should be to get to 10K so I get the swipe up option. Then I might start getting paid for posts, which would obviously be bloody fantastic, I mean who does not want to make easy money? I am being super-duper cautious about taking what my new insta family say too personally – whether it is good or bad. Vanity or bitterness are ugly traits.

I unblock Simon and prepare a text,

ME: Hi Simon, how are you? I am still so upset about what you done but I can't stop thinking about you. We need to talk, forgive my last text. My words were harsh and your penis is well proportioned lol, I think that's why I can't stop thinking about you. Msg back pleaseeee Ellie xx

His ego is so huge that he will be soaking up the compliment like a sponge in dirty bath water. Like clockwork my mobile beeps. I have changed his contact from sexy to a more appropriate name.

TWAT: Hi babes, yeah wow your text was explicit. Is Tuesday calling for some of the big man. S x PS: I am really sorry Ell's I like you, you are fun.

ME: Oh my god, you know me too well. I just can't get our passionate Tuesdays, out my head. E x

TWAT: Happy to oblige. See you soon babe x

ME: xxxx

Ugh he is so shallow and transparent. What alarms me most? He believes I will go back for more sex after everything he has done to me. He wasn't bad, but he wasn't that great either. He has branded me as dumb, which will make my plan easier. It crossed my mind to DM my angry followers and sign up for the vodka drinking, shot to the kneecaps, wolves eating, men show. But how would that benefit me? What I most need right now is money. And if my plan goes as intended, Mr Twat will be paying the remaining £990 of my birthday balance today. Then all the fumbles in his bed will not have been in vain. I will merely be an underpaid sex worker that cashed in after the action.

"Morning Ellie."

I jump. Wanda is first to greet me coming out of the lift in her floral calf length skirt, blouse and brown waistcoat. I fear on the next staff night out I may tell her if she wants to be taken seriously, she must address her wardrobe.

"Hi Wanda, thanks for signing off my flexi day yesterday. Sorry again for any inconvenience." I can't make eye contact. Eye contact will result in me blushing or worse laughing.

"No problem Ellie, I had a rat infestation once, was an awful experience, took trained men two days to exterminate them all." Wanda said seriously.

"Wow, two days," I could have pitched for two days flex, damn it. I had planned on using excruciating period pain but when I called Wanda, I saw a group of rats on the TV causing mayhem in an angry tenant flat. I spontaneously went with rats.

"Jazz checked your high importance emails and you have a backlog of notes to type up from yesterday's team meeting."

Wanda snaps back into office manager mode when Mr Brown thunders past like the incredible hulk on *his* period.

"Thanks Wanda."

"Are they all away?" Wanda inquires taking her seat.

"The rats?" she prompts waiting for an answer.

"Yes, yes… well no. One more rat left." I answer watching Simon stride in without a speckle of remorse.

I sit down at my desk, breathe in and give Simon the biggest sultry smile I can muster up.

"Did the cat eat your gym bag again Ellie?" Jim asks.

"It was a rat this time." I wink.

Benny knew the truth. Matt and secrets do not mix. He gives me a soft smile then emails me.

BENNY: So now do you see why I don't like Simon? He targeted you through Matt. Poor Matt is feeling awful. My poor Matt was shaking and crying knowing he deliberately came into the coffee shop that day. We decided he wanted an Epic Fail Number 2. You have been so popular on YouTube Ellie. He maybe wanted to make more cash? He looks like he doesn't even care. WHY ARE YOU SMILING AT HIM???? I am texting Matt.

ME: aw god you sound like Matt. Calm down already – I need your help today. I have a payback plan.

Jazz arrives looking pretty in a baby pink shift dress. She throws herself towards me, hugging me tight. I get the low down and a delicious jam filled doughnut (last night's weigh in was cancelled so I can afford the calories). Sam was back with Jill; he feels guilty for not telling me in a more appropriate setting. He wants to call and apologise but Jill has forbidden him to speak with me again. I 'embarrassed' her screaming she was a tramp. *If the shoe fits.*

"Hope they are very happy together!" I screw my face up and stick out my tongue.

Bob cheating has taught me one thing – I can bounce back from anything. Normally I would be crying my way through a boxset in between essential shopping trips for alcohol and sugary snacks – not this time.

It is almost 5PM. I have flirted shamelessly on email all morning with Simon before enjoying lunch and giggles with Jazz. I got our happy eager waitress to take a photo of us - eating our salads, sunglasses on laughing, not a care in the world. I posted it on Instagram, tagging Jazz. I pray Sam sees my photo and knows I'm swimming – zero sinking for this fat whale.
"Thanks Wanda," she passes me the stationery cupboard key and I sign the diary. We have a strict stationery procedure – sign key in, out and note what items we took. All thanks to a temp secretary stealing almost five hundred pounds worth of stationery shit over a month. She maybe, would have gotten away with it for longer if she hadn't gotten greedy. One day she pocketed enough black ink to ring alarm bells with Wanda. It is more hassle getting a box of pens for my team than nipping out for my lunch.
The stationery cupboard was out of sight down the hall and next to a meeting room that rarely gets used after 5PM.
I give Benny a wink. His timing is everything. Even a second too late could be disastrous – I will not be able to go through with fulfilling Simon's fantasy of a BJ in the cupboard. I walk down the hall giggling like a teenager, praying it works. Simon made four figures off of my Epic Fails video, which is now sitting at almost five million views. I am entitled to £990 of that.
I swing around on the big swivel chair; the room is small with metal shelves on every wall labelled in alphabetical order. Wanda's stationery cupboard is more organised than my life.
Like clockwork the door opens slightly.
"Hi babe," Simon takes another look behind him and slides in, closing the door quietly. Confidently he strides over and starts kissing my neck passionately. His aftershave is overpowering. I gag.
I jingle a key standing up, unravelling myself from his groping hands and wet lips. "I need to lock the door." I go over and pretend to lock the door. I turn back with a wide smile. He is sitting frothing at the mouth on the black leather swivel chair, trousers and boxers at his ankles. His manhood hard and ready.

I walk as seductively as I can walk with a sore stomach. I over ate on the cookies Dave brought in. His wife made them from scratch. Think I may hire her to bake for my cheat days. Thinking about cookies, I move behind eager Simon and massage his shoulders. I run my hands down his chest unbuttoning his shirt.

"Come on Ellie, time is of the essence," he takes my hand and gently pulls me round to do the job I had promised.

"Close your eyes," I whisper in his ear, giving his lobe a little nibble. He shudders and closes his eyes grinning ear to ear as I make my way to the front.

The door opens quietly. His eyes are still closed, trousers still at his ankles, penis rock solid. I move aside to let Benny take a photo.

"What the fuckkkk!" Simon opens his eyes as Benny is giving a head to toe examination. videoing at the same time.

He scrambles out of the chair, face bright red, flapping about, jumping to pull up his trousers. His wallet and keys fall out his pocket.

"What the fuckkkk. You crazy bastards!" he screams again trying to fasten his belt, flustered.

Benny gives me the thumbs up. I jump out the room and we lock Simon in the stationery cupboard. My heart is pounding, my hands shaking.

"Check your phone *babe*," I instruct, forwarding on the photo and video of him flapping to save his dignity.

"You fat fucking cow," he whispers angrily, aggressively trying the door handle.

"So here is the deal, *babe*. You call the restaurant where you filmed me. Pay my outstanding balance of £990 or, we will, anonymously share this photo and video on the work server."

"Ginger bitch!" he kicks the door.

"Ohhh *babe* don't you know the rhyme, sticks and stones can break my bones? You know the rest get FUCKING DIALING. And, for an added bonus, if you do it in the next three minutes, I won't forward them onto real estate sales executive Lana Nightingale. Yes, you heard me your fiancée who you LIVE WITH in

Edinburgh, cat called Percy, number 07556 88..."
"OK OK OK, relax Ellie" he speaks with a change of tone. The aggression has gone. Panic has set in.
"Amazing what you can learn online if you dig a little deeper." It took me a little over two hours to track this information down.
"If I pay this we are done, photo, video deleted never to be mentioned again?" Simon is now begging, which delights me.
"Yip...tick tock." I check my mobile. Two minutes left.
"Hi, hello, hey. Tim did you say? Yes, hi Tim, I'm ok thank you. I am calling to pay the outstanding balance for a Miss Ellie Benson please."

36

Therapy Session six – Thursday the 11th of June

Birthday Balance – ZERO! Cheers Simon, you cockroach.

Instagram Followers – 8913

Happiness Ranking – 8/10

They say forgiveness is the key to happiness. Six weeks ago, I would have stubbornly disagreed but today I see some truth in it. *Holding onto anger is like drinking poison and expecting the other person to die.* Wise words Mr Buddha. Doubt Buddha would approve I took it upon myself to dish Simon his karma, but it helped speed up my forgiveness process. And while I have made a complete fool of myself to millions of strangers throughout the globe, it also exposed Bob for the cheat he is. I feel stronger than I have in a long time, and although I astonish myself admitting it - I really do forgive him. I actually thanked his cheating ass in my gratitude journal last night. Six weeks ago, I would have preached there is more chance of me shagging Tom Hardy than forgiving Bob - but with my blinkers of hatred removed I realise if he hadn't cheated, I would have lived a lie. I am not the sort of girl Bob desired, and I would have robotically kept trying to please him, by being someone I am not.

Sam on the other hand I forgive but miss. I had got used to his blunt words and caring ways, dry sense of humour and friendship. I push Sam out of my thoughts, no dwelling shall be done and as Mrs Withering kindly reminded me in the hallway, *there are plenty more fish in the sea* – should I dive in 'the sea' despite sharing the same hair colour the fish would think Ariel had swallowed Ursula.

"Beautiful Ellie, my favourite influencer, how are we today?"

"Hardly," I gush turning a little pink. I will never, ever think of myself as an influencer.

Sarah is the most delightful human being on the planet. Unflawed and genuine.

"Trust me Ellie, it may be unexpected. But you are definitely influencing people with your real, honest unfiltered posts, it's quite refreshing…"

"Ellie, the unexpected influencer," Dr Kendrick says joyfully. She smiles holding open her door in a floral shimmery yellow dress with puffed sleeves. It is less formal than her normal attire.

"Aw Sarah, I shall miss your face! You my lovely, are a happy tonic." I sit down my glass of water with crushed ice and mint leaves to hug her tight. I will miss her, and the water. Six weeks ago, I was hungover and dreading my first session. Today I wish I could teleport back to session one.

"Ellie, just out of curiosity what's your last article on? I am excited to read it next week!" Sarah asks.

"It was supposed to be a cinema trip on my lonesome but I have decided to go for a jog tonight instead. Thinking of signing up for a 5K." This reminds me to Google converting KM to miles so I know what I'm up against. The cinema would be the easy option. Think I am going to watch that recommended movie, 'Brittany Runs a Marathon' for motivation.

"Have you never jogged Ellie?" Sarah asks taken aback.

"Nope, not deliberately anyway. Run for the bus if needed, last time I actually ran was in high school – and again it was forced!" I laugh, Sarah joins in amazed at my lack of jogging. Her phone rings, she gives me her happy smile and skips back to her desk.

"A 5K sounds fantastic Ellie, please come in." The Doc stands aside with a welcoming hand gesture, guiding me to her safe haven.

"How are you feeling Ellie? I must say you look different today," she speaks warmly, sitting and crossing her legs elegantly.

"I feel different, eight out of ten today I would say!" I chuckle and plonk myself down. Visually, I am not that different; hair in a messy top knot, black dungarees with a white t-shirt underneath, I haven't shed away hundreds of pounds or changed my make-up routine... however, I definitely feel different.

"Tell me about your week so far. How has it been?" Doc asks prompting me to leave no stone unturned.

Week in and out I have stripped my soul bare to Doc, she has seen the very worst and the very best of me. Again 'visually' not the very worst - she has not seen me naked, unshaven after a weekend of binge eating and drinking. Although she credits '*me*' for the changes, I can't thank her enough for opening my eyes to the potential hidden within me. I trudged through my twenties believing that getting married and having kids will start my journey of fulfilment, the time when my habit's will change and my life will become 'better'.

My eyes are drawn to a shiny red frame. There is a wall of multi coloured frames, randomly placed, each with different quotes...

"No one can make you feel inferior without your consent." I read out loud.

"It's true Ellie. No one can *make* you feel anything."

I fill Doc in on everything, leaving nothing out. She doesn't say she agrees with the stunt I pulled on Simon, but I am certain when I leave, she will be laughing about it. I told Sarah too, so hopefully they can have a laugh together.

We are going to do some hypnosis to cement 'I AM ENOUGH' into my thirty-year-old head and hopefully a sprinkle of encouragement for my Aunt Patsy's speech. While I am never going to be able to erase my Epic Fails video, therapy has helped me correct how I speak to myself. I am divorced, but it does not make me damaged goods. I may be overweight, and yes, I am going to be healthier, but I am still a fucking goddess with my curves in all the right places. I may be an underpaid secretary but that is not my final destination. I have family and friends that love me, and one day I will meet my prince. But when he does appear one thing I now know for sure, he will be welcomed into my life because I want him, NOT because I need him.

37

I use the cuff of my black cardigan to wipe away the tears.
"Stop, stop, stop" I hit Matt on the leg. My stomach is aching from chuckling. I catch my breath.
Ruby is buckled over. She's trying to mutter 'sorry' but can't stop giggling. She holds up her hands shaping them to form a heart.
"You have to start somewhere." I shrug defeated. I join in laughing again.
Matt holds up his phone. My round, sweaty, bright red face is his new screen saver.
I went for a jog last night. Borrowed Jazz's Fitbit so I could record my Olympic time. Managed to jog (non – stop) 1K in eleven minutes. Felt so smug owning and actually wearing running trainers, I decided to do an insta story. Worst mistake ever, too busy focusing on looking up to my mobile, I missed the branch sprawled across my path. My phone flew to safety landing on the grassy bank (thankfully) and the video uploaded on my Instagram stories (regrettably). By the time I realised my fall had been captured, from an upside-down angle, and shared with my 9001 followers it was too late, I had an influx of DM's concerned about my wellbeing. I limped my dignity, sore grazed knees and sweaty arse back home. Before attempting to shower and clean my running injury I took a photo from my thighs down - grazed, knees embedded with stones, dirt and blood followed by my muddy black and red trainers.
I posted the photo on Instagram and shared to my twitter page – Running IS fun. 1K in 11 mins #itwasuphill #it'sismeellieb #youhavetostartsomewhere #runningepicfail #iamok #thankful
I use all the appropriate emojis and promise myself that before

the year is out, I WILL run a 5K, even if it kills me. Given my insta story, death is a possibility.

"Aw hen, me and Benny couldn't move." Matt laughs again. He's now sprawled out on Ruby's sofa.

"Think about the content for next week's article!" Ruby encourages with a thumbs up.

"Every cloud." I add sarcastically.

I feel happy, laughing really is the best medicine, especially when it is with my best friends. The sun is setting, the sky over The Clyde is magnificent. Ruby's balcony doors are open, tacos have been prepared and the prosecco has been poured. Jamie is at work and Matt has managed to untangle himself from the new love of his life, so it is just the three of us. We have gathered at Ruby's for an overdue catch up and I have brought the multiple outfits I ordered online. I desperately need advice on what one to wear tomorrow, nerves are beginning to set in and I am kicking myself – why oh, why, did I agree to speak in front of two hundred people? Thanks to my fresh wounds I can't wear the short black dress I thought was the winner.

We take a boomerang of our glasses clinking (never gets old) with the sunset in the background. I post it on my Instagram feed with the caption 'Cheers to my favourite humans.'

"Seen as we are clinking glasses anyway…Ellie, fan-tas-tic news - you have a permanent weekly column for The Daylight Gazette! Spoke to Rick, cute guy...if I wasn't engaged." Ruby jokes, she is obsessed with Jamie.

"Hot Rick couldn't praise you enough, readers are loving the fresh, funny, relatable stories. He wants to spice it up with photos and maybe do an interview here or there on local heroes for added content. We are meeting with his right hand, Zoey next week to look at your contract. Same rate, paid monthly." Ruby is beaming. She really is the girl that everyone wants on their side. She champions other people succeeding.

"That's an extra grand each month. Holy shit," I can't contain myself. I scream loudly. Birds resting on a neighbour's balcony flap away terrified from my outburst. A small bird drops a shit on their pink bushy pot plants (sorry). I am jumping up and down, flapping with the excitement of a toddler meeting Santa. I will be able to catch up with my council tax, pay off my credit cards. And treat myself obviously. Maybe once I'm up to date with my debt I could splurge out on a monthly visit to Doc and Sarah.

"Just to think Ellie, six weeks ago you were a fat, blubbering mess about to embarrass yourself globally and spend the night in jail." Matt chirps in.

"MAAAATTTT!" Ruby screams.

"WHAT, just pointing out how fabulous things are now. Well, you are still carrying more weight than ..."

"MATT, shut up!" Ruby threw her hands up frowning.

"It has been a whirlwind. Six weeks ago, I was living in rock bottom's basement. Now I'm making my way to the attic. Ruby has said yes to the dress, and Matt has found someone other than us to put up with him." I clap.

"What can I say, I have a big ding dong," Matt smirks.

"OK, on that note," Ruby rises to her feet and tops up our glasses. "Come on let's see what outfit you are going to dazzle in tomorrow Miss columnist," Ruby strolls back into her living room. Her silver silk dressing gown floating behind her.

"Well come on *big cock* – I need some of your, brutal honesty, minus the fat shaming." I drag Matt to his feet.

"Call me Matt Gok big cock Wan," he adds, taking it too far, as per.

38

The venue is spectacular. Aunt Patsy decided on a black and white theme, my idea of a Hawaiian bonanza was shot down after I mentioned wearing a hula skirt and drinking my cocktail straight from a coconut. *Her loss.* The event organiser has done a magnificent job though, ensuring it looks classy, not trampy. Black silky seat covers, around the beautifully set circular tables. Centre pieces of black vintage trees entwined with sparkling lights. A sparkling white marble dance floor and my favourite of the whole entire set up – A HUGE DISCO BALL!!! I have every intention to be shaking my booty, Shakira style, under this bad boy later on. I wonder if when I am sixty, I would be able to fill a room with people (that I actually know) to celebrate. Doubt it. Clearly my dear Aunt has gone for quantity over quality. She is greeting person after person, air kissing and laughing, so far, all I've seen are tuxedos, ball gowns and air kissing. Other than the obvious family members, I don't recognise a soul. So many unfamiliar faces, god, I wish I wasn't talking. I make my way back to the VIP position of the 'family' table right next the dance floor.

My dad refused to wear a tux. His suit jacket is now off and he is loosening the navy-blue tie I picked out. Mum agreed a black tie is for a funeral, and Aunt Patsy is very much alive, air kissing another stream of unfamiliar guests - pouring in like mice to a cheese trap.

"Hey Dad!" I squeeze his shoulders, sit down and sip my bubbly – I am allowing myself two small glasses of Dutch courage before my speech, then it's green lights to the dance floor. I have been so bloody good the past couple of weeks. Not sober Sally, but not pished out my face, I congratulate myself and take another sip. I have been seated in between my parents. Aunt Patsy may as well have made a huge fricking sign to say *She is single, any desperate bachelor DM my red headed niece on @itismeellieb.* I pull out my cards. I have written my speech down carefully with sharpies (in case of drink spillages prior to it). Apprehensively, I read over them in my mind

"Excited?" asks my dad joyfully, tapping his foot to the 80's pop background music. His cheeks turning rosy red from the tepid air and straight whisky mum has turned a blind eye to.

"Ecstatic!" I sulk with heavy sarcasm.

My mum is in deep conversation with my cousin Joel. He looks like a cute overweight penguin. His tuxedo has that 'shrunk in the tumble dryer' look, his thick floppy black hair and child-like grin is somewhat adorable. He is lovingly rubbing Tiffany's belly; I shudder thinking it was once my prickled cactus arse he was rubbing. Tiffany is almost four months gone and only looks like she's swallowed a tennis ball. My mum's glamourous pink lippy and forced wide smile is masking the jealousy shooting out her aura. Her eyes stay fixed on Tiffany's small bump. Tiffany talks about how she is planning to use no pain relief and have a quiet, water birth...at home. I congratulate her with my reservations. I have never squeezed a child out my vagina, but I am pretty sure given the in-depth description from Tiana, quiet births are not standard. Especially with NO pain relief, in water at home. It will be like a scene from Jaws. I shiver.

"You are glowing Tiffany; Joel is one lucky guy." I jump in as I see my mum sadden. It would be *my fault* if she was to cry, as it's *my fault,* she's not likely to be a gran anytime soon. Tiffany is glowing, and Joel is lucky - Tiffany is beautiful kind and loyal.

"Thanks Ellie," she smiles.

I love her that little bit more knowing she stood up to my Aunt Patsy too. How I would have paid to be a fly in the co-op that day.

"Let's get the party started eh?" my uncle Raymond arrives like a whirlwind plonking himself to the left of my dad.

"So how is my favourite niece?" Uncle Raymond asks, saliva flying in all directions. He straightens up the hair piece, that he 'doesn't wear'. If you could sit a small brown rug on top of a round red peanut – you get the picture.

"ONLY niece, and I am fine, thank you - you?" I ask. I love my uncle Raymond but I have never liked him.

"Nice set of racks Ellie, you must be an awful cook still being single and all, husband one, tick when's number two coming along eh eh?" he lets out a loud jolly laugh. No one joins in.

And just like that I remember why I do not like my uncle Raymond. He turns his attention to Tiffany, comparing her future birth to his willy squeezing out kidney stones. I almost throw up when he pulls a clear plastic tube from his inside pocket and gives it a shake. The kidney stones, three in total rattle for us all to hear, and see. Boak.

Mum scolds my dad for inviting his younger sibling. "Oh, dear lord, seriously Albert, why did you send him an invite?" she asks crossly.

"It is the, *family,* table dear," my dad comments. He stopped being embarrassed and apologising on behalf of his brother from an early age. *No reflection of me* he told my mum when Raymond got caught pumping his plus one at their wedding, in the toilets of the church.

"Unbearable, that's what you are Raymond!" my mum says through gritted teeth as he breaks wind loudly. Unapologetically, he raises his hand with a smile to claim the stench circulating.

He inhales a whiff intentionally. "Here, here old gal. One of these never came out your rectum?"

I was mortified when I broke wind in yoga, no not Raymond – his hand is still up like he's waiting for a high five.

"Enough now Ray, come on," my dad chirps in shaking his head.

A young waitress is trying to hold her breath while sitting down the fresh bread rolls and butter.

"It was her…" my uncle Raymond jokes pointing at my poor mother marching away furiously. I try not to laugh; it would only serve as encouragement for his bad jokes.

There is a little stage behind the marble floor with a microphone now being tested. A DJ in his late thirties, is all set up, looking dapper in a dark grey suede suit and a spiky blonde Mohican. He taps the microphone. The room falls silent.

"Ladies and gentlemen. May I say you are all looking fantastic this evening," he raises a glass. The room cheers.

"Welcome to the double celebration of Patricia Hudson, sixty years young and retiring from financial corporation - Global Bling, after thirty years of service." he raises his glass, again. The room cheers, again.

"If you can all please take a seat and welcome the beautiful birthday girl to the stage." DJ asks offering a hand to help Aunt Patsy up the few stairs. She blushes, loving being referred to as a *beautiful girl*. Once upon a time, on a bus, a thoughtful teenager stood up to offer the 'old burd' a seat. That was four years ago, and she has not been on a bus since. Patsy prides herself on her flawless appearance.

"FOR PATSY!" Uncle Raymond bellows out unprompted raising his glass. I am no mind reader but I can tell my dad is now questioning why he invited his brother – although he will not admit it to my mum. My mum is heading back to our table with uncle Brian. Brian is welling up like his wife is about to be awarded with an OBE as she takes to the stage. Aunt Patsy does look stunning in a black puffy ballgown, not unlike her second wedding dress except in black. Her hair is pulled tight in a French roll held perfectly in place with an obscene amount of hairspray. It is rock solid; I had a poke when we arrived.

"I am overwhelmed with gratitude and happiness seeing all my loved ones here tonight, thank you from the bottom of my heart. Throughout our meal, a few of my nearest and dearest will be coming up to say a few words. Then it's cake, drinks and dancing till dawn. Have a fabulous evening, I love you all so much," she waves like the queen greeting spectators at Buckingham Palace.

The last of the stragglers start to arrive filtering in, most likely with their excuse in place to leave straight after we sing happy birthday. My eyes dart to the gifts at the reception table, now overflowing with what I presume, are bottles of champagne in glitzy gift bags. I will 100% be knocking a few on the way out as payment for my speech.

All of a sudden, the room goes still, my heart beats faster, I feel nausea. I can't decide if that's from uncle Raymond recurring farts or if it is because a familiar face has just entered the now, dimly lit, ball room.

Why is he here? I suck in my stomach and excuse myself to go to the loo.

39

Aunt Patsy is cuddling the lady he arrived with. It's hard not to stare at her in a high, Marge Simpson style bun and plum lipstick. Thankfully her hair is white and not blue or I'd think I'd been teleported to Springfield. I was planning on ignoring him, but it's too late, my Aunt is waving and screaming my name. I glance over my shoulder, just in case I am lucky enough for another 'Ellie' to swoop in and save me. Nope, not that lucky.

"Yo, helloo," I slide over and greet them with the goofy coolness of your stereotypical dork.

"Norma, this is my niece Ellie, Ellie, this is my dear friend and retired work colleague Norma, and her dashingly handsome son."

My Aunt stands aside, displaying me like a prized goat.

"Over complimentary." I mutter, pulling my best resting bitch face.

He holds out his hand and flashes me a wink. "Hi Ellie, I'm insensitive Sam. It really is a pleasure to meet you."

"Hi insensitive Sam. I'm Ellie, divorced, loud mouth." I shake his hand weakly. My stomach is flipping like a roller-coaster on crack. He is in a suit with a bow tie, hair is sleeked back, eyes dark and inviting. I am trying so hard not to make eye contact. This would be so much easier if he was rotten. Why does he have to be so visually fine?

Norma and my Aunt start gossiping about the CEO of Global Bling, bringing his mistress as a plus one. Presumably his pregnant wife is at home, oblivious he is dipping his dick in a piece of meat a decade younger than herself.

"Sorry," Sam whispers. I forgot how energised I felt in his presence. The line from Notting Hill comes into my head – I am just a girl, standing in front of a boy, asking him to love her. I resist the temptation to laugh, *or worse* say it.

"It's OK." I shrug off his sorry, pretending I was over it. Lie.

"You look phenomenal Ellie." Sam admires my figure hugging, floor length black velvet dress (thank you spanx). V neckline to show ample cleavage (as Uncle Raymond pointed out) with sleeves just above my elbows to hide the bingo wings. My tan is on point, my tattoo almost healed, and I had my hair and make-up professionally done. Smokey eyes with big lashes and bold red lips. My hair stylist has pinned my hair so it's falling down one side in elegant loose curls.

"Thank you, you look dashingly handsome yourself." I mock my Aunt. I knew I looked beautiful, so I said *thank you*, as opposed to a humorous, flippant remark to tear myself down. I may not be the prettiest girl in the room, and I'm definitely not the thinnest, but for the first time in months, I looked in the mirror tonight and loved my reflection. I don't think I have ever felt as glamourous and confident in my own skin.

I AM ENOUGH I repeat Dr Lacy Kendrick words and gather my thoughts.

"What will Jill say if she finds out you are speaking to me?" I gasp taking the piss. Hand over my mouth, face of horror.

"Jill, who?" he smiles cockily.

"Eh wifey Jill!"

"Ahh that Jill. I filed for divorce. Turns out I want to swim and she was a ball and chain around my ankle." Sam raises his eyebrows with a grin.

I beam. "Is that so?"

"It is." Sam takes a small step towards me. I freeze, unable to move. He slowly tucks a strand of hair behind my ear and runs his hand down my cheek. His eyes fixed on mine. I have goosebumps in areas I didn't think got goosebumps.

"And now I am going to pass you over to my cousin Ellie. Hello Ellie." Joel is tapping the microphone, scanning for my whereabouts. Fuck, I have missed his poem. He has been working on it for months, a love letter to his mother. No wonder Tiffany has issues with her mother-in-law. Joel would still be breast fed if

Patsy was lactating.

I give him two thumbs up. His broad smile confirms he is unaware I missed every word.

"Fuck. Wish me luck." I can't decide if it's helping my nerves Sam being here, or multiplying them.

"You don't need luck. You are fantastic, just be *you*." Sam encourages. I am unsure if he is being sarcastic, but I have no time to debate it. *Just be me.* Being *me*, has gotten me into several very unhealthy predicaments.

I collect my cards, kiss my mum's cheek and make my way to the stage.

Butterflies are having a party in my stomach, there is a full orchestra going on in there. I greet the DJ and make my way to the microphone. All eyes are on me, Sam offers a reassuring smile and a wink. The sexiest wink I have ever seen. I am picturing him naked...Focus Ellie. Focus. I look at my cards.

"Hi ladies and gentlemen, it's such a pleasure to be standing here tonight. You are all looking beautiful," I pause as Uncle Raymond screams for staff to hide any Champagne towers. My dad gives him a stern warning and signals for me to carry on. "There are people in life that you look up to, people that inspire you, people that push you to be a better person. Patricia Hudson, is one of those people and I am truly blessed to call her my Aunt. I would like to take this opportunity to say thank you Aunty Patsy. Thank you for being, well - you." My words start a wave of hands clapping, guests are nodding in agreement, some people are even standing up. My Aunty Patsy is basking in the love. I pause to clear my dry throat, and take a sip of the cold bubbly.

"One of my Aunts admirable qualities are her standards. They have always been high. I mean, who else goes through husbands like socks to find Mr Perfect." My joke goes down like a led balloon with Patsy but a ripple of laughter is crossing the room. "Not that I can judge," I quickly add. "I'm already one husband down," I admit, chuckling. Guests laugh again, with Uncle Raymond shouting, *best epic fail ever.* "With that said, I have a huge amount of respect for my Aunt, she knows her worth, and settles for nothing but the best – I know this, because my Uncle Brian, is the best of the best," I raise my glass to him. He is crying. "Patsy has spent three decades at Global Bling, why? Because it is the best financial company. She has always strived to live her fullest life. Accomplishing greatness, while leaving a trail of magic everywhere she goes. I think all of us could do with being a little bit more Patsy." She is now standing, centre of attention, on the dance floor, hands in prayer position thanking me. Joel looks pissed off, like I have out shone his poem. Or, his patience with Raymond has dissolved. I hold my Champagne flute above my head. "Everyone please raise your glass to Patricia Hudson. Happy 60th you beautiful human, I have no doubt you will live retirement to the max. Now cheers to getting shit-faced and having a memorable, (but not my birthday night memorable) night!" Everyone is clapping loudly. I expect this is what it would feel like to collect an Oscar.

My mum is grinning ear to ear, I'm sure I see a tear. I have made her proud and more importantly not embarrassed the Benson name.

I can't see Sam though. My eyes are scanning the room like a robot zooming in on a target. I am pretty sure if Joel hadn't rudely interrupted us, he would have kissed me. I want that kiss.

My mum is still clapping as I reach our table. "Well done darling, perfect, you looked beautiful up there." Mum congratulates me and breathes a sigh of relief.

"Smashed it Ellie!" Dad gleefully raises his glass of whisky.

"If I wasn't your uncle," Raymond adds inappropriately, through a slur of beer.

I thank Tiffany for taking videos and photos on my phone, and jump on Instagram. My followers have shot up again. Six weeks ago, I had 241 followers and lived at rock bottom drowning my sorrows daily to mask the burden of my shitty life. Fast forward six weeks, I have reached *my* (Ruby's) goal of 10K followers, which is unbelievably, mind blowing, yet humbling. My mind has never been in better shape. My figure, not so much, but

Rome wasn't built in a day. I post a short video and full-length photo of me –

"Happy 60th to my awesome Aunt Patsy. An inspiration! I vow to be a little more Patsy – Cheers to raising your standards, knowing your worth, and grabbing life by the balls. #it'sis-meellieb #selflove #youareenough #raisingmystandards #igot-thisshit #plussize #lovetheskinyouarein

I check my notifications. Sam has tagged me in a photo. His first Instagram post is of me! -

Well done Ellie. Smashed it! #beautiful #itisellieb

A full-length, filter free photo, it is a good photo too. Better than Tiffany's poor attempt to make me look a stone lighter. It's all about the angles. It would be a bonus to have a boyfriend that could take nice photos from considerate positions. Even better a boyfriend that would, ungrudgingly, take a hundred photos just to make sure you get that perfect one. *Concentrate Ellie, you haven't even seen his penis and you are fantasising about posing for photos on the canals of Venice.*

My heart misses a beat. I cannot wipe the smile off my flushed cheeks. I feel a pair of hands wrap around my waist. I turn around.

"You hash-tagged!" I throw my arms around his neck and tilt my head up to meet his eyes.

"Crazy to think six weeks ago I was arresting you. You say the wrong thing ninety percent of the time, you swear more than necessary, you are a tad strange – a good strange…"

"Fuck don't hold back Sam!"

"You are also kind, caring, thoughtful, hilarious, an all-round beautiful human being. Inside and out."

"I –" Sam locks his lips on mine before I can say anything. Christina Perri, One Thousand Years is playing as Patsy & Brian take to the dance floor. I am lost in the music and the kiss - the most natural, warm, gentle, sensual kiss I have ever had, I am floating.

In a moment of magic, excitement flickers through my mind – I feel happy and grateful. I am grateful Bob cheated, I am grateful I got arrested and I am grateful my video has voted me #1 Rude Tube of 2020 so far. Most of all, I am grateful for the new, stronger, confident, version of myself that is emerging

Maybe everything does happen for a reason, and life is mere moments of serendipity. But through reflection, the past six weeks has taught me every decision you make has a ripple effect, sometimes good, sometimes bad. But if you embrace new opportunities with open arms and a healthy dose of self-love, your dreams may be closer than you think.

DAYLIGHT GAZETTE

Our fun, fabulous, witty columnist, Ellie Benson, shares her experience of trying Yoga for the first time! #Elliebdoesyoga

Ever been to a yoga class? I went for the first-time last week. Nobody warned me about flatulence. Downward dog after a plate full of baked beans is a very, very, bad idea. Fellow yoga goers gawked at me like I actually SHARTED. FYI – I did not. Flatulence aside, I would highly recommend yoga… The story behind me going to yoga is a different laughing matter altogether.

I found my husband in a compromising position with another female shortly after our wedding day. In the months that followed I was on an emotional roller-coaster, hating the ride yet unable to jump off, before reaching the destination better known as *rock bottom.* On my birthday the emotion I chose was rage. And we all know that rage combined with alcohol is a recipe for disaster. Imagine my delight when I saw my ex-husband proposing to that same naked female on MY thirtieth birthday and wait for it, drum roll…what should have been our first wedding anniversary. *Who knew rock bottom had a basement eh?*

My reaction to this life defining moment can be viewed courtesy of YouTube Epic Fails. I am that 'Fat Red Head' racking up views like a dancing dog, for my explosive, embarrassing outburst. PLEASE NOTE – All actions have consequences.
My consequence however is a bitter sweet one. A block of therapy sessions with an American, kick ass therapist, hell bent on baring my soul so I emerge the best version of myself. For five weeks I have to try something new. First on my 'new to do' list was yoga!

I would urge any females battling with negative inner voices to give Yoga a bash. Not only is it a work out like no other. Suitable for all shapes and sizes, it helps you switch off and focus on the most important person you communicate with. YOU.

Much Love, thanks for reading!
Ellie B x

Any yoga fart-ers out there? Please share your funny yoga experiences and tips for newbies! Don't forget to tag @itismeellieb #itismeellieb #elliebdoesyoga

DAYLIGHT GAZETTE

Our fun, fabulous, witty columnist, Ellie Benson, shares her experience of going on her first blind date! #Elliesblinddate

Do you have a friend that insists they know what's best for you? Or more specifically WHO is best for you? One of my childhood friends credits himself as a matchmaker – his match making confidence stems from orchestrating several high school romances – over a decade ago.

I reluctantly gave my friend the green light to organise my first blind date. Once the date had been set, panic kicked in. I googled how to get rid of cellulite FAST after catching an unpleasant glance of my derriere in the mirror (just in case things got steamy).

My panic escalated when I could not find a quick cellulite fix. Then I asked myself - are blind dates still a thing in this techno obsessed, information hungry world? Prior to meeting any new man for the first time, whether it be a dating app or through a friend, I would have followed a simple, yet essential, pre date search.

1. Google name – say silent prayer he's not a wanted serial killer.
2. Social media stalking to dissect every area of his life and appearance. (Best to buy alcohol for this time-consuming task, scrolling through Facebook, Instagram, Twitter, Linked In etc.)

But with no name, I could not complete the above. Filled with butterflies and no expectations, I anxiously ventured to the new sushi restaurant to meet my mysterious man. Armoured with red lippy and stubborn cellulite my stomach was doing somersaults, similar nerves compatible to my first kiss - awkward experience involving braces and way too much saliva.

When I locked eyes with Mr Blind Date, I was astonished to see he wasn't a stranger at all. He was a new work colleague... Do you believe in fate? Serendipity? Everything happens for a reason? Or are you a realistic survivor, gathering the facts, following science? I sit somewhere in the middle. Was it love at first sight? NO - We had already shared at glance at work with zero sparks, but it was a surprising coincidence.

While I wouldn't be looking out your wedding hat, one thing this blind date has taught me - is that pushing yourself out your comfort zone

can be good.
And no, he *didn't* see my cellulite...yet!

Much Love, thanks for reading.
Ellie B x

I would love to hear about your blind date experiences. Has anyone actually married their blind date? Or was it a laughable, awful experience. Pease share and don't forget to tag @itismeellieb #itismeEllieB #elliesblinddate

DAYLIGHT GAZETTE

Our fun, fabulous, witty columnist, Ellie Benson, shares her experience of getting a tattoo for the first time! #Elliegetsatattoo

Research shows that 40% of Glaswegians are believed to have some sort of ink. I decided it was time to join the Glasgow gals and get ma-self a tattoo! I have seen my fair share of tattoos; in fact, I am sure I could drum up some late-night business for the gang at 'Tattoo Fixers'. The most memorable tats I saw were in the girl's bathroom. That time in the evening when enough cocktails had been consumed to bare your soul to a new 'bestie' in the club toilets. Only to wake up the next day fearful as shit, wishing you hadn't shown a random stranger the dick on your left arse cheek (PS: zero judgment from me, Sara - toilet bestie of 2017).

Trudging to the tattoo shop, part of me was grateful I was single, or I may have been tempted to confess my love by branding myself with a name. Imagine I had got my ex's name on my body? Shit. That would have added to the long list of things he fucked up. I would have had to select chunky barbwire to erase him. Or maybe just a big X.

I have never willingly had any needle near me. And I was shitting myself at the thought of it. I ventured to Terrific Tatts, where I was greeted warmly by a tall muscular gentleman. The shop was bright and enticing, outstanding art work displayed everywhere. I met the owner, Michelle, who drew the most amazing piece of art in front of my eyes. After seeing my ear, eye and lips overlapping into each other I immediately screamed 'yes' like a bride to be crying 'yes to the dress.'

The following day I popped paracetamol, prayed for my pain threshold to be higher than I expected and ventured to Terrific Tatts. Two hours and twenty minutes later I lost my tattoo virginity! I did not cry with the pain, but I did swear through water eyes on several occasions.

Shout out to the artistic genius that is Michelle! Thank you for my ink – Love it!

Thanks for reading,
Much Love
Ellie B x

Do you have an interesting tattoo experience to share? Good or bad! Do you wear your tattoo like a badge of honour, showing it off for all to see? Or is it tucked away behind clothing whilst you pray your application for tattoo fixers will be accepted? Please share and don't forget to tag @itismeellieb #itsismeellieb #elliegetsatattoo

DAYLIGHT GAZETTE

Our fun, fabulous, witty columnist, Ellie Benson, shares her experience of getting a spray tan for the first time! #Elliebspraytan

Hello beautiful people! I bet the majority of ladies reading my column (thank you very much) have had a spay tan? If you are nodding your head then I am jealous, I wish I had taken the plunge years ago. I was crippled with nerves at the thought of exposing my water melon breasts, rolls of tummy and stubborn cellulite! So much so, that on several occasions I had booked a tan and then cancelled it, fearing the therapist may die of repulsion.

Now millions of people are aware I am a curvaceous size 18, with bouncing breasts (thank you Epic Fails) I decided to book that spray tan! My work colleague recommended a beautiful salon in the heart of town. You walk into a welcoming upbeat atmosphere, with chirpy people and happy music. I got a patch test and booked my tan for the following day. As a vampire ginger; my skin can be sensitive.

Twenty-four hours later I was standing in a pair of paper pants. I think dental floss would have covered more. I was modelling an unflattering black hairnet and my feet were stuck to disposable flip flops. I vowed in this moment of nakedness I would cut out my secretive mid-week takeaways.

My beautiful friendly therapist Lisa, does not look even a tad fazed by my hanging DD boobs and large nipples. I clock a few straggling ginger nipple hairs and felt my cheeks turn pink! I started mumbling my boob concerns to Lisa, but she was busy plugging in a machine and brushes over my nipple hair panic. She unrolls a plaster resembling a bandage cuts it to shape and places it over my scabbing tattoo. Five minutes later I had been sprayed a golden brown! It was cold, quick and strangely satisfying.

We all have our body hang ups and insecurities, no matter our shape or size. For a long time, my fluctuating weight has dictated my mood, and limited me trying new things. I am on a journey to embrace my imperfections and love me for me. 'Feel the fear and do it anyway' as Susan Jeffers says. I am glad I popped 'get a spray tan' on my therapy to do list. I can't recommend this salon enough. Spray tan will be my new norm!

Golden goddess √

Look slimmer √
Teeth appear whiter √
Body confidence √

Thanks for reading
Much Love
Ellie B x

To tan or not to tan? Golden goddess or oompa loompa? I would love to hear any funny tanning experiences. Or tan tips! Any tan virgins still out there? Please share and tag @itismeellieb #itiismeellieb #ellieb-spraytan #fakeitdontbakeit

DAYLIGHT GAZETTE

Our fun, fabulous, witty columnist, Ellie Benson, shares her experience of jogging for the first time in adult hood! #Elliebcouchto5k

I know it sounds ridiculous but the last time I intentionally ran was at high school. If *intentionally* includes being screamed at by Mr Samson to move my hippo hips or I'd get detention. I have also attempted a pathetic jog to catch the bus on several occasions. Each time the bus pulled away before I could climb on all red and sweaty.

Every evening I have been doing a gratitude journal (an order from my therapist) and it has become apparent (with my gratitude to sugary snacks and prosecco) that I need to ramp up my health. Not just to shed the pounds but for mind, body and soul! I am bombarded on social media with the benefits of running. In truth I have always been embarrassed about the thought of running. My over active brain imprinted embarrassing images of me jogging along like a sloth bred with an elephant. But with my new found body confidence (aka not giving a fuck) and commitment to try new things I thought why bloody not! After downloading the NHS couch to 5K app I treated myself to a pair of inexpensive running shoes, borrowed a Fitbit and set off to the park.

For those who follow me on social media you saw first-hand my jogging 'Epic Fail'! Shoe lace. Trip. Fall. Skint knees – mobile flying through air uploading the video for all to see on my insta stories. I was sent a DM from a delightful gentleman advising - I am an attention seeking fat mess that should be eradicated. Six weeks ago, this message would have catapulted me into a binge drinking/eating rampage while crying that I am indeed an overweight train wreck. Not now. Not anymore. Is it hurtful? Of course! No one likes to be insulted but my six-week therapy has taught me the most important lesson of all – the way you talk to yourself really bloody matters! Self-love is not selfish or arrogant it is vital. You can't pour from an empty cup!

While attending to my bloody knees imprinted with gravel, I received a message from a friend. *Hey Ellie, awesome you ran (and fell lol) but hey you still ran! As Will Smith quotes - Self-discipline is the definition of self-love!*

That hit home. Self-discipline = self-love. I am not quite at 'Britany Runs a Marathon' level but I am sticking with the couch to 5K. I shall be taking my body, curves and all, around the park. My shoe laces will be firmly tied and I shall be giving it 100%!

Thanks for reading
Much Love
Ellie B x

I am so grateful for your kind words throughout my therapy journey while trying new things. Is anyone else doing couch to 5K? Would be super curious to hear about running stories, tips and how you keep motivated! Please tag @itismeellieb #elliebcouchto5k #runnersofinstgram #sanitynotvanity

ACKNOWLEDGEMENT

To my husband, Jan, thanks for being nothing like Bob or Simon! You are my rock - I love you!

To my beautiful friend and Glasglow Girls Club founder, Laura, thank you so much for editing Ellie, you are bloody awesome!

To Victoria - without you there would be no Ellie! You are the voice inside my head, pushing me to be the best version of myself and never give up! Thanks for reading and re- reading all my work patiently. Thanks for the long walks, cafe trips and lengthy calls, for all the laughs, tears and goal setting under new moons! You are a kick ass, beautiful human.

Printed in Great Britain
by Amazon